MW00823774

CHILDREN OF THE SHIP

CHILDREN OF THE SHIP

DOUG BRODE

CHILDREN OF THE SHIP

Children of the Ship © 2023 Doug Brode
(Excerpt from) Shelli © 2023 Doug Brode

Published 2023

Cover Design: Enchanted Ink Publishing
Formatting: Enchanted Ink Publishing

ISBN: (Paperback) 978-1-7372255-2-2
ISBN: (Hardcover) 978-1-7372255-3-9

Library of Congress Control Number: TX0009235077

Alien Sky Publishing – First edition 2023

ALIEN SKY★
PUBLISHING

Dedicated to my children, **Hayden** and **Leia**

PART I

THE FINAL INCIDENT

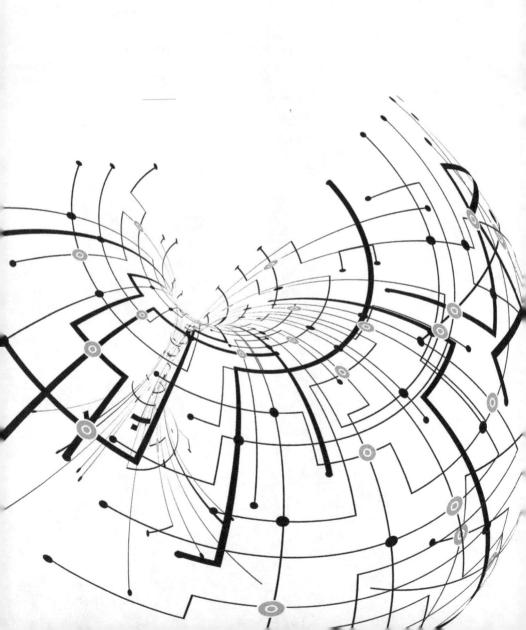

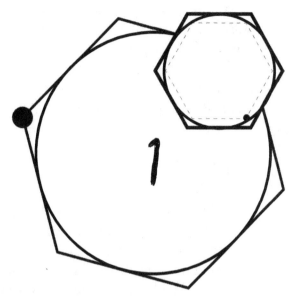

Blackwood, Oregon. 2038

The house squeaked in its joints. Even with the windows shut, air seeped in, walls breathed, and floorboards creaked. Casey Anderson had grown accustomed to such noises. Living at the edge of town, a mere arm's throw from the surrounding tree line, she'd come to expect an occasional odd groan echoing about the old house. Casey sat in bed, clutching her laptop, as she waited for the noises to settle. They didn't.

The rattling grew louder, closer.

Brushing aside her dangling blonde hair, her ears prickled at the reverberation of shrieking floorboards just beyond the open bedroom door. Without turning, she pressed her right palm against the closed window behind her, checking for wind. The glass remained steady, warm to the touch. No sign of a draft.

A thick rasping sound poured from the doorway, like labored breathing. Human breathing. Yet, she was alone in the house. Her husband, Jacob, had taken their daughter out for dinner and ice cream.

As the creaking wood outside her doorway continued its approach, the noises reminded her of the heavy footsteps her father used to make all those years ago, just before he'd enter her bedroom. Casey rubbed her eyes and shook off the memory. He was long dead, and she didn't believe in ghosts. Like a mantra, she repeated that thought over and over as the rasping breath drew closer to her open door.

There are no such things as ghosts, Case. There are no such things as—

THUMP!

The house shivered; the bed rattled beneath her. Casey stared, unblinking, at the outer hall, half expecting someone—or something—to peek around the corner. She opened her mouth to call out, but her voice caught in her throat. Stealing a glance at her computer, she noted the time: 9:15 p.m. Jacob had only left an hour ago, and he wouldn't be home yet. Besides, Casey would have heard his car outside. She always did. Living in a small town, the tiniest whispers carried far.

And screams, her mind urged. *Screams carry even farther.*

THUMP! THUMP!

The drumming sounded like footfalls ascending a staircase. Finally, Casey found her voice.

"Jacob?"

No answer. She closed the laptop and slid her left leg off the bed.

THUMP! THUMP!

"Hon?" she called again with a wispy tone. "This isn't funny."

Casey hesitated, trying to decide if she should make a run for it. If there was a burglar (*or an axe murderer,* her mind whispered) in the house, he now knew precisely where she was. *Good one, Case.*

The thumping stopped, replaced by a creaking whine that put her remaining nerves on high alert. Houses creaked all the time. She knew it, and she knew how they sounded. This was different. These noises weren't random. They stopped and started, winding their way closer.

Dragging her other leg off the bed, she inched toward the gaping entrance. Casey's eyeline dropped to the floor just beyond the doorway, checking for shadows. A haphazard pile of laundry in the outer hall made a black hump along the hardwood floor. Inky, clumpy black. If anyone was standing outside, she would see his shadow.

Unless . . .

Casey stepped closer and then stopped on the balls of her feet.

Someone is hiding directly beneath the overhead light.

She glanced around the bedroom for a possible weapon. To her left, a vacuum cleaner sat propped beside the wall. Casey imagined herself using its elongated handle like a spear against an attacker, then laughed at the thought. It was a nervous laugh. Still, the knotted tension in her shoulders relaxed. With a lunge, she took the last three steps to the doorway.

CRRRREEEEEEEAAAAAK!

The sound was no longer outside. It was coming from within the bedroom. From behind her.

Spinning about, her eyes darted toward the noise's source. Along the wall, a yellow, craggy line cut its way from the floorboards to the ceiling.

CRREEEEAAAAAKKKK!

At the bedroom's entrance, a second crack splintered the door from its hinges. Yellow light seeped out, like blood from an open wound. The door tumbled with a loud THUD.

Casey screamed. Without thinking, she jumped over the fallen door, headlong into the waiting hall. Alarms blared in her skull, pulsing behind her eyes. Casey spun back toward the fallen door and the bedroom's cracked wall. Lingering, she questioned whether to try and move the heavy door by herself or wait for Jacob to return. When the cold floor sent a shiver up her legs, sending gooseflesh rippling across her arms and chest, she snapped out of her daze and ran downstairs to the living room, where she planned to wait with the lights on until Jacob returned.

By the time Jacob's car pulled up, Casey's nerves, and the house, seemed to have settled. When they went upstairs to survey the damage, the cracks weren't as severe as her imagination had allowed. Less than half an inch thick, they spiderwebbed from the floorboards to the ceiling but produced no strange yellow light and no creepy noises. The bedroom door, however, was still broken off its hinges. Jacob assured her he'd call their landlord in the morning.

"Weird," he said, "but nothing worth losing sleep over."

Suppressing a shudder, Casey chose to believe him.

A few hours later, she awoke to the sound of screams.

Her eyes blinked open in the dark, staring at her rumpled pillow. When the scream came again, laced with panic, she bolted out of bed. Glancing back, she noticed Jacob peek out from beneath the heavy covers.

"You know it's your turn," she said.

"Would you mind, babe?" he groaned, ducking back under the blanket.

"Fine," Casey replied, stifling a yawn. "*You* sleep while *I* slay the monsters."

Lumbering along the chestnut wood flooring, she headed down the hall toward the sounds of soft sniffles. Sarah had obviously had another nightmare. It was the fourth in as many days. Casey wiped the last remnants of sleep from her eyes as she entered Sarah's bedroom.

"Mommy!" Sarah shouted as soon as Casey turned on the light. The sound of relief in the seven-year-old girl's voice was evident, as if she'd been saved from the jaws of certain death. Or, at least, Casey thought, saved from the oppressive loneliness that accompanied every child's darkened bedroom. Remembering her own fright not so long ago, Casey sat on Sarah's bed and offered a compassionate smile. Sarah jumped into her arms, pressing her small body against Casey's.

"It's alright," Casey said, wiping away her daughter's tears. "It's OK."

"I ate him, Mommy!" Sarah whimpered. "I ate him alive!"

Casey patted the young girl's sweat-soaked hair. "Ate who, honey?"

Sarah shook her head. "I don't know who he was, but he kept screaming and screaming while my teeth were ripping—"

"Hold on," Casey interrupted. "Be honest. What *completely inappropriate* movie did Daddy show you this time?"

At the mention of his name, Casey heard Jacob approach down the hall. Casey turned to the door as her husband stumbled into view, dressed in his boxers.

"It wasn't me," he said even before his feet had entered the room. "Honest."

Noting the way his voice pitched, Casey eyed him until, at last, his shoulders sagged. "King Kong," he admitted in a barely audible voice.

Casey blinked. "Are you kidding?"

Jacob came over and sat on the bed. Sarah leapt into his lap. "It was the old black-and-white version. I didn't think she'd get nightmares from it."

"It wasn't from the movie, Mom. Really," Sarah said, hugging her father.

"Next time," Casey said, glaring at Jacob, "*you* come in while *I* hide under the covers."

Suddenly, the overhead lightbulb flickered once, twice, and then exploded.

CRRREEEEEAAAAK!

Along the ceiling, cracks formed, releasing a thick cloud of dust and debris. Chunks of plaster rained down. Sarah shrieked. Casey was about to join in, but then the floor tilted beneath them. With a lurch, the bedframe collapsed, and the walls bent inward.

In the darkness, Casey pictured the house eating them.

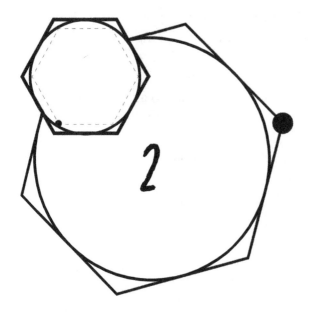

2

In total, *three* strange incidents had occurred in the town of Blackwood.

The first took place over a forty-eight-hour period. Something had arrived in the woods. A giant spaceship of unknown origin. The ship hadn't crashed or landed; it had simply *appeared*. Pine trees snaked in and out of its structure, as if the mile-wide craft had always been a permanent part of the Oregon landscape. When the spacecraft arrived, it brought a red mist with it that infected everyone in the town below. Everyone, that is, except two children: fourteen-year-old Jacob Anderson, and his little sister, Samantha. They hid and watched and saw everything. Over the next two horrible days, the town stood guard around the ship, like human shields. When the ship finally vanished, the townspeople claimed they could only recall fragments of what had happened. But Jacob never forgot. He remembered what he'd seen, and worse, what he'd done to survive.

The second Blackwood incident occurred ten years later. Only this time no one took much notice. There was no flying saucer in the mountains and no creepy red mist permeating the town. Instead, the second incident revolved around a single missing person. Or, rather, the *finding* of a missing person. Casey Stevens, a woman who'd seemingly vanished off the face of the earth four decades prior, was discovered strolling along the side of the road, wrapped in a plastic shower curtain and nothing else. Despite all the time that had gone by, Casey had aged less than ten years. It was all very strange, to be sure, but after the first incident, this one didn't merit nearly the amount of attention or anxiety as it might have otherwise. Casey's reappearance was soon forgotten by everyone in town except the now grown-up Jacob Anderson, who'd discovered her beside the road. Shivering beneath a plastic sheet, confused and afraid, she swore she had no memory of where she'd been or any idea how she looked as young as she did despite such a significant passage of time. Casey did, however, reveal one thing of note: she was pregnant.

The third and final incident came eight years later.

In October.

Hunched on his hindquarters, Jacob checked for damage. The south side of the house had sunk a good three feet into the ground, and a sewer stench permeated the area. He assumed a drainage pipe must have ruptured. When his boots melted into soggy earth, he stepped back, kicking off what he *hoped* was only mud. The smell alone made their house uninhabitable.

Inside, he heard Casey shouting, trying to rally Sarah off to school. For once, he welcomed the sounds of morning chaos. It kept his mind off persistent questions, such as what could cause a home nestled 2,500 feet above ground level to suddenly sink? His thoughts continued to churn as he heard a vehicle rumble up the driveway.

Sheriff Austin climbed out of his Ford Bronco and surveyed the scene. Even with half his face hidden beneath oversized sunglasses, his expression darkened as he approached. No surprise, considering the sheriff owned the place. Jacob and Casey were only renters. Most of the time, that had proven to be a bone of contention between the couple. Jacob hoped to settle down while Casey refused to lock herself into staying in Blackwood for the long haul. Six years later, they were still renting. Stuck in the mud, just like the house. They'd planned to pack up and leave Blackwood, with all its bad memories, at least a hundred and one times. But Sarah had school, and Jacob owned a business, so they'd stayed. "For now," they'd said. "Only for now."

"Jeeezuus." Sheriff Austin groaned, plugging his nose at the stench. "What the hell happened?"

"You got me," Jacob replied. "We were in Sarah's room when suddenly the whole damn structure just fell out from under us."

Austin glanced toward the front door. "Everyone alright?"

"A little shaken up," Jacob said. "But yeah, we're fine."

"Good." The sheriff leaned down where the foundation had sunk beneath the clumpy ground. When he stood back up, he supported his back, as if bending over had strained it. Jacob wasn't sure how old Sheriff Austin was, but Casey had mentioned she'd gone to high school with him back in the 1980s, which would put him somewhere around seventy. If Austin ever suspected who Casey really was, though, he'd kept his thoughts to himself. At one time, Jacob's wife had been a minor mystery about town. But that was years ago, and no one in Blackwood was ever eager to explore mysteries. Or the past. Not since the ship.

"Well," Austin said, "you can't stay here. Not for a few days at least. I'll have Lenny come over with his boys and give me an appraisal."

Jacob considered that for a moment, wondering where they would stay for the next few nights. Behind him, the front door sprang open. Casey was putting a too-large pink backpack around Sarah's shoulders as they hustled over to her silver Camry. It was, as Jacob had pointed out on multiple occasions, a thoroughly impractical car for that high up in the mountains. But Casey had insisted. She figured it would fit in nicely when they moved to Portland. Whenever that might be.

"Morning, Sheriff," she said with a heavy note of exacerbation.

"Hey there, Case." Austin leaned down low enough to make eye contact with Sarah. "Hiya, Sarah. Heard you had quite a scare."

"Not as scary as the beast," she said, a shiver running up her little body.

The sheriff paused, catching Jacob's eye.

He shrugged. "Just a nightmare."

Austin made his lips into an "O" shape and nodded. "Well, we all get bad dreams now and again. It's our mind's way of keeping us on our toes."

Sarah frowned. "Why would my brain worry about my toes?"

"It's an expression, hon," Casey said. She pecked Jacob's cheek, then pulled Sarah toward the car. "Come on; we're going to be late for school. Again."

"Wouldn't want that," Austin said, waving as they climbed into the car.

After Casey's car pulled away, Jacob turned to the sheriff. "Any idea where we might stay?"

Austin rubbed the back of his neck, thinking it over. Then his police radio squawked to life.

"Hold on a sec," he said, walking back to his vehicle.

Hearing the sheriff on the radio, Jacob paced back and forth, inching closer to the Bronco. He didn't consider it eavesdropping, nor was it idle curiosity; it was his job. Having spent six years working for the *Portland Gazette* as a field reporter, he'd eventually bought Blackwood's tiny paper a couple years back. While newspapers were a dying breed almost everywhere else, people in Blackwood weren't in such a rush to turn all digital, all the time. Not that the business was all he'd dreamed it would be. But it was his. All his. And that meant the world to him. Jacob was editor in chief, lead columnist, and, when necessary, field reporter. Most of his articles dealt with lumber prices, the occasional obituary, and from time to time, a story with a little more substance, like local politics or the church's seasonal fundraising events. Today, though, he thought as he edged closer to the SUV, might be different. Jacob might have a real story on his hands. And not simply one about his house sinking into the ground.

"Yep, yep, I'm on my way," Austin said before placing the radio receiver back in his vehicle. When he turned, he caught Jacob's curious gaze and sighed. "I suppose you wanna come along?"

"Depends," Jacob said, trying not to sound overly eager. "What's up?"

"Animal mauling."

Jacob paused, immediately recalling Sarah's horrible dream and what she'd said about tasting someone's blood. It was simply a coincidence, he reminded himself.

"Geez, a local?"

Austin shrugged. "No idea. His features are . . . obscured from the wounds, according to Mike. He's on the northern summit with the body now." They both paused, glancing toward the mountain to the north, covered in shadow. Austin's voice tightened. "So, are you tagging along?"

It wasn't really a question. Jacob hopped in his truck and followed the sheriff out of his yard.

Halfway out of town, though, Jacob's foot lifted off the gas, slowing his approach. The far side of the northern summit had, in recent years, garnered the name "Wicked Woods," and for good reason. No one ever went up that way anymore. Not even hunters.

Why would someone be stupid enough to go up there at night?

His fingers trembling against the steering wheel, Jacob forced himself to push down on the gas. After all this time, he was returning to where it had all started. The northern summit.

Where, once upon a time, he'd seen an alien spaceship.

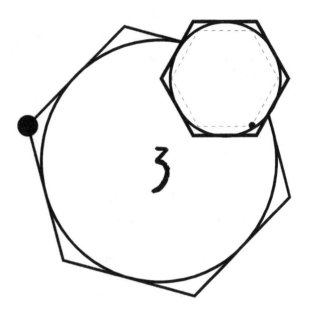

3

The walls moaned like horrid ghosts were hidden behind the paint and the plaster. The noise put Casey's teeth on edge as she threw Sarah's clothes into a suitcase. After dropping Sarah off at school, Casey had swung back home to grab a few essentials. It had seemed like the reasonable thing to do, back when she was standing in the school parking lot, warmed by the morning sun. Now, however, rummaging for clothes on the second-floor landing, with the outside light dim and the shadows seemingly moving about on their own, Casey was having second thoughts.

The floorboards let out a crackling scream beneath her tennis shoes as she rushed to fill the suitcase. Once the clothes were done, though, she still needed to grab Sarah's iPad, which reminded her to also grab the PlayStation downstairs and Jacob's laptop in their bedroom. Funny, she thought, as she tried to keep her mind focused on the job at hand rather than the house's groans, how essentials meant something completely different back in the 1980s. Over the decades she'd been missing, the world had become consumed by electronics.

Now that she had been back for a while, even Casey had to admit she'd grown accustomed to always keeping a phone in her pocket. Though "back" was a relative term, as she had no idea where she'd been or what she'd done over the four decades between 1985 and the day she woke up, naked and pregnant. In all that time, Casey had only aged about ten years while everyone else had grown old. The how's and why's of it all were questions she'd long ago decided she probably didn't want answered.

Zipping up the first suitcase, Casey moved into her own bedroom and got to work on the second. The room shuddered, causing her to brace herself against the closet doorframe as she scrounged around for shirts, pants, and underwear. Eyeing the mess dripping out of the closet, she noted how the fallen clothes had taken up a good quarter of the bedroom's floor. She had meant to get around to cleaning eventually. Now it would have to wait. Casey smiled. Maybe this would be like a small vacation.

Then a loud CRASH made her jump.

The dresser's mirror had fallen down, shattering glass at her feet. In that instant, a memory flashed behind her eyes, showing her in vivid detail the last night she'd seen her previous fiancé, Arthur, alive. The night their old cabin had shaken, the windows bursting open, blazing with an emerald light that had engulfed the cabin. Her innards had tightened, as if ensnared by an invisible hook. She'd felt her bare feet leave the ground, her body spinning as it lifted toward an emerald light in the sky. It was the last thing she would remember for over forty years.

Now she worried it was happening again. Whatever *it* was.

A violent shudder ran across the second-floor landing. Clutching the suitcases in both hands, she wobbled out the door and headed downstairs. Three steps down, the house lurched. Casey went sprawling, though she never felt herself tumble down the staircase or land with a crash. Instead, she found herself standing in a dark place that stank of mildew and earth.

A red light blinked overhead, and a piercing noise made her cover her ears. An alarm. It blared so loudly that it blocked out her other senses. Turning around, she saw an ironwork elevator descending toward her. Casey's gaze darted this way and that, taking in what few details her limited eyesight could perceive. She appeared to be underground, though how or why eluded her. Glancing down, she noticed a white lab coat draped over her body, as if she were playing doctor. Then a voice from behind her cut through the sirens.

Casey . . .

Overhead, a fractured shape hung like a twisted origami sculpture. Sharp edges protruded from every angle, seemingly metallic and razor sharp. What the shape was, she couldn't tell, but something about it seemed familiar.

Come . . .

The way the strange structure was twisted and torn open reminded her of jagged teeth, jutting up and down like a wicked grin. Then the grinning shape spoke.

You can't hide . . . Not from me . . . Not from yourself.

Casey awoke, lying prone at the bottom of the staircase. A crimson smear dripped from her forehead, burning her eyes. The floor beneath her creaked and yawned, splintering with spiderwebbed cracks. A yellow light glowed from under the floorboards. It made her nauseous, and her stomach twisted. She wanted to vomit, desperate to look away from the pale yellowness pouring through the wood paneling. The light swallowed her as the inner voice returned.

You . . . can't . . . hide . . . forever . . .

Casey forced her eyes closed, shutting out the light blazing through the floorboards. Blindly, she reached for the front door. At her feet, the floor bent and buckled. Finally, her fingers found the front door. With a wrench, she twisted the knob and flung it open. Half running and half wobbling, Casey flew out of the house.

Fresh air slapped her face and filled her lungs. Stumbling past the porch, she collapsed in the front yard. The sweet smell of grass and morning dew washed away the vomit burning at the back of her throat. A few more gulps of air, and the world slowly stopped spinning. Birds chirped overhead, signaling that the nightmare, or whatever it had been, was over.

Casey sat up, wiping a glob of blood from her brow and cheek. Swooning, she struggled to rise. Her head throbbed, threatening to split open. Turning back toward the house, she studied the innocent-looking white front door. Beyond it, two suitcases lay only a few feet inside. Eyeing the spilled suitcases, she considered what she'd gone through to get them in the first place. She needed to go back inside. Just for a moment. It was the fall, she told herself, and not the house, that had caused the hallucinations.

Except when she tried to move, her feet refused to budge. Casey wasn't going back inside that house. Not ever.

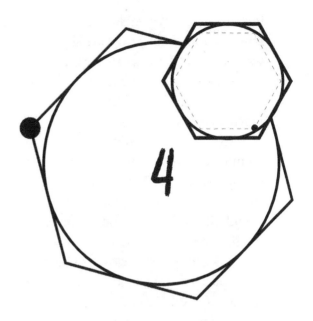

4

Jacob's mind whirled from the sickening stench invading his nostrils. Everywhere he looked, blood oozed. It dripped from tree branches and splashed along the grass. At the center lay a corpse—at least what little remained of one. If not for the abandoned white van parked a few feet away, Jacob wouldn't have even recognized the body as human. The vehicle's engine was still running, and its headlights punctuated the horror of what he was seeing, magnifying the colors so that the entire forest seemed to be caked in red.

"Whatever did this," Deputy Mike Hodges said, "it sure as hell wasn't no mountain lion."

Jacob swallowed. "Bear?"

Sheriff Austin ran a tape measure along the ground. "No, no," he said, more to himself than to Jacob. "It's a cat print, alright. Though these impressions are crazy big."

That got Jacob's attention. He edged his way across the bloody field. "How big?"

Austin shook his head, rechecking his measurement. "Seven

inches long, nearly eight inches wide." He moved to a second set of impressions. "Rear prints are slightly smaller, so it carries most of its weight in the front, whatever it is."

"How big would a mountain lion's print be?"

Austin shrugged. "About half this size. Three and a half inches maybe. Four, tops."

Jacob's revulsion diminished as his curiosity grew. It didn't take a Pulitzer prize-winner to realize there was a story here. And judging by the size of the paw prints, a big one. Rummaging through his jacket, he took out his phone and began snapping pictures. When the sheriff glanced over, Jacob assumed he'd be told to stop, but instead, Austin simply gestured along the path.

"Take some more closer to the van," he said. "We'll need to send those pics off to the wildlife department."

Jacob nodded as he walked about, taking photos.

"And watch your step," Austin added. "This is still an active crime scene."

"Geez, Austin," Hodges said, "looks like a straightforward hunting incident to me. Some animal musta got the jump on him."

"If this man was a hunter," Austin replied, "where's his rifle?"

Jacob paused, glancing back. So overwhelmed by the gory scene, he hadn't taken in all the details. He couldn't help wondering what else he might be missing. With that thought, his attention turned to the van. Stepping over large swaths of crimson-stained grass, he stopped at the vehicle's rear double doors. Hesitating, he glanced back at Austin, who gave him a sharp nod. Using an abundance of care, Jacob grabbed the van's back latch with his shirt, just in case fingerprints were needed to identify the body.

Swinging the doors open, however, took his mind far away from the body or the blood-covered forest. Inside, a glowing bank of lights and screens greeted him, offering what appeared to be topographical maps of Blackwood and the town's surrounding mountains. Along the graphs, red blips marked specific points throughout the region. Jacob was so transfixed by his discovery that he didn't notice Austin and Hodges on either side of him until Hodges whistled in his ear.

"Someone call Darth Vader," the deputy said. "I think we just found his van."

Austin climbed inside, studying the various screens and controls. "This guy spent a pretty penny on all this fancy equipment."

Hodges followed the sheriff inside, running his fingers along the keyboards.

"Hold up." Austin stopped him with a wave. "It's evidence."

"Evidence of what?" Hodges asked, still convinced this was a hunting trip gone terribly wrong.

Austin ignored the question. "Whoever this guy was, he's certainly not local." Glancing at the monitors, he scratched the back of his neck. "I've never seen anything like this stuff."

"I have," Jacob said, his voice barely above a whisper. He'd recognized the fancy machines and onscreen maps the moment he'd opened the van. Admitting to it out loud, though, had taken a mighty effort. He felt his stomach doing somersaults.

"Where?" Austin asked, his eyebrows arching.

Jacob hesitated. Hodges had only moved into Blackwood a few years back, and some things simply weren't discussed with outsiders. As if understanding Jacob's concern, Austin turned to his deputy. "Get on the radio," he said. "Have the doc and someone from state wildlife come out here ASAP."

Once Hodges was out of earshot, Austin waited for Jacob to continue.

"I've seen this kinda stuff before," Jacob reiterated, "back during, well . . . you know . . ."

Austin shifted uncomfortably. "During the incident."

Jacob shuddered at the sheriff's mention of what was known as the "Blackwood incident." An image of his father's chest exploding replayed behind his eyes. Even now, after almost two decades, Jacob could still feel the shotgun's recoil slam into his shoulder. He could smell the burst of gunpowder, and he could see his father's body fall out of view.

"Jacob," Austin said.

Shaking his head, Jacob pushed the images back into the recesses of his mind. When he spoke, though, his voice cracked. "The Army team that came up back then had long black trucks filled with screens and maps just like these."

Austin crawled out of the van to get a better look at the bloody mess spread across the grass. Among the gore, half of a human torso jutted out from behind red-stained foliage. "So, you're suggesting our friend here was military?"

"Military, government, same thing."

The sheriff nodded as he paced around the mysterious animal tracks. "And now they're back."

Jacob sighed. "Or they never left."

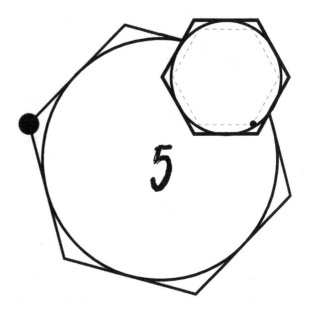

5

What the hell is wrong with her?

    Noelle Reese watched Casey stumble out of her home and fall to the ground. She lifted a rifle scope to her eye, trying to get a clearer view from behind the tree line. Her index finger skimmed the rifle's trigger.

It would be so easy.

"Report," a voice boomed through her headset, as if someone, somewhere, had been reading her thoughts.

Drifting the scope off Casey, she surveyed the house's outer damage. The lower right side had sunken beneath a pile of mud. Noelle sighed into her microphone. "Yeah, it's a sinkhole, alright. The eastern side of the house is dug in pretty deep. Three, maybe four feet."

"And the asset?"

She suppressed a low growl rising in her throat. Asset. She hated that term. It made Casey sound invaluable. What was worse, Noelle knew that she was. More important than Noelle, at least to those on the other end of the radio. She watched Casey struggle to get back on her feet. A red stain marked her forehead.

"She's injured," Noelle said, worried her smile could be heard through the mic. Swinging the rifle over her shoulder, she let out a long, slow breath, resigning herself to what would come next. "I'll check it out. Stand by."

Noelle trudged back to her truck, stowed the weapon, took out her earwig, and flipped on a ball cap. *Time to go to work.* She drove around to the main road, Carson Creek, and then looped back up toward the house. By the time she'd arrived, Casey was heading to her car.

"Hey, Case," Noelle said, pulling over. "Everything alright?"

Even with her face pale white and blood seeping above her brow, Casey smiled warmly, as if glad to see a familiar face. "Oh, hey, Noelle. Yeah, I'm fine. I, uh, I just tripped down the stairs."

It was obvious she was holding something back, but Noelle didn't press. Info gathering wasn't the same as interrogation, though Lord knows Noelle would have preferred that route a year ago, back when she'd first landed this assignment. It would have saved everyone a hell of a lot of time. But orders were orders. Like all the agents at Watchtower, Noelle had a personal stake in this. Both in Casey and in finding the lost ship. Supposedly, Casey didn't remember anything that happened before she was found eight years ago. Noelle didn't buy that for a second. Casey remembered. Maybe not all of it but certainly some. Every time Noelle looked at Casey, she couldn't help wondering what this seemingly ordinary, middle-aged woman remembered about Major John Reese, Noelle's father. Both of them had been inside the ship, but only Casey had come back. Noelle planned to find out why, one way or another.

But not today.

Her smile struggled to widen. "That's a hell of a gash ya got there," Noelle said. "Hop in. I'll take you to the clinic."

Casey waved her off. "No, don't be silly. I'm fine to drive. Besides, my shift is about to start."

Noelle laughed; it almost sounded genuine, even to her own ears. "Someone else can serve up the burgers today, Case. You're not driving anywhere with an open head wound." Noelle's tone hardened slightly. "Get in the truck."

Casey glanced back at the house, and her eyes watered. Whatever had happened in there, it'd obviously shaken her up something fierce. With a huff, she relented. "Yeah, sure. Alright."

As Casey went around the front of the truck, Noelle noticed the glove compartment was still open, her microphone wire spilling to the floor. She shoved the radio inside and shut it just as Casey climbed in.

"Thanks," Casey said, blushing as if embarrassed. "This is really nice of you."

"Please," Noelle said, her throat tightening as she thought of her father, "don't mention it."

Despite half the town working up at the lumber mill at that time of day, downtown Main Street was bustling with activity. People swarmed the two-lane street. Ahead of the crowd, police and ambulance lights flashed. Forced to park half a block from the clinic, Noelle led Casey the rest of the way on foot. She put her arm under Casey's shoulder, pulling her unsteadily along the crowded sidewalk. At first she tried to calmly nudge past the people. When that didn't work, Noelle resorted to shoving her way through. At last they arrived at the apex of all the excitement: the clinic. But when she pulled at the door, it didn't budge. Locked. Trying to ignore the rumbling bystanders behind them, she pounded on the door until a nurse peeked through the glass.

"I'm afraid we're closed for a bit," the nurse said with a strained smile that made Noelle's blood boil.

"She's hurt," Noelle snapped, yanking Casey and her blood-covered forehead into view. The nurse's eyes rose to meet Casey's wound, then worked their way back to Noelle. Even with a bloody wound at her doorstep, the nurse's bland expression didn't offer much hope. Noelle cringed inwardly, suddenly wishing she'd brought along her sidearm. Then a man came up behind the nurse and unlocked the door.

It was Casey's husband, Jacob.

Flinging the door open, his complexion was as pale as Casey's, and his clothes were covered in dirt and red-black stains. Blood. He pulled his wife inside while Noelle tried to work out what the hell was going on. Before she could ask, Jacob threw a barrage of questions at Casey. "Are you OK? Jesus, what happened to you? Why'd you go back to the house without me?"

Noelle followed them inside before the nurse shut and locked the door. Behind the front desk, a rush of movement, accompanied by panicked voices, caught her notice. Above the din, the local sheriff's usual laid-back drawl rose to a fevered pitch.

"Don't tell me to calm down, Doc!" Sheriff Austin shouted, blinking out of view, then vanishing into an office. A door slammed behind him. Curious, Noelle inched closer, then paused and glanced back at the nurse. She was busy helping Jacob clean and bandage Casey's wound. For once "the asset" being the center of attention seemed to have paid off. Noelle snuck past the counter, heading toward the office that Sheriff Austin had gone inside. She'd planned on listening in. Halfway to the door, however, something else pulled her away.

A wretched, coppery stench overwhelmed the clinic's habitually sterile odor.

Her gut twisting, Noelle followed the smell. Blood. The odor was strong enough for her to expect to find a lot of it. But whatever her imagination might have conjured before she made her way around the corner, nothing could have prepared her for what she found. All the training in the world couldn't have covered it.

It wasn't a body per se, simply pieces of one.

Spread out across a six-foot-long metal table lay what could only be described as slabs of meat wrapped in shredded cloth. Ribs punctured the redness, revealing a torso, while fragments of bone and tissue on either side suggested arms and legs. There was no sign of a head.

Struggling to ignore the gore, Noelle kept her focus on the shredded clothes. Though ugly with stains, she recognized what was left of the man's brown-and-blue patched shirt.

Hawthorne.

He'd been a geologist who spent his time studying soil samples, tracking the sinkholes outside of town. At least, they had been only occurring outside of town, until now. After last night's damage to Casey's home, the disturbance had officially crossed into town. Now, looking over the gory remains through watery eyes, Noelle feared they had an even worse problem on their hands, one far more imminently dangerous. After glancing around to make certain she was still alone, Noelle pulled out her phone. She tried to stop her fingers from shaking as she dialed, but it was a losing battle.

"Hawthorne's dead," Noelle said when the call connected. "Looks like an animal attacked him."

"What kind of animal?" the voice asked, its normal stoic flatness pitched with surprise.

Instead of answering, Noelle asked her own question. "When did he last report in?"

There was a brief pause before the voice replied. "02:30"

Noelle checked her watch. *Less than ten hours.*

Surveying the remains, she suppressed a shudder. Hawthorne had been over six feet tall and almost as wide. Whatever had done this to him had been big. Huge. And strong. Noelle's throat tightened, and her mouth became a desert.

"I . . . I think something came through."

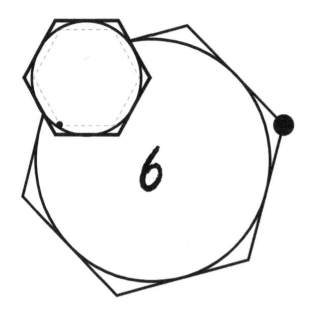

6

It's called a hypersphere . . . a voice echoed, rattling around Casey's head. *A three-dimensional representation of a fourth-dimensional sphere.*

As strange as the words sounded, even more unnerving was that the voice was her own. Through a groggy fog, she recognized this as one of her "lost episodes," as she called them. Over the years they'd come and gone. It was as if a blank white page had suddenly revealed a dim impression. Not words or a clear image but a hint of something not fully erased from her mind. Worse was the nausea that always followed. After having been haunted for so long by fractured sounds and images that she could never piece together, Casey no longer welcomed such revelations. She didn't want to know what had happened to her. The past, she had decided, was better left where it belonged. In the past.

Casey's head swam as the nurse bandaged the bloody gash that ran along her temple. The sting of antiseptic pulled her away from the fearful memories just out of reach and back to the present. Back where it was safe and familiar. Casey sat in the clinic's waiting room with Jacob beside her, holding her hand. His handsome, round face offered a crooked grin, which usually made her feel better. But not now. Recalling the images she'd seen in the house, the fractured origami of metal looming over her, made her fingers tingle in his soft embrace. Had that been a figment of her imagination? A memory? Again, she had to remind herself not to push too hard for an answer. Some truths were better left unknown. Casey blinked, pushing back the echoing voices, and forced her lips to match Jacob's smile.

"I'm alright," she assured him. "Really."

"You look like shit."

"Thanks, babe." Her smile slowly became real. "You always know what to say."

"It's my super power."

The nurse made a guttural sound in reply, as if she didn't think much of his bedside manner. Her response only made the two lovers laugh louder.

With the bandage applied, the nurse stood. "You're lucky you don't need stitches." The odd tone in her voice didn't make Casey feel very lucky. If anything, the nurse seemed more confused than relieved. "I could have sworn the cut was deeper a few moments ago."

Jacob and Casey shared a subtle look. This had happened before, or at least something like it had. A couple of years back, Casey had cut her hand on a pair of gardening shears. But by the time they'd made it back to the house, the wound had begun to close. Like the nurse, they'd thought the same thing. The wound had been deeper.

As Jacob's eyes moved across Casey's head wound, she could practically see the wheels spinning behind his curious gaze. Hoping to push aside any further inquiry, she let out a long, loud sigh, signaling to Jacob not to push the subject. Like her repressed memories, this was simply another question that Casey didn't need answered. Not today. Probably never.

Then the sheriff barged in, halting her internal conversation before it could progress further. His face was beet red and covered in sweat. Casey couldn't help but be glad that someone looked worse than she did, though when he spoke, she regretted her sense of relief.

"Wildlife ain't coming," he said, the words sounding heavy in his throat. "Something about a fire north of Portland. They've got their hands full."

"So, I guess it's up to us," Jacob said.

That got Casey's attention. "What is?"

The sheriff nodded. "I'll put together a hunting party, and we'll go out after dark. Based on the time of death, whatever this thing is, it seems to hunt at night."

"Wait," Casey interjected. "What are you talking about?"

"Someone was killed up on the northern summit," Jacob replied.

"You mean . . ." Casey paused, hearing Sarah's voice in her head. "Eaten."

Jacob wrapped his arm around her. "Just a coincidence, babe."

"What is?" Austin asked, tilting his hat back and arching an eyebrow.

Casey shot Jacob a hard look, hoping he'd get the message. He didn't. Jacob shrugged and offered his best aw-shucks smile. "It's nothing. Sarah had a nightmare is all."

"Oh, right." Sighing, Austin let the air out of his gut. "You mentioned that before."

"Who was killed?" Casey asked.

"No idea," Jacob replied. "He wasn't local."

"His name was Vincent Hawthorne." Noelle appeared behind the counter. "He worked at my store."

The nurse spun around, pointing a crooked finger at her. "No one gave you permission to go back there!"

"Oops. My bad." Noelle rolled her eyes and slumped in a chair beside Casey.

Austin cocked his head, more curious than upset. "How long did he work for you?"

"About three months, give or take. He was from Portland, I think. Not sure where he was staying though. Logger's Inn, probably."

Jacob leaned over, curious, his reporter hat on. "Any idea what he was doing out on the northern summit in the middle of the night?"

Noelle shook her head. "Nope. But whatever killed him must have been fucking huge. A grizzly, maybe? I mean, Vinnie was a good six foot two inches at least. Barely cleared the front door."

Casey caught an odd glance between her husband and the sheriff. Something about Noelle's statement seemed to bother them. Perhaps it was Noelle's tone. She didn't seem nearly as frightened or as sad as one might expect. Still, Casey just assumed it was her way of coping. She could understand that. Better to bury one's feelings behind a cocky demeanor than go blubbering in front of a bunch of men.

"Did you ever see Mr. Hawthorne driving a white van?" Jacob asked. Casey noted an undercurrent in his voice. His face was soft and easy, but the tension was there, behind his eyes.

Noelle didn't seem to notice. "Naw, I don't think so."

"You sure?" Austin asked, his tone even sharper than Jacob's.

Noelle slumped forward, hanging her head. "Maybe. I don't know. Honestly, I never paid much attention." She looked up. "Why?"

"No reason," Austin said with an abruptness that quickly ended the conversation. He turned to Jacob. "I'll start calling around and get some guys ready for tonight."

While the men talked about wild animals and hunting parties, Casey's mind circled back to Sarah and her nightmare. What was it she'd said, exactly? "I ate him alive." Casey's stomach twisted at the memory. "He kept screaming and screaming while my teeth were ripping . . ."

"But I'm a flower!"

Seven-year-old Sarah was having a traumatic day. First, a freak accident had tilted her home into the ground like a surreal seesaw. Second, she'd just gotten the worst news of her young life. Despite all this, Casey had to smile. She only wished her own childhood had had such problems.

Jacob leaned across the dinner table. "Honey, haven't you ever heard the saying, 'There's no such thing as a small part'?"

Sarah's fork hit her plate, and her jaw gaped. "Again, Dad. I'm. A. Flower!"

"Is it at least a speaking flower?" Casey asked.

"Worse," Sarah replied, her dour expression darkening even further. "I have to sing."

"You love to sing, hon," Jacob said, smiling broadly and trying his best not to eye the plate of uneaten food still laying before him. Casey figured he was good to go for one more round of this before sinking his head and retreating to his hungry stomach.

"At home," Sarah protested. "Not in front of a thousand people!"

"Oh, I wouldn't worry about that," Noelle said, sitting down with a plate of hash browns. "I mean, how many parents even live in Blackwood?"

Jacob nodded, as if Noelle had arrived at the perfect answer. "Of young kids? Maybe a hundred, tops." He turned his smile to Sarah and bit a piece of bacon. "See? Now that doesn't sound so bad."

Instead of showing relief, tears formed in Sarah's eyes, and her lower lip quivered. "You mean . . . no one's going to come?"

As if recognizing that he'd lost, Jacob gave up the ghost and focused entirely on his breakfast-for-dinner. Casey wrapped her arm around Sarah, her voice soft and even. "We'll be there, honeybun, front and center."

"Me too," Noelle said, grabbing a biscuit. "I wouldn't miss it for the world."

"See?" Casey wiped her daughter's eyes. "Now it will be a hundred and one."

Once Sarah's tears had vanished and she returned to her food, Noelle asked her what the play was.

"Rapunzel," Sarah replied, her voice sour. "Jannie Doohan got the part because *she's* super talented. That's what our teacher said. Jannie's *special*."

Casey took her daughter's hands in hers. "You're special too, honey. Everyone is. Just wait. Someday you'll find out what your specialty is too. I promise."

Sarah tilted her head, thinking that over. "What are you special at, Mommy?"

Casey paused, unable to come up with a quick response.

"Your mommy's special at being a mommy," Jacob said. "And a wife." He kissed her cheek.

As Casey considered what he'd said, she felt her face flush. Not from anger but disappointment. He'd probably thought he was coming to her rescue.

"Sorry about the late-night breakfast," Noelle said, as if noting the awkward moment. "It's all I had in the fridge."

"Are you kidding? Bacon and hash browns is my favorite meal," Jacob replied. If she hadn't known better, Casey might have figured he was flirting with the younger woman. But she knew her husband, and indeed, this probably did beat anything she'd have cooked up at home. Noelle had been nice enough to offer them a place to stay until their house was repaired. They didn't know her all that well, but it was either there or the local inn. Free room and board had won out.

Thankfully, Jacob had gone back and gotten their luggage while Casey had picked Sarah up from school. A mental image of a fractured black monolith whispering to her still rattled through her skull.

Come . . .

The voice had sounded low and gravelly. Worse, she'd recognized it somehow. Whatever the dark origami shape had been, she felt as if she'd known it intimately—and it her.

Glancing around the table at her daughter and her husband, who by then had returned to the subject of the play and Sarah's role in it, Casey decided that right then that she wouldn't want to be anywhere else. A mile from her home and the pale yellow light, Casey felt safe.

Across from her, Noelle held up a bottle of beer and nodded in a silent toast. Casey returned the gesture and tried to forget about the voices and images still rattling in her brain.

You can't hide . . . Not from me . . . Not from yourself.

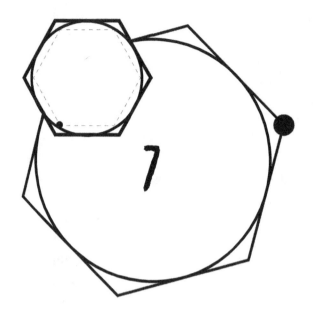

7

Everyone, on occasion, finds themselves staring up at the night sky. Sometimes they might notice a star that seems to shine brighter than all the others. Their eyes track away from it, scanning other stars, as if to confirm their comparative dimness, before inevitably returning their gaze to the pinprick of light that blazes so brilliantly. At first, most assume it's a plane. Only, it doesn't move. Then they imagine it's a planet. But it's perhaps a bit too low in the sky. Systematically, the viewer crosses off potential answers until eventually their mind begins to conjure the most fantastical explanation possible: that they are witnessing something truly astonishing. An honest-to-God UFO. The real deal, hovering just above the horizon. An alien vessel.

Jacob used to look up at the stars and have such thoughts. But not anymore. Not after the ship arrived, leaving a trail of death and nightmares in its wake. After that, Jacob kept his head down and his vision planted firmly below the horizon. Especially at night.

Glancing left and right at the string of hunters trudging up the mountain beside him, he noticed none of them ever glanced up beyond the tree-lined ridge either. The higher along the northern summit they climbed, the more nervous the burly bunch seemed to grow. Jacob eyed the dozen or so rifles dancing about him, swinging left, then right at every tick or rustle hidden within the darkened greenery. He doubted their growing anxiety had anything to do with the creature they were pursuing. It was the place.

Scanning the rocks and foliage above them, he tried to estimate how far they were from "the site." That's what he called it, at least. The site where the ship had appeared, blazing with emerald light. Worse were the sounds it had offered. Not outwardly audible but rather a din of whispers that had constantly scratched inside his skull like an itch he couldn't reach. The closer he'd come to the enormous craft, the louder the cacophony thundered in his head. Although the forest was now silent—*dormant*, his mind corrected— Jacob had refused to go back that far up since. No one had. Jacob figured they were still about a mile south of the site, but that was more than close enough to give everyone, even the rough and tumble local hunters, the willies. Scanning the hardened faces around him, Jacob realized that Sheriff Austin had picked this group for more than one reason. While everyone in Blackwood could hunt, all these men had been there eighteen years prior, during "the incident." They knew what had happened, and they also knew how to keep their mouths shut. Even Jacob, a reporter, knew what to say and what not to say. Some things, after all, needed to remain secret.

"Over here!" the sheriff's voice sounded from behind inky black bushes.

As the men quickened their pace, rounding the foliage, Jacob began to doubt his decision not to carry a firearm. Of course, he had good reason, though that offered little comfort as he stumbled over rocks and crashed through scratching branches. Behind him, pitch blackness threatened to swallow him whole. Jacob moved faster.

The hunters had stopped and circled the sheriff, studying something on the ground. Had they found another victim? Nudging his way through the ranks, Jacob felt his feet crunch against something. The men were standing around a large patch of snow, roughly seven feet long, extending straight across the grass like a piece of carpet.

Charlie, a foreman at the lumber mill, scooped some snow in his palm, then peered up toward the distant mountaintop. "How far down from the peak do you think we are?"

"Far enough," another man replied. "No way that snow came all the way down from the top."

"Well, wherever it's from," Austin said, chewing the inside of his cheek as if it were tobacco, "God doesn't paint in straight lines." His finger traced through the air, following the narrow white shape. "Looks more like something from a snow machine."

"Out here?" Jacob asked, glancing around. "Who'd lug a snow machine all the way up here in the middle of the night, then turn around and leave?"

Austin gave him a sharp look. At first, Jacob assumed the sheriff wanted him to be silent while he thought out loud. Then, when Austin followed the glance with a subtle nod, Jacob understood. The van. Maybe there was a connection. Before he could take that idea any further, though, a sharp breeze cut through his jacket.

"Sheriff . . ." Charlie began.

"Yeah," Austin replied, turning toward the bitter wind. "I feel it."

Spinning around in search of the source, the men lumbered along the rocky slope, momentarily forgetting the reason they were up there. Jacob hadn't, though. His eyes darted about, peering behind various shoulders at the surrounding darkness. He half expected to find gleaming eyes staring back. But all he saw were silhouetted trees and pine branches. Above, the moon was gone from view. Another shiver ran up his spine, only this time it wasn't caused by a breeze. Clutching his flashlight, Jacob kept himself positioned between the armed hunters.

Yep, he decided, *shoulda brought a gun.*

Even if he never fired the damn thing, at least the weight of it in his hands would have given him a hell of a lot more comfort than a simple mag light.

The brittle breeze returned, slapping Jacob's thoughts aside and turning the air frigid with another violent gust. He trailed closely behind Charlie, using his back as a shield against the onslaught. Hidden behind the bulky man, all Jacob could make out was a monolith of brown leather directly in front of him. When the men stopped, Jacob bumped headlong into Charlie, though if the foreman noticed, he didn't turn around to acknowledge it. Jacob peeked out from behind him, trying to see why everyone had stopped.

They'd found a cave. Snowflakes swept out of the mouth like a blower set to high, twisting and twirling before descending at his booted feet. Inside the cave, something gleamed. Jacob raised his flashlight, joining the others' dancing beams as they swept across the ten-foot-wide opening. While the sparkling reflections inside gleamed brighter, the black mouth remained concealed in shadow. Sheriff Austin warily eyed the white flecks blowing out of the entrance.

One of the men to Jacob's left voiced what everyone else was thinking: "That ain't natural."

Jacob found himself nodding in silent agreement with the others. They exchanged glances, first toward the cave and the billowing snow, then back at each other. After a long, frightful pause, Jacob cleared his throat.

"Maybe we should head back and wait for a geologist."

That idea seemed to split the dozen men into two camps. A few nodded in agreement, but most others kept their gaze fixed toward the blackness waiting beyond the breach. Neither group, however, seemed eager to enter.

"You fellas stay here," Sheriff Austin said. "I'm gonna have a look."

Instinctively, Jacob wanted to grab his arm, pulling him as far from the surreal cave as possible, but he didn't.

"I'm coming with," Charlie said. Beside him, two others nodded in agreement.

Jacob stepped back from the entrance as the four men went inside. He watched their flashlights blaze along the cave's open mouth, across hanging icicles that reminded him of jagged white teeth. As if the cave was eagerly waiting to consume its new visitors. Their light beams grew faint, then died behind a curtain of black.

The rest of the men stayed put, lingering outside. While he waited, Jacob rubbed his palms against his pants, pacing. His gaze drifted back and forth, studying the cave's orifice. Snow crunched under his boots, the sound of it accentuating the silence and his own cowardice.

He cursed inwardly. *Some reporter.*

Inhaling cold air through gritted teeth, Jacob suppressed a shiver that ran from his legs to his spine and made his shoulders quiver. He knew he had to go inside. The longer he waited, the more he'd regret it later. The news story, which had begun with hunting a mysterious creature, had now taken a turn toward the bizarre. But it was a story nonetheless.

With a violent shake, he threw out his body's nervous tingles and trudged forward. While the others watched, Jacob entered the cave . . .

And was instantly swallowed in shadow.

A fresh gust of cold frost knocked him back, as if protesting his arrival. Jacob continued forward, sweeping his flashlight across the ice-covered walls. Gleaming reflections of blues and purple sparkled. Jacob touched one of the walls, feeling the thickness of the overgrown ice, before he slowly peered up, finding dagger-like icicles jutting toward his skull.

Jacob crouched low, edging across a slippery surface while struggling to keep his balance. Twisting the flashlight around, he watched as streams of frosty breath escaped his lips.

Snow pouring out of a cave in the middle of October. Nothing about this is right.

His mind raced, attempting to come up with an answer—any answer—no matter how unlikely. Jacob considered that perhaps this was frost from the mountain peaks far above that had somehow been trapped inside the earth. He knew how ridiculous that sounded, but it was the best he could come up. Strangled voices ahead urged him to pick up the pace. Blue-black walls curved to his right, Rounding the corner, Jacob was relieved to find light beams dancing about to greet him.

"Figured you'd show up eventually," Austin said, lowering his rifle.

Sheepishly, Jacob shrugged. "Couldn't let you boys have all the fun."

As brave as his words might have sounded, his quivering voice gave him away. Glancing at Charlie, Jacob noticed that the giant foreman appeared equally pale and frightened. Seeing the large, outdoorsy man openly afraid did nothing to calm Jacob's rising anxiety. Despite the frigid conditions, he was sweating beneath his heavy layers.

Strength in numbers only applies when the majority aren't shaking in their snow boots. Sucking in cold air through chattering teeth, Jacob followed the group deeper into the cave.

"You ever seen anything like this, Sheriff?" Charlie asked.

Austin shook his head. No one had ever seen anything like an ice cave in the middle of October, especially so far down from the peak. Jacob's mind drifted back to the *other* unnatural event all those years ago. He couldn't help wondering if perhaps there might be a connection between the ship and the cave. With an absent shaking of his head, he pushed the idea aside. Ice caves in the middle of autumn were peculiar to be sure, but they didn't rise to the level of an alien spacecraft suspended in the trees. No, he assured himself, whatever event might have caused the phenomenon in the cave was still natural. Odd, yes, but natural. Then he peered around the next corner, and he changed his mind. Everyone stopped cold.

What they had found was most definitely *unnatural.*

"You're all seeing this, right?" Jacob asked, his voice shrill.

"Seeing it, yes," Austin replied. "Believing it? No."

Jacob peered into a jagged opening in the cave wall. Standing over six feet tall, the opening appeared almost as wide. It looked like a zipper had been pulled down across the rock-ice surface, revealing another world beyond. Bright sunlight poured through the crack, pushing away the cave's ominous shadows. Only, this light brought no warmth.

Beyond the crack lay an impossible vista. Above was a gray sky and puffy clouds. Below was an enormous blanket of ice and snow, covering a wooded mountainside. Perhaps it was Oregon, perhaps not. Jacob couldn't tell. And all things considered, it didn't matter. Whether it was another part of our planet or an alien world on the opposite side of the galaxy, he couldn't have been any more amazed.

Several men gasped. A couple raised their weapons, cradling them like children might Teddy bears. Even Sheriff Austin lost his usual stoic grimace, his jaw slackened along with his flashlight and his firearm. The unmistakable scent of seawater filled Jacob's nostrils while frigid air reached out from the opening, embracing him in a cold, invisible blanket. His mind told him to back away, to turn and run, but his feet refused to budge. Standing frozen with a mixture of fear and astonishment, his eyes watered from the landscape's blinding brightness. Still, Jacob's body refused to turn away. On either side, Charlie and the other men seemed to regain their senses. Without a word, they spun around and ran back the way they'd come, leaving Jacob and the sheriff alone at the unnatural entrance.

Sheriff Austin, however, didn't retreat. Taking a ginger step forward, then another, he approached the opening. Lifting his gloved hand, his fingers reached for the open sky beyond.

Jacob yanked at Austin's coat, pulling him backwards. "Don't."

Eyeing the ground, Jacob found a small rock and picked it up, then tossed it through the opening, watching it cross into another world. It landed in a white puff of virgin snow. Whatever it was, it wasn't an illusion. Unfortunately, while his experiment might have seemed to prove that the view was indeed a doorway of some sort, that only urged the sheriff closer. There was an eagerness in his eyes that Jacob hadn't noticed before.

With a single lunge, Austin stepped out of the cave, thrusting himself into the tundra. Jacob blinked, trying to process what he was seeing.

The sheriff stood on the snowy peak, turning around and around, looking up and down and every which way, as if trying to take in the enormity of it all. Tears streaked down his craggy cheeks, though whether due to the blinding sunlight or the awesomeness of what he was experiencing, Jacob couldn't decide.

"Sheriff?"

Austin stomped about gleefully, knee high in snow, then burst out laughing.

"Sheriff?" Jacob called again, his tone rising. "Come back!"

Suddenly, the sunlight dimmed, and the cave grew darker. The gaping entrance along the wall grew smaller, replaced by ice and frost. As if noticing something had changed on his own side as well, Austin's smile slackened. Leaping forward, he reached out for Jacob. Too late—

The wall sealed shut. Jacob stood alone in darkness, too stunned to react.

Once his brain was able to fully process what had just happened, Jacob began pounding against the solid ice-rock wall. He screamed and screamed until his voice grew hoarse. His shoulders shrank as a shiver ran from the bottom of his spine all the way to the back of his skull.

Sheriff Austin was gone.

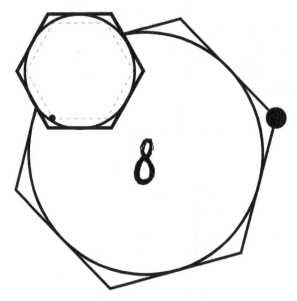

One year earlier

On the third floor of Quantico's federal holding facility, Noelle Reese lay in a gray cement cell, studying tiny cracks running along the ceiling. The squeak of a door opening accompanied a burst of outer light, announcing her newest visitor. A man in his late forties or early fifties entered. After having been interrogated for the last three days, Noelle didn't even bother to sit up.

"I see we're making ourselves comfortable," he said. When she didn't glance in his direction, the man continued. "My name is Joseph Burke."

Noelle sighed, rolled her eyes his way, and then went back to studying the ceiling.

"Congratulations," Burke said, unperturbed by her lack of interest. "Most spies usually wait until they graduate as special agents before trying to hack our systems."

"I'm not a spy." Noelle sat up and curled her arms around her knees.

Burke sat on the concrete floor and leaned against the wall, as if they were lounging on the beach. "But you did use the federal database to access top-secret military files."

"Tried to," she admitted. "It didn't go very well."

He eyed the four gray walls. "Clearly."

"I just want to find out what happened to my father," Noelle said. "I have a right to know."

"Maybe you do, and maybe you don't. Either way, you've been looking in all the *wrong* places."

She studied his rumpled suit, round wire glasses, and receding hairline. "Federal agent or federal lawyer?"

"Theoretical physicist," he said with a shrug.

She laughed. "OK, I admit it. I didn't see that coming."

He matched her smile, as if taking it as a sign to continue. "Like you, I've also lost a family member to . . . *unknown variables.*" Burke stood. "My grandparents, Max and Ruthie Burke, worked at Area 51 back in the late fifties, studying the ship. My grandad, Max, died because of it."

"What are you going on about?"

"*The spaceship,*" he said. "The same one your father boarded seventeen years ago right before he vanished off the face of the earth."

Noelle blinked, then blinked again. She couldn't have heard that right.

Cocking her head to the side, she gave him another look. He didn't *look* crazy. Still, this guy was basically talking about little green men. She glanced at the door behind him, wondering if the guards outside were having a laugh. Before she could come up with a snide rebuttal, Burke drew something metallic from his coat pocket.

The small shape dangled hypnotically in front of her. Military dog tags. Snatching them from his fingers, she read the words imprinted across the dull metal: *Major J. Reese.* Her eyes widened, then glistened with tears. Stroking the dog tags, she cleared her throat and met his gaze.

"How'd you get these?"

Burke grinned. "By looking in the *right* places."

Thirteen months later, Burke had lost his smile as he peered stoically from behind Noelle's laptop screen. Along the edges of the screen, pieces of large, oddly curved machinery hinted at his strange surroundings. The place they called "Watchtower." Considering its bizarre origin and the purpose for which Watchtower had been designed, it seemed an apt title, though now the tower wasn't used for spying through keyholes of time but rather to keep an all-seeing eye on the current inhabitants of Blackwood. Most especially, Casey Stevens, now known as Casey Anderson. What the government hoped to discover, Noelle was never told, and she didn't ask. She was there to find out what had happened to her father. But after a year working undercover as a store owner, she hadn't found any answers. Partly because Casey didn't seem to recall anything about the ship or her ordeal during the years she'd been missing. More to the point, because Burke hadn't *allowed* Noelle to push Casey for answers. "Observation only" had been the rule of the day, as it had been *every* day Noelle had been stuck in Blackwood. At first she'd assumed the assignment was a blessing, as it kept her out of federal prison and promised to provide the answers she'd so desperately been seeking since childhood. Now it felt like the worst kind of prison sentence, one where the walls were invisible, and the answers dangled just out of reach. Burke had promised a lot. So far, though, he'd delivered nothing. Tonight more than ever, her working prison sentence seemed more dreadful as the answers lay curled upstairs, sleeping with her daughter. Noelle's dark complexion showed her frustration clearly through the other end of the computer screen. Burke nodded sympathetically, but to Noelle his crooked frown was as false as his words.

"Just keep her safe and sound," he said, "and the answers will come."

"You've been saying that for over a year now, Burke," Noelle replied through gritted teeth. "At least try to come up with some new material."

The screen replaced Burke's visage with a topographical map of the mountain, an image of the enormous, one-hundred-story Watchtower beside it. At the top of the diagram, a series of boxes indicated the town of Blackwood. Connecting the two locations, a series of jagged lines ran through the ground and up the mountain's interior, almost touching the town's location. The computer-drawn tunnels reminded Noelle of red and blue veins running along a wrist, peeking out just beneath the flesh. Except, these weren't veins, and what pulsed inside was far more deadly and unknown than simple blood cells.

"Are the tunnels still growing?" she asked.

"No idea," Burke admitted, his own concern now clear to see in the corner of the screen. "Hawthorne's last report indicated a growth rate of just under a half mile a day. If that rate stays consistent, they could reach the town by tomorrow. Or they may simply stop at the town's edge. We just don't know."

"When are you sending up Hawthorne's replacement?" Noelle tried to keep the impatience out of her voice, but it was a losing battle.

"I'm working on it," Burke replied. "But as you know, I try to only recruit those like ourselves, ones who have a personal connection to the ship, or this place."

Noelle cursed inwardly. *Yeah, because we're easier to control. Who needs a large government budget when you can dangle long-lost answers in front of someone like a bucket of water in the desert?* Again, her fingers absently rubbed the dog tags hidden beneath her shirt. She cleared her throat. "We need someone out here ASAP. The damage to Casey's home wasn't extensive, but it could be the first sign of one of the tunnels breaking through. Not to mention whatever killed Hawthorne."

The geological map vanished, and Burke's visage filled the screen once again. He shook his head. "Don't let your imagination get the better of you. Chances are it was simply a mountain lion."

Noelle leaned closer to the screen, her chin almost touching the laptop while her eyes bored into his. "That was not a mountain lion. Or a bear. Something tore him apart, piece by piece."

Burke brushed her concerns aside. "It could have been any—"

The screen blinked out, along with the house's power, plunging the living room into blackened shadow. Chunks of moonlight created wedged shapes along the hardwood floors and baby-blue plaster walls. Noelle rose off the couch and felt the ground quiver beneath her bare feet. Bracing herself for a sudden lurch, she half expected the house to sink into the ground, like Casey's had. But for the moment it remained steady. Instead, sprinkles of yellow light shone through tiny cracks along the floorboards, as if someone were running flashlights underneath. Only there was nothing under the floor. No basement. No lower level. Nothing but dirt and earth.

CRRRAAAACKKKK!

The sound was worse than the house's tremor. It put her teeth on edge and made her mind swim. A shudder ran along the floorboards, up her feet and legs, and twisted her gut before crawling up her spine and wiping her mind clear of anything beyond the impending threat, though what the threat was remained unclear. Spinning about, she glanced across the darkened living room, searching for signs of imminent danger. And then she found it.

Jagged splinters cut across the wall like invisible knives slicing along the surface. More pale yellow light shone through, brighter than moonlight. The cracks continued to spread across the room, moving toward the staircase. Noelle tried to remember how close her sidearm was from her current location. She had a 9mm tucked away in the kitchen cupboard and another stored in her bedside table. Noelle wanted to feel the comfort of a weapon in her palm. The desire was neither logical nor practical, but the idea thundered loud enough in her mind that her body urged itself into action. Slipping on tennis shoes, she bolted for the kitchen and found the weapon. As she'd hoped, the weight of it in her right hand brought a momentary feeling of comfort.

With a heavy sigh, she returned to the living room, ascending the staircase. Below, moonlight vanished from view, and all that lit her way was the jagged yellow lines that continued to spread toward the second floor. Noelle didn't need to guess where the rippled, torn edges were headed. The guest bedroom.

Her heart rate quickened along with her footsteps as she rushed up the steps. As if reacting to her quickened pace, the cracks formed faster and deeper, slicing through the plaster wall, and beating her to the bedroom door. The door buckled and whined. Wood splintered as wicked lines cut across its surface. Like knives cutting through a soft pumpkin, the lines seemed to form odd shapes. Her right hand tightened around her weapon while her left turned the knob. Swinging the door ajar, a pale yellow glow poured out, blinding her.

Engulfed in light, Noelle entered the bedroom.

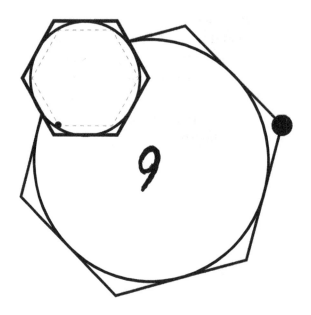

9

G one?" Deputy Hodges' eyes bulged from their sockets. "What do you mean, *gone*?"

"He stepped through the portal, or whatever it was," Jacob stammered, falling to his knees in exhaustion after his run out of the ice cave and back into the safety of the forest. "Then the wall closed and he . . . he was just gone!"

The hunters stood silently on either side of Hodges. To his right were those who had remained outside the cave; to his left were those who had gone in. Although none of them had seen the wall close, sealing Sheriff Austin's fate, the hunters to Deputy Hodge's left had at least seen the strange portal. Their pale expressions seemed to back up Jacob's account enough for Hodges to think twice about running into the cave himself. He lingered at the edge, his feet just outside of where the crystalline floor began at the cave's threshold. Jacob couldn't tell if Hodges believed him, but either way, he hesitated to run in and check for himself.

Huddled together around the cave's mouth, each man glanced at the icicle-covered entrance, as if it were an open, screaming mouth with long glassy needles for teeth, daring them to enter. No one did.

"Well, shit," Hodges said, "We can't just leave him in there."

Jacob shook his head. "I'm telling you, he's not inside the cave."

Hodges seemed unable to comprehend what Jacob was saying, or at least he wasn't willing to fully embrace such a ludicrous idea. "People don't just up and vanish!"

"He didn't vanish!" Jacob shouted, more out of fear than frustration. "He walked through the fucking wall into some kind of—I don't know—portal or something. I saw him standing under bright sunlight, knee high in winter snow."

"That's . . ." Hodges paused, drawing his words out, as if his mind was trying to make up what to say next. "That's . . . just . . . not . . . I mean, that's—what you're saying simply doesn't make any fucking sense."

Jacob straightened his back and tossed his thumb over his shoulder toward the frigid cave. "Go on in and look for yourself!"

Hodges didn't budge. His eyes rolled up in his head, as if trying to either come up with a solution or simply slow things down long enough to think clearly. In either case, Hodges came up short. He turned his back on the cave and pulled out his cell phone. "I should call this in."

One of the hunters who'd gone inside the cave, Charlie, shook his head. "You ain't getting any reception out here. We'll need to get closer to town."

Hodges hesitated, glancing again at the cave's icy mouth. "I can't leave. You go and—"

Something darted out of the surrounding foliage. In a blink of an eye, Charlie was gone, along with whatever had taken him.

His screams echoed through the trees as he was dragged about by an unseen entity. Hodges and the hunters raised their weapons and placed their backs to each other in a circle. Jacob lingered to the side, trembling at the cave's entrance. Everyone had been so consumed by the cave and the sheriff's disappearance that they'd forgotten why they were out there in the first place. As Charlie's screams faded to a soft gurgle, however, the remaining men realized just how much danger they were in.

Watching the hunters swing their weapons about blindly, Jacob stumbled backwards, inching farther into the cave's gaping icicles. While the cave was far from safe, it had to be better than standing out in the open. Or so he hoped.

Foliage shook soundlessly about the frightened hunters. Under the shadowy canopy, Jacob couldn't see their sweaty faces, but he could smell their fear on the soft breeze. And, he assumed, so could their attacker. Whatever it was, the thing had moved faster than Jacob's eyes could register. One minute, Charlie had been standing right beside him. The next, a black thing had burst from nowhere and taken the burly six-foot-something foreman back into the woods without a single shot fired. The creature had to be huge. And fast. And strong.

None of those thoughts gave him any comfort. Judging by the way the remaining men fidgeted, their rifles spinning about aimlessly, it seemed they had similar concerns. After what seemed an eternity of haggard breaths shattering the surrounding silence, Hodges stepped away from the group, eyeing the bushes on either side of them.

"Charlie?" his voice was so soft, even Jacob, hunched only a few feet away, had trouble hearing him. If the foreman were still alive somewhere in the dark, there was little chance he would have detected such a quiet plea. As if thinking along the same lines, Hodges raised his voice. "Charlie!"

Still no reply. Not even the sound of birds chirping or branches snapping. The forest was dead silent, and the silence was even more haunting than Charlie's screams. But where Jacob's vision was dulled by blackened leaves and stoic trees, his other senses seemed to kick into high gear. The scent of sweat and musty earth wafted his nostrils. And something else. It was a smell he couldn't quite place, but an image of damp fur came to mind. Precious moments before he heard the rustle of leaves and snapping twigs, the scent grew stronger.

Closer.

Jacob ducked behind the cave's curvature just as a blackened thing burst through the woods and leapt at the deputy. This time the hunters were ready—or so they thought. Gunfire shattered the silence like ear-piercing thunder. Muzzle flashes lit up the woods. Jacob caught a glimpse of a giant gleaming mouth shaped by two long, curving fangs—ripping and tearing through the mass of men.

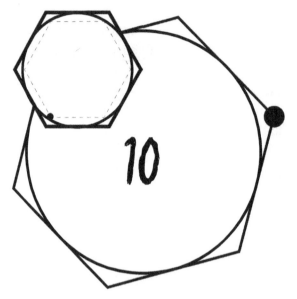

10

Hours earlier

Soon after dinner and long before they'd cleaned the dishes, Sheriff Austin knocked on the door of Noelle's house looking for Jacob.

Casey's husband had tried to put on a brave face, but it didn't go well. His shoulders sagged as he followed the sheriff out. Just before he left, Casey tried to offer up a few words of encouragement, but they fell flat. She knew what was bothering him, but she wasn't eager to dredge up the past. While she didn't know every detail about the incident almost twenty years ago, she knew enough.

Her fiancé, Arthur, had returned to Blackwood hoping to find her, only to end up vanishing himself. Several others had died, including Jacob's father. How he'd died was the reason Jacob never owned a gun, never went into the woods, and never, ever, went hunting.

Until tonight.

She hoped the trek out into the woods, searching for whatever had killed that man, might bring him some closure.

By the time the dishes were done, it was way past Sarah's bedtime. Casey laid beside her in the dark, assuring her that everything would be fine.

"I'm not scared," Sarah whispered, and it even sounded like she meant it. Still, something seemed to be bothering her. Sarah hadn't been loud or difficult to put to bed, and that in of itself was strange enough. Casey assumed it was because Sarah wasn't sleeping in her own bed, so she lay beside her, hoping to help her fall asleep.

After a pause, Sarah's voice returned in Casey's ear. "She's not your friend, Mom. Not really."

Casey turned around on the pillow, finding her daughter's gaze amidst chunks of shadow. "Who?"

"Noelle."

Casey chuckled. "Don't be ridiculous, honey. She was nice enough to let us stay here."

A long silence lingered between them like a looming golem. "She's not being nice," Sarah said finally. "She's watching us."

Casey glanced at the cracked doorway, a sliver of light spilling into the pitch-black room. No one was standing there. "It's been a long day, hon. Let's get some sleep."

Undeterred, Sarah continued to push. "She blames you for something."

Casey rubbed her daughter's small head, trying to comfort her. When that didn't seem to work, she decided to placate Sarah's imagination. "What could she possibly blame me for?"

"I don't know, but she does." Sarah rolled away. "She hates you."

She hates you. Those words sprang to mind the moment Casey's eyes snapped open, and she found Noelle at the bedroom door, pistol in hand.

While instinctively shielding her sleeping daughter with her body, Casey took in the larger, more otherworldly threat, which quickly became apparent. Cracks streaked across the walls like jagged snakes, cutting through plaster and wood to reveal a yellow light from within. The sight of it made her nauseous, as if the light had reached inside her gut and tossed her dinner contents about. Nothing about that light appeared natural. Whatever it was, Casey knew instinctively that it posed a far worse danger than the woman at the door or her raised pistol.

Noelle stepped into the room, but then a crack widened from the walls down to the floorboards, tearing the floor apart in a ragged design. Almost instantly, the gap widened from one foot to three. Noelle hesitated in the doorway, as if unsure whether to make the leap or not. Instead, she tucked her firearm in her waistband and threw out her arms.

"Jump!" she screamed over the house's thundering quakes.

Casey grabbed Sarah in a bundle of blankets and edged closer to the end of the bed. Below, the crack in the floor widened even farther. From within a yellowish luminescence grew blindingly bright, engulfing Casey's vision.

Staring into the light, Casey's stomach lurched. Her teeth rattled in her gums, as if threatening to tumble out in a shower of bone. For a moment it seemed impossible to focus on anything above the din of nausea. Then Noelle's plea broke over the house's disturbing creaks and violent whines.

"Jump!"

No longer able to see beyond the sickly light, Casey closed her eyes, took a deep breath, and leaped off the bed and into the light.

Then, as if an invisible switch had been thrown, the world went black.

When Casey landed on her knees with a hollow thud, she found herself alone, no longer cradling Sarah. The emptiness in her arms ached as she spun about, searching for her daughter. Lifting herself off a shimmering, metallic floor, her jaw slackened at the view around her. She wasn't in Noelle's house or anywhere else even remotely familiar. Casey was standing in a gray corridor. Through the curved walls, pulsing light reflected at odd angles, casting shadows that seemed to move with a life of their own.

"Sarah!" Taking a step forward, the pain from her fall sent fire up her knees to her thighs, causing her to stumble. "Sarah!"

Undeterred, she forced herself to rise and continue forward. Panic setting in, the thundering in her chest grew as rapid as her breath. Under any other circumstances, the shock of where she was or how she'd gotten there would have been foremost on her mind. But right then, all she cared about was finding her little girl. With each step down the mysterious hallway, her breathing grew faster until her head was swimming from the rush. Swooning on wobbly legs, Casey leaned against the curved wall, trying to catch her breath and clear her mind enough to continue.

When the cobwebs around her thoughts began to dissipate, Casey noticed that the sounds of her breathing seemed distant and hollow. Again, she called for Sarah. This time she noted how dim her voice seemed in the long corridor, as if it had been swallowed by the sheer size of the strange environment. While her mind attempted to work out how she had gotten from Noelle's bedroom to this . . . this *other place*, her body continued forward, unwilling to halt the search.

"Saaarrraaaahhh!" Casey screamed so loud it took out the last of her lung capacity.

Eventually, too exhausted to continue, she stumbled backwards and crumpled to the floor. Tears welled in her eyes as the full desperation of her situation settled in. Fear sat in her gut like a boulder, weighing her down. She reached up to the slick wall for purchase but found none. Reeling onto her knees, Casey choked back the next wave of tears and forced herself to rise. Wherever she was and whatever was happening didn't matter. All that counted was finding Sarah. One foot in front of the other, Casey pushed away any other thoughts beyond her daughter and focused on the mission at hand. After a few more steps, her legs grew stronger, and her walk turned to a run.

The distant sound of her rushing footsteps grew increasingly disorienting in her eardrums, but Casey pressed on, curving around the corridor's bend and into the next hall. It looked no different, though it seemed colder, as if she'd suddenly stepped from a warm beach into a meat locker. Casey stumbled to a halt.

Meat locker . . .

Something about that idea sounded familiar. But where or when she'd had such a thought eluded her. Like a dangling morsel just out of reach, the idea teased her appetite for answers. Adding to the confusion, the enormous, freezing tunnel felt vaguely familiar.

I've been here before. That realization made her flesh shiver far more than from the cold.

Over the last eight years, she'd come to terms with not knowing what had happened to her. Yet, standing in the corridor, she knew for certain that this was where she had been. Perhaps not the entire time but certainly for some of it. And although she couldn't recall when or how, she knew without a doubt that the last time she was there she'd felt afraid and alone. Just like now. Except this time it was worse because her daughter was gone.

Is she even in here? Casey hesitated as she let this idea play out in her mind. *Maybe Sarah's still back at the house with Noelle. Safe. Maybe I'm the only one missing.* After all, she reminded herself, this had happened before. Snatched from her home. Alone.

Her heart rate slowed for the first time since arriving in the mysterious corridor as this fresh concept grew into a newfound hope. It warmed her chest and settled her nausea. There didn't appear to be anyone else there except her. Whoever—or whatever—had brought her there might very well have only wanted Casey. But why?

Continuing her pace unabated, the assuredness that she'd been there before grew stronger with every step until she found herself standing at a crossroads. Two hallways stretched out to the left and the right, both darker than the one down which she had already ventured. In the distance, twinkles of shimmering light waved enticingly. Would one of them offer an escape? Rocking back and forth on the balls of her feet, she couldn't decide which way to go. Again, a tickling feeling of familiarity itched at the back of her mind while a silent thought urged her to go left.

Casey ignored it and went right.

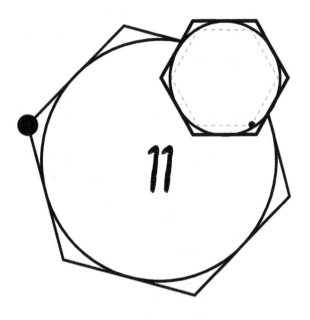

11

One moment Noelle was perched in her doorway, urging Casey to jump across the bright yellow gap and into her arms for safety. The next she found herself anywhere but someplace safe. She was trapped in a tight cocoon of white with fluid drenching her skin and a tube running up her nose and mouth. Even before trying to move her body or escape whatever she was trapped inside, her first instinct was to reach down in search of her firearm. Surprisingly, she found it still nestled in her waistband. Relieved, she grasped the weapon with her right hand, then used her left to push against the tightness confining her. It appeared to be a sack of some sort, flexible but strong enough that any pushing or prodding had little to no effect. Noelle decided to try her gun instead. Forcing it through the gelatinous liquid, she pressed the muzzle against the sack's membrane-covered surface and pulled the trigger.

Noelle spilled to the floor. Her skin and clothing covered in goo, she yanked tubes from her face and inhaled, only to choke on a gasped breath. A mixture of toxic stenches and moldy odors assaulted her senses. She flopped onto her stomach and vomited. Trembling more from fear than the frigid onslaught, Noelle remained on the floor. She checked her arms and legs, making sure she wasn't injured. She appeared to be unharmed. Physically, at least. Her mental state, on the other hand, was another story. She tried to joke to herself about what she would tell a therapist someday about all this. Instead of alleviating any tension, however, the thought only soured in her gut. Some things simply couldn't be laughed off. As she spun onto her back, gazing up at the odd sack-like form she'd just escaped, the horror of her surroundings set in.

Row upon row, thousands of similar white sacks covered in red-lined membranes dangled from an unseen ceiling far overhead. Each sack contained a vague outline of every conceivable human size and shape. A large man, a thin woman, even small children. Noelle shuddered at the ghastly view, struggling to her feet as more and more ghostly silhouettes peered back, unmoving, as if frozen in place. It took all of Noelle's willpower not to crumple back to the floor and scream. She couldn't help but wonder why she was awake while all these others slept. Then an even more immediate concern sprang to mind. While Noelle had a nagging suspicion as to where she might be, it was nothing more than mere guesswork. She assumed she'd fallen through the yellow light into an underground tunnel, and this was the other side. A bit like Alice in Wonderland, she thought, except, the creepy, scary version. While Watchtower had never confirmed what had created the tunnels in the first place, she knew they contained doorways to other times and other places. The past and the future. Hawthorne had told her as much. If that were true, then this was clearly not the past. Noelle was in the future.

Turning on her heel, she headed along rows of hanging sacks. Keeping her eyes glued to the gray floor, she tried to ignore the frozen figures dangling on either side. A strong aroma of something akin to spoiled milk invaded her nostrils, growing stronger as she slipped between rows, searching for an exit. Careful not to touch any of the hanging sacks or their horrifying contents, Noelle instead focused on the growing stench, following it like a mouse might to moldy cheese.

That's what she was, Noelle decided, a mouse in a maze. And if this was the future, then she needed a way back to her own time. She wasn't looking for an exit sign or even a doorway; she was searching for the yellow light. If it had brought her there, then perhaps it might lead her back home. It was a long shot, but it was the only idea that came to mind. And a goal, any goal, seemed better than none. Passing a third, then a fourth row of swinging sacks and silhouetted figures, Noelle began to wonder if there would ever be an end in sight. She paused, glancing back the way she'd come, and wondered if she should try going the other way.

Suddenly, a hand grabbed her mouth, yanking her backwards. She fell, sprawled between swaying sacks. Drawing her weapon, Noelle spun. The weapon's barrel stopped between two familiar green eyes.

Casey Anderson was staring back at her, holding her finger to her own lips. "Shhhh!"

Noelle hesitated before lowering her gun. If Casey noticed, she didn't slow down long enough to show it.

"At least now I know this isn't a dream," Casey said, glancing about.

Noelle cocked her head. "What?"

"I just . . . I thought maybe this was all in my head," Casey replied. Noelle could tell there was more to her reaction, but she didn't press. Under the circumstances, she had to admit she might have thought it was a dream too, if not for what she'd learned from Watchtower.

"No," Noelle said, holstering her gun. "This isn't a dream."

Instead of asking where they were or how'd they arrived, Casey grabbed Noelle's shoulders, pulling her closer. "Have you seen Sarah?"

Noting the fear in the woman's voice, Noelle shook her head. Until then it hadn't even occurred to her that she wasn't the only one who'd fallen into the other side of the yellow light. But if Casey was there, so was Sarah. And whatever issues Noelle might have had with Casey, she wasn't so coldhearted as to include a seven-year-old girl in her vendetta.

With a resigned sigh, Noelle waved for Casey to follow. "Let's try this way."

They snuck along another aisle of silent bodies and hanging sacks, following the stench to its source. As Noelle had hoped, the aroma brought a breeze with it, pressing against them from a distant, darkened shaft. There was no yellow light, but it was at least an exit from that room. Shifting her gaze beside her, she noted the pained expression on Casey's pale, sweat-covered face. She was desperate to find her daughter. Just as desperate, Noelle added inwardly, as she was to discover what had happened to her father. Absently, her fingers went to her collar, fingering her dad's dog tags. Maybe her own answers might be hidden somewhere up ahead. However, as she passed a human male locked in a silent scream behind a red membrane, Noelle prayed that neither Sarah nor her father were there, encased in liquid cocoons. Frozen and afraid. Any fate, even death, would have been better. Without a backward glance, she led Casey out of the room and away from the suspended horrors.

The tunnel before them opened into a vast, empty hall with walls curving far overhead into archways. It reminded her of a church or a cathedral, although if this were a place of worship, it was certainly for no god she recognized. Dark gray walls with a shimmering floor below created distant echoes from their footsteps. Sound itself seemed distorted, as if pausing too long between their footfalls and the thin reverberation their feet caused against the surface. A part of her wanted to speak to discover how the odd effect might reverberate when amplified by their voices, but the tightness in her gut kept her silent. Worse than the odd sound was the scent of spoiled milk that had now grown strong enough to invade her closed mouth. She could taste the wretched air on her tongue, causing her throat to contract and spasm from a gag reflex. Casey didn't seem to notice or care. Consumed by finding her daughter, the strange woman with the mysterious past looked far more alert and focused than Noelle had ever seen her before. She wondered if perhaps some piece of Casey's lost memories might be bubbling to the surface, and if so, whether those memories would be a help or a hindrance. There were already too many unknown variables. As much as Noelle might want the answers that Casey's dormant memories contained, she felt it best for the docile middle-aged waitress to remain as ignorant as before. Right now Casey was happy to follow her lead, but if she regained her memories and all the knowledge that came with them, Noelle doubted she'd be able to lead her along on an invisible leash quite so easily. No, she decided, best that Casey stay in the mental dark just a while longer, until they escaped.

If we escape, she corrected herself.

Beside her, Casey gasped. Turning, Noelle followed Casey's surprised stare to an opening in a distant wall. Beyond, giant shapes expanded and condensed, like breathing lungs. Stepping closer, they made out the distinct shape of machinery mixed with what appeared to be living, breathing tissue. It was a grotesque sight, mixing gray machinery with pink-fleshed organic material. A hodgepodge of elements not quite discernible but close enough that their combination froze the blood that was flooding Noelle's brain. Her spine went rigid as her eyes drifted off the horrid machinery toward two rows of tall gray figures. Connected by wires from their mouths to the enormous organic machine, they looked like strings of spaghetti being shared from the same bowl. The figures did not move or turn in their direction as Noelle and Casey approached. Noelle's basest instincts, her lizard brain, wanted to turn back and search for another route. But Casey had already marched ahead, desperate to find Sarah.

They stopped at the edge of the room, staring in disbelief at the sleeping figures that stood erect on either side of the machine. Tracing the wires from the breathing machine to the gray being's mouths, Noelle wondered if it was somehow feeding them. If so, what sort of food would such creatures eat?

Worse were the gray creatures themselves.

Although she'd read enough reports to know what these beings were, and more importantly, what they *were not,* seeing them in the flesh was a shock to the system. The sight of their gray scaled bodies with no genitalia and large bulbous heads shaped around oval black eyes caused the back of her skull to throb with silent warning. While familiar, to see these things up close overwhelmed her senses and caused her to step back. The reports she'd read had called the gray beings "seekers." Not alien but human in origin. The next evolutionary step for humankind. That thought, more than any other, made Noelle's skin crawl and her head swim. Casey, however, didn't show any signs of wonder or disgust. Without hesitating, the woman reached out and touched the closest seeker, running her pink nails across its gray skin.

"I've seen them before," Casey said, turning to Noelle. "They're . . . human?"

Noelle nodded. "So, you do remember."

Casey withdrew her hand and stepped away from the dormant creature. She shook her head, as if fighting back bad memories. "No . . . no . . . I don't . . ." Her voice died in her throat.

Noelle considered prodding her further but decided against it. It was neither the time nor the place. She pulled Casey away from the figures, leading her deeper into the room.

"Come on," she said, trying to snap Casey out of her wandering thoughts. "We need to keep looking for Sarah."

Casey's expression soured, as if she'd momentarily forgotten about her own daughter. "Sarah . . . yes . . . yes!" Her pace quickened. Rushing past the sleeping creatures, they headed toward a shimmering light at the rear of the chamber. A light at the end of the proverbial tunnel.

Noelle felt her heart lift in her chest as the light blazed with a sickly pale yellow glow, the same as the one that had brought them there. At last they'd found their exit. But would Casey be willing to leave without Sarah? Noelle ran through various options in her mind as they closed the gap between them and the bright luminescence. She couldn't leave Casey there, not when she still held all the answers Noelle needed. So, either she would have to stay there until they found Sarah, or she'd have to force Casey back through the light. A blow to the back of the head would subdue her enough for Noelle to carry her the rest of the way, but that would mean abandoning a young child in that awful place. Could she do that?

Thankfully, Noelle never had to discover the answer.

Ahead, a small silhouette stood with her back to them. Sarah. In front of her, suspended ten feet off the ground, a naked old woman with hundreds of wires pouring out of every inch of her body hung suspended, like a spider in its web. The image was so startling that Noelle momentarily forgot about Sarah and stared agog at the hideous old woman. With only a thin layer of flesh wrapped about her skeletal frame, she appeared more like a living mummy than an old woman. Beyond old. *Ancient.* Black liquid pumped from her body through the tubes and into a series of breathing machines.

Unconcerned by anything but her daughter, Casey dove forward, wrapping her arms around the little girl. Sarah didn't turn. Didn't even flinch. Gazing up at the old woman, the child pointed upwards. "That's me, Mommy."

If Casey heard, let alone understood, Sarah's words, they seemed to have no effect. "I'm here, honey," she said. "Mommy's here. Everything's going to be alright."

"Mom . . ." A withered, faint voice said from above. It wasn't the little girl. Unattached by the emotion of the scene, Noelle understood before Casey did. Again, the old woman spoke. "Mommy?"

All color drained from Casey's face as she gazed up at the ancient thing. Her body shuddered as her mind seemed to slowly put the pieces together.

The living mummy, with wires pouring from its body, was little Sarah, all grown up.

Casey stood, clutching her daughter. Her lips opened and shut, unable to find the words.

Suddenly, the pale yellow light returned. Noelle felt the light before she saw it. A fiery warmth blazed across her face while shades of yellow peeked into her peripheral vision. Stretching around them, the light burned brighter, engulfing her vision. Through closed eyelids, stars formed, so many that her skull felt like it was on fire. Distantly, she heard Casey and Sarah scream. Their voices trailed off, then died.

At last the light seeping through Noelle's eyelids grew darker, and the stars receded.

Hesitantly, Noelle opened her eyes, terrified of what she might see next.

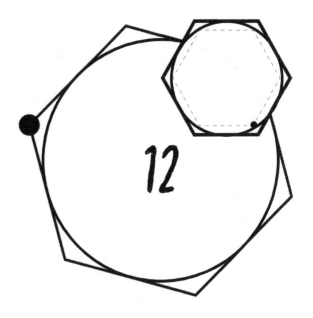

12

Jacob lingered at the mouth of the cave, hidden behind hanging icicles that spread over him like shimmering spears. Peeking through the frozen obstacles, he watched in horror as a huge shape tore through the hunters. Though his view was obstructed by the forest's canopy shadow, a cacophony of screams and bursts of gunfire punctuated the frenzied chaos.

Amidst the cluster of darting silhouettes, the largest belonged to a great beast, catlike in shape, though twice as large as any lion or tiger Jacob had ever seen. And even then, only on television. But this was in the flesh, mere feet away, and whatever it was, the creature was ferocious in its assault. Huge taloned paws swatted several men aside with a single blow while twin elongated fangs flashed from its jaws, only to vanish into the shoulder of one of the hunters. With a twist of its neck, the beast flung the man across the woods. In that moment, revealed through fractured moonlight, Jacob saw the thing that was quickly slaughtering the hunting party. Still, his mind protested what his eyes revealed.

What he saw *could not exist.*

Screaming inwardly, his body shrank even lower into the cave's entrance, terrified that the beast might see him. Beyond all reason or explanation, the near-mythical creature reared its enormous fanged mouth in a roar. Through shafts of moonlight, Jacob stared, dumbstruck, at the supposedly long-extinct beast, covered in blood and dirt.

The sabertooth tiger threw its thick neck backwards and let out a blood-curdling roar.

Before Jacob's mind could fully catch up with what his eyes revealed, something flung out from the chaos, tumbling to the ground only a few feet away. A torn arm twitched amongst the grass, its fingers still clutching a pump-action shotgun. Jacob eyed the weapon for what seemed an eternity, trying to decide whether to chance venturing out of the cave or not. Was it worth the risk? In quick reply, his mind answered: *What's the alternative? Lying on your belly while everyone else is torn to shreds?*

Yes, he admitted. After all, he was safe right where he was, at least for the time being.

But what about after the others were all dead? Would the creature leave? Or would it pick up Jacob's scent and stalk him into the cave? With a shake of his head, Jacob pushed the cowardly, shameful thoughts aside. He couldn't just watch them all die. He had to act. Though, so far, he hadn't yet found the will or the strength to stand, much less move. A shrill scream broke through his rambling thoughts, urging him into action.

Pushing forward on his haunches, Jacob crawled from the cave, scrambling toward the bloody arm and its weapon. He kept his eyes low, focused on the blood-covered shotgun, not wishing to look up at the carnage on display only a short distance beyond.

As soon as Jacob had crawled beyond the shadows of the cave, he felt naked, exposed, in the lighter shadows that the high treetop canopy provided. Every inch closer to the torn arm seemed to take a lifetime while the screams grew more fevered and desperate. His heart thundering in his chest, Jacob scrambled through the grass, reaching for the shotgun. Grasping the barrel, he drew it to himself, along with the arm, its fingers clutching the handle in a death grip. Usually, such a thing would have revolted him to the point of stopping in mid-act. But right then, Jacob's terror far outweighed his revulsion. With a heavy shake, he dislodged the fingers and freed the weapon. The dismembered arm dropped to the ground with a wet smack.

Jacob rose, wobbling on shaky legs that bent and twisted beneath him. Raising the shotgun to his shoulder, a memory flash of the last time he'd held a shotgun came to mind. The night he'd been forced to shoot his own father. After all these years, he could still feel the faint echo from the recoil slamming against his shoulder. Spreading his legs wide apart, Jacob raised the weapon and focused on the nightmare before him.

The beast tossed another victim aside before it turned its enormous snout toward Deputy Hodges. His rifle empty, Hodges drew his sidearm, firing wildly at the creature, though seemingly missing every shot. Jacob took that lesson to heart and inhaled a slow, steady breath. Pumping a shell into the chamber, he carefully lined up his shot. Before firing, he decided to take another long step forward, closing the distance between himself and the beast by a third. At this close range, he doubted he'd miss. If he did, it would be Hodges who would pay the price. Jacob heard the deputy's revolver click over and over, its chambers empty. Whether or not Hodges had landed any shots, Jacob couldn't tell. Just how many rounds would it take to kill a thing of this size? Remembering the recoil from the last time he'd fired a shotgun all those years ago, Jacob leaned into the weapon. He needed to make this shot count. He might not get a second.

The beast swatted its large paw at Hodges, knocking him to the ground. It loomed over him, its bloody teeth dripping across the deputy's terrified face. It was now or never.

BOOM!

The volume of the shotgun's blast was more jarring than the recoil. It made Jacob's eardrums scream with a clanging ring. He pumped in a second shell and fired again before seeing if the first shot had had any effect. As it turned out, the first round had hit the creature in its right rear leg, tearing off a chunk of its hindquarters. But by the time Jacob had reloaded and fired a second shot, the sabertooth tiger had already vanished into the foliage. Smears of blood across enlarged leaves left a trail behind, as well as evidence of Jacob's successful attack, though it didn't bring him much relief. If anything, Jacob's heart rate only climbed while he spun the weapon about, scanning the surrounding trees for any sign of movement. After a drawn-out breath, he lowered the weapon slightly. The beast appeared to be gone. For now.

Deputy Hodges lay crying on the ground like a newborn having just escaped its mother's womb. Jacob rushed over. Gibbering incoherently, the deputy's words slurred with no meaning beyond fractured syllables. Jacob shook him, trying to snap him out of it, to no avail.

Glancing across the wooded field, Jacob noted multiple men struggling to rise, seemingly as disoriented and as terrified as Hodges. Eyeing splotches of gore along the grass, with hints of limbs and intestines spread about like confetti, Jacob knew he wouldn't have fared any better if he hadn't hidden in the cave. That thought, and the guilt that accompanied it, burned him from within. Still, he reminded himself, Hodges and the others were only alive now because of him. Because, in the end, he'd acted. He may not have been a hero, but, he assured himself, he wasn't a coward either.

Suddenly, a huge shape burst from the trees and hobbled toward him. Jacob spun, raising the shotgun.

CLICK!

The chamber was empty. The beast paused several feet away, as if waiting to see if the firestick would cause more injury. Jacob pumped the shotgun and pulled the trigger again.

CLICK!

His arms dropped, cradling the useless weapon like a club as the beast recognized it was no longer in danger. Its paws clambered forward. Approaching him.

Jacob spun and ran full tilt, back into the cave. The sabertooth was hard on his heels.

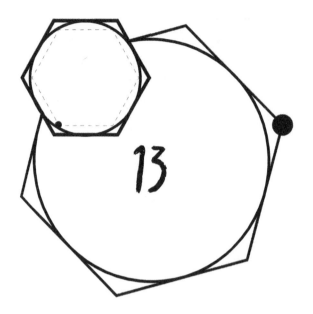

13

Under any other circumstances, the creature would have caught up to Jacob before he had entered the cave, but because it was wounded, Jacob had a slight head start. It was a slim lead and growing shorter, as evidenced by the sound of the creature's loud, rapid breathing echoing along the icy walls. Jake was still clutching the empty shotgun as he ran farther and farther into the cave. The tunnel curved to the right, leading him back toward where the portal had been. Would he too get trapped in some other place, like the sheriff? Hearing the rapid breathing close behind, Jacob wasn't sure which fate would be worse. As his lungs burned and his legs grew numb from exhaustion, he decided that, yes, being eaten alive *would* be worse. Much worse. Leaning forward, Jacob ran faster, trying to gain every inch of distance possible.

Although slowed by its injury, the beast kept coming. Even wounded, it didn't seem to tire. Jacob didn't pause to look back, though his mind painted a picture of the snarling, vicious animal pouncing through the ice cave, its mouth open, long teeth wet with blood, anticipating its next meal.

Him.

Snapping Jacob from his nightmarish vision, a light appeared up ahead, just after the next turn. It blazed with a yellowish glow, filling the icy cavern with a warm luminance. With no other option, Jacob used the last of his strength, racing toward the light. Half running and half sliding, he skidded around the turn too fast and tumbled to the floor, falling mere inches from a new portal that had sprung to life. A vast desert of ochres and brightly lit hues blinded him. But that wasn't his concern. Rolling onto his back, Jacob turned just in time to see the monstrous tiger come around the corner. Its pace slowed as it eyed him, as if expecting more of a fight than Jacob had offered. Lying on the floor, Jacob held the empty weapon higher across his chest in a feeble defense. As if knowing its prey was defeated, the beast seemed to grin, exposing its elongated teeth to the portal's light.

Then it leapt.

The weight of it alone took Jacob's breath away, causing him to exhale in a pained gasp as the thing crushed him. More from instinct than conscious thought, Jacob swatted at the beast's head with the butt of the shotgun. Instead of landing a blow, however, the creature bit down on the gun, pushing its fangs down toward Jacob's face. A disgusting mixture of blood and saliva poured over Jacob's eyes and into his mouth. Retching from the taste of it, Jacob spun, kicking his legs about madly beneath the huge animal.

More from luck than skill, Jacob hit the creature's wounded hind leg. It yelped in pain.

Thrashing about, the thing's talons clawed desperately. Jacob felt its claws cut through his jacket and pants, though he couldn't guess at the severity of his wounds. Tilting his body to the right, he pulled the shotgun up and over and then kicked outward, sending the tiger scrambling off him and tumbling into the portal. A mad swarm of blowing sand and flying dust whirled about the creature as it struggled to right itself.

However, if Jacob had hoped the portal would shut immediately, closing the beast off from him, he would have been sorely disappointed. The animal regained its footing, spinning back toward the portal. Toward Jacob.

With no more fight left in him, Jacob remained on the floor, eye to eye with the beast. Awaiting the inevitable. Again the creature pounced, lunging back into the cave.

Then an explosion of noise erupted behind Jacob. Deputy Hodges and several hunters appeared, firing at the beast. Blood splattered out from the desert world and into the cave's icy realm, drenching Jacob in a gory mess.

The sabertooth tiger stumbled back against the onslaught, reeling onto its hindquarters, before its huge head fell backwards into a mound of swirling sand. So transfixed by the beast's dying moans, Jacob didn't notice the portal sealing itself until the wall closed completely, sending the cave back into cold shadow.

It was over.

Stunned silence permeated the dark chamber, broken only by the hunters' heavy, ragged breathing. Sitting upright, Jacob was relieved to find that although his jacket was hanging in shreds, his chest appeared relatively unharmed. His right leg, however, burned as if on fire. Pulling himself to his feet, he noticed a series of gashes running down his thigh. Deep cuts drenched in blood. The beast had left its mark.

By the time Jacob and the hunters had wobbled out of the cave and surveyed the damage, four men were confirmed dead, and another two were missing, their bodies lost somewhere in the darkened woods. Deputy Hodges took charge the best he could, having the hunters scan the area with their flashlights, to no avail. After no one could get a phone signal, they decided to head back to their vehicles and call for help. Most were able to hobble along on their own accord, Jacob included, though some needed help making it back down the slope toward the dirt trail half a mile down.

Every step was agony. Jacob bit his lip, careful not to moan or complain. The memory of having hid within the cave while the others were being slaughtered ate at his gut and caused far more discomfort than his bleeding leg. Still, the farther they walked, the more he felt his head swim from lack of blood. Finally, he was forced to pause halfway down, taking off his shirt and wrapping it around his wound. Hodges stopped and helped, still silent with shock. When it was done, a solemn nod was as close to a conversation as either of them could manage. Jacob just hoped the makeshift bandage would be enough to stop his blood loss until they got back to town. Either way, compared to some of the other men, he'd gotten off easy. Too easy, he thought. Most of the men had long gashes across their bodies, a couple across their faces. Jacob was glad for the lack of light, as each wound he saw only deepened his feelings of guilt.

Having made their way back down to the dirt path, Hodges led them to their trucks. Seven darkened vehicles awaited them, with Jacob's parked in the rear. He'd been the only one who'd come alone. The remaining hunters piled in two trucks, abandoning the rest. Jacob and Hodges continued down the line, flanked by empty vehicles that seemed to punctuate their losses. At the end of the line, the deputy paused in front of his SUV, hesitant to open it. He'd driven the sheriff up there, but now he was heading back without him. Choking back a sob, he grabbed his police radio from inside and reported in. Jacob didn't bother to linger and listen, instead hobbling to his own vehicle. It wasn't until he heard Hodges shout something that Jacob stopped. Not wishing to look back the way he'd come, he peered over the ledge, toward Blackwood.

Only there wasn't any sign of the town.

A blanket of darkness lay sprawled below like a black pit cradled at the bottom of the mountain. Where were all the lights? The entire town couldn't be asleep yet. Where were the lit windows or car headlights? Where were all the streetlamps?

Reaching into his bloody pants pocket, he pulled out his phone and dialed Casey's number. There was still no signal. Hodges and the others approached on either side of him, peering over the cliff at the black void below.

No one said a word. No one needed too. They were all thinking the same thing:

What now?

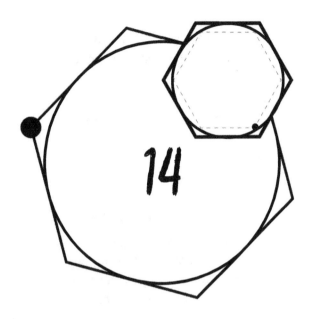

14

"That's *me*, Mommy," young Sarah Anderson said, pointing to the old woman.

It seemed to take an eternity for Casey's mind to catch up with her daughter's assertion. Turning her gaze away from Sarah, she stared at the withered figure dangling overhead. Casey couldn't even begin to guess how old the woman was, though judging from the apparent fragility of her bones and skin, she appeared to be well over a hundred and possibly much older. As Casey's thoughts caught up with Sarah's words, the truth solidified in her mind. *That's me, Mommy.* Casey knew Sarah was right. It was the familiarity of the ancient woman's eyes that provided the first proof. Emerald green, just like hers and Sarah's. But it wasn't the color so much as the emotion behind those wet green eyes.

Then the ancient woman spoke with a paper-thin rasp. "Mom . . ."

Casey felt the connection, with all its horrific connotations, crystalize in a single moment. This old, decrepit *thing*, barely human anymore, with dozens of tubes protruding from her frail body, was Sarah. Or at least a future Sarah. How, or why, this was possible wasn't foremost on her mind. Nor was when or where they might be. Instead, the first anguished thought that burned from the back of Casey's skull to the front was a single, sad question: *Is this what becomes of my precious baby girl?*

Before Casey had time to speak or scream or voice her horror in any other way, a pale yellow light sprang up around her, engulfing them in blinding luminance.

Then there was darkness.

A scent of wood and dust tickled her nose, waking Casey from what she prayed had only been a dream. When her eyes opened, and she found herself lying on a strange floor, her hopes quickly dissipated. A burst of white light announced Noelle's closeness as the young woman scanned the area with her phone's flashlight. She used her left hand to survey their surroundings while clutching a pistol in her right. Why did she have a gun? A vague recollection of something Sarah had said earlier came to mind. Something about Noelle not really being their friend. And there was something else, though Casey's brain was too foggy to recall what it had been. *A warning*, her mind whispered. But what had Sarah said?

Casey bolted upright. *Sarah! Where's Sarah?*

As if reading the concern on her face, Noelle panned her flashlight to the corner of the bed. "She's over there."

Only then did Casey realize they were back in the upstairs bedroom. Sarah was lying on the floor, crumpled in a fetal position at the foot of the bed. A wave of warm relief flooded Casey's senses as she pulled her daughter close. Noelle scanned the girl's back with her flashlight, as if checking for cuts or bruises, not finding any. With a sigh of relief, Casey turned Sarah over. Suddenly, her relief vanished, and a new horror set in. Sarah's once-beautiful round face was pale with red lines spidering out from her eyes and crawling across her cheeks and lips. At the center, her eyes stared outward, unblinking. Noelle's flashlight crept upward, revealing black pits where Sarah's eyes should have been. Gasping in horror, Casey's first thought was that the little girl's eyeballs had been scooped out, leaving her ocular sockets empty and hollow. But upon closer inspection, Casey noted the wet curvature of the black forms lying within her sockets. Sarah's eyes were still there, yet somehow they'd turned completely black. The dark orbs at the center of Sarah's face didn't move or turn in recognition. Casey pushed her head down to her daughter's chest. A steady heartbeat answered.

"She's alive," Casey said, though her words held little relief. "What's wrong with her?"

Noelle moved her phone's flashlight back and forth, checking for any response from Sarah's eyes but found none. "I'll call a doctor."

She tried dialing 911, but there was no signal. Turning on her heel, she went to the bedside lamp and flipped the switch. Nothing happened. "No signal, and the power seems to be—"

The rest of her words turned to a groan as she glanced out the window and stopped cold. Hearing the note of terror in Noelle's voice, Casey lowered Sarah's head to the floor and stood, following Noelle's shocked gaze.

Outside the second-floor bedroom window, there didn't appear to be any stars or silhouetted treetops. The sky was a thick swath of utter black. Noelle, who was standing closer to the window, seemed to notice something else through the glass, but before Casey could approach, Noelle spun around and grabbed her arm.

"Get Sarah," Noelle said. "We need to leave."

"I don't think I should move her—"

"Right now!"

Relenting to the urgency in Noelle's voice, Casey lifted Sarah in her arms and wrapped a pink blanket around her. A craggy broken line still cut across the hardwood floor, though the gap was not nearly as wide as it had been. The pale light, with its odd visions or dreams, was gone. Casey lunged across the gap in a single bound. Then Noelle used her phone's flashlight to lead them down the staircase. The darkened house groaned with each step. Halfway down, the structure tilted. Casey felt her body twist uncontrollably over the railing. Sarah began to slip through the blanket and fall over the side.

Noelle caught them both, pulling Sarah and her shaken mother back from the brink, then pressed them against the wall. In the tiny singular light from her phone, Casey realized Noelle's facial expression and body posture had changed before her eyes. It was as if she were seeing an altogether different woman for the first time. The simple smalltown store clerk had seemingly been replaced by a stronger, commanding presence. Perhaps it was simply the situation. Still, the thought lingered. Her eyes dropped to Noelle's waist, finding the gun tucked into her jeans. Eyeing the weapon, Casey tried to recall what Sarah had told her. "She's not your friend," she had cautioned. "She blames you for something."

What could she possibly blame me for? Casey pushed the question aside. Whatever was happening to Sarah right now was all that mattered. *Keep it together, Case.*

Cradling Sarah close to her chest, she followed Noelle downstairs. Below, the darkness shimmered. Black water, several inches thick, covered the floor. More water dripped out from cracks along the walls. Like bleeding wounds.

"The pipes burst," Noelle said, though not nearly with the amount of concern that Casey thought was warranted. Splashing through the slowly rising water, Noelle raced to the front door and flung it open, only to recoil from what she found.

Curious, Casey stepped off the stairs and into the freezing water. She ignored the shiver running up her body and instead focused on a clumpy black substance filling the doorway.

Outside, there was no lawn or street. Not even a horizon line. In their place stood a wall of brown earth. Jagged gray rocks jutted out beside torn tree roots and mounds of dirt, some of which tumbled inward. Before Casey could process what was happening, Noelle slammed the door and leaned back against it, her fingers shaking as they fumbled with the lock.

"Was that *dirt*?" Casey asked. "What the hell is happening?"

"Isn't it obvious?" Noelle asked, pushing against the door. "We're buried underground."

Stunned, Casey struggled to work up a response. "That's . . . that's impossible."

Noelle grimaced. "Tell that to the mountain of shit blocking our exit."

Once satisfied that the wall of mud wouldn't come crashing through the door, she let out a heavy sigh. Below, water continued to rise while the sound of grinding pipes echoed behind the walls. Finally, Noelle turned around, surveying the darkness with her phone's light. "We need to find another way out of here."

Again, her commanding tone startled Casey. *Whoever this woman is,* a little voice said at the back of Casey's mind, *she's not who you thought she was.* Stepping back onto the bottom step, Casey wondered if that idea was simply her imagination or a result of what Sarah had said, seemingly a lifetime ago.

Something about her isn't right, and you know it. She did. But how did she know?

Casey didn't believe in telepathy or any sort of second sight. And yet, something in her mind seemed to click as colored light blossomed around Noelle like an aura. A dark purplish hue. When Casey blinked, the aura was gone, but her unease remained. Perhaps it had only been her imagination. In fact, maybe this whole crazy situation was one long nightmare. If so, she couldn't wait to wake up.

One look at Sarah's horrific visage, however, and Casey knew this wasn't a dream. She held Sarah close and shivered.

Noelle bolted from one room to the other, searching for a possible escape. Even when she was out of view, Casey heard her wet splashes through the darkness. Casey sank to the bottom step, exhausted. Then something else caught her eye.

A yellow glow seeped through sunken floorboards, casting a strange luminance along the water.

"Noelle . . ." she called out.

When Noelle returned, Casey pointed to the yellow crack beneath the water's surface. "What do you think is down there?"

Noelle shook her head. "Nothing either one of us wants to see. Trust me."

Again that inner voice at the back of Casey's mind whispered, *Don't trust her.*

"You sound as if you know what it is," Casey said, choosing her words carefully.

Noelle fidgeted with her phone. "I'm sure someone will be along shortly to dig us out."

She hadn't answered the question. Casey decided to press. "Houses don't sink into the ground."

"Yours did," Noelle replied. Then the aura returned. This time it was red, edging around Noelle's form. The emotion that most connected the color in Casey's mind was not fear but anger. Whether real or imagined, the different colored auras seemed to reveal emotions that others wished hidden. This time Casey was certain it wasn't her imagination.

"You think this is somehow *my fault*?"

"It is!" Noelle shouted. "This is all happening because of *you*!"

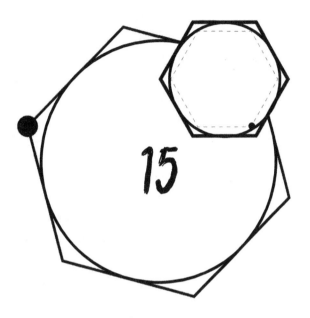

15

A motor caravan snaked through pitch darkness, winding down the base of the northern summit and heading toward town. Jacob's truck was third in line. He kept one hand on the wheel while the other continued to try and get a phone signal. So far, no luck. His gaze dropped to the speedometer, and he grimaced. The caravan was going under twenty miles an hour, taking each dark turn in careful stride. Unable to go any faster, his knuckles whitened around the steering wheel while his face flushed red. So consumed with his own worry and frustrations, he hadn't noticed the truck up ahead skid to a halt until he was almost upon it.

Jacob jerked the wheel, careening off the road. Rocks and debris peppered his windshield.

Lurching to the right, his pickup truck stopped mere inches from a giant pine. His headlights illuminated every tiny detail crisscrossing the tree's bark, as if to accentuate how close he'd come to a head-on collision. If his heart hadn't already been working overtime, that would certainly have done the trick.

Shoving his door open, Jacob crawled out and headed back to the road. Behind him, more vehicles skidded and stopped in similar haphazard fashion. Several heads popped out from various windows, all basically asking the same thing, though using different words.

"What the hell's going on?"

"Everything alright up there?"

"What stupid motherfucker thought it would be a good idea to stop in the middle of the fucking road?"

Jacob wondered all three, but he kept his thoughts to himself. Making his way around the two lead trucks, he found Hodges's empty SUV parked in front, angled across the narrow road. Had he hit a deer? If that was the case, all things considered, it might not have been worth halting everyone in their desperate attempt to get home. Not to mention they'd left behind half a dozen dead bodies back on the summit. Friends and neighbors who needed to be retrieved before any animals discovered their remains. *Normal, present-day animals*, Jacob added, still reeling from the shock of what they'd fought against and barely survived.

Hodges and one of the hunters stood with their back to him as Jacob approached. Their headlights illuminated little in the pitch blackness ahead. It seemed to Jacob as if the men were simply staring into a long, black void. When he stopped between them, he realized just how true that thought was. Jacob was peering into nothingness.

It wasn't until his left foot slipped over empty air and Deputy Hodges pulled him back that Jacob finally understood what he was seeing—or, rather, what he wasn't seeing. Tilting his gaze downward, the ground simply vanished in a line at his feet. As his eyes adjusted to the strange sight, fragments of images peeked out from the darkness below, offering both a shape and a relative size to the oddity before them. A giant, bowl-shaped crater, at least a couple of miles in diameter, perhaps wider, stretched out farther than their eyes could perceive. Glancing to his left and right, Jacob noted the pale, slack-jawed expressions of the men around him. Only then did he realize they were standing on the edge of town.

Blackwood was *gone*.

In its place lay a deep depression in the earth, far wider and deeper than they could make out from their current vantage point. Instead of hesitating, this time Jacob was the first to act. Concern for his wife and daughter burned him from the inside as he bolted forward, racing down the crater's curvature. At first he heard Hodges and the others urging him to stop, but soon enough they followed. As steep as the drop was, it wasn't a sheer cliff. Jacob was able to scramble and slide a good quarter of a mile down the slope before he saw the first sign of what remained of Blackwood.

Only, it wasn't a sign; it was a cross.

He recognized the top of the Lutheran church. Its spire was the tallest point in town. Now it lay half buried in mud and rubble.

Jacob quickened his pace. Rushing down the remaining slope, he jumped onto the flattened earth where the town should have been.

With a sudden explosion on either side of him, jets of spraying water and plumes of blazing fire burst about in a mad network of mingled elements. While the water drenched him, the fire illuminated a clear path forward. More flames, presumably caused by broken gas pipes, sprouted up and soon dotted the entire haphazard landscape.

Jacob followed the fiery trail.

Behind him, the hunters' shocked gasps and desperate pleas broke the silent darkness. Each man, concerned for a family member or friend, ran off in different directions in hopes of finding their loved ones. Everyone except Hodges, who quickly caught up with Jacob. With no family of his own, the young deputy seemed to have decided to stick with him.

"We didn't see anything hit the town," Hodges mumbled, more to himself than to Jacob. "How could we not have seen something fall from the sky big enough to crush an entire town?"

He pulled at Jacob's arm, his eyes wide and full of fear.

Jacob didn't stop; he needed to find Casey and Sarah. Trying to recreate a map of Blackwood in his mind's eye, he assumed that if they'd come from the northern summit, then Noelle's house would be less than a mile to the south. He continued, not running but not pausing either. He raced through showers of spraying water. Nearly invisible rocks and sliding mud made the journey slower than he'd have liked, but nothing was going to stop him from finding his family.

Close behind, Hodges kept pace, continuing his rambling. "We'd have at least heard it," he said, his voice sounding like a child's. "I mean, an asteroid would have—"

"This wasn't caused by an asteroid," Jacob said, more from annoyance than out of any interest in conversation. "This isn't an impact crater."

Hodges eyed him sideways as they stumbled along. "What makes you so sure?"

Jacob pointed toward the curvature of the depression surrounding them. "The church's steeple wasn't destroyed. Nothing hit this place from above. The ground sank beneath them."

Before Hodges could offer a reply, ghostly figures emerged from the surrounding gloom. Still reeling from shock, the surprise appearance of someone right in front of them caused the young deputy to reach for his weapon. Jacob stopped him with a wave. He recognized the first figure. It was Martin Quinn, the butcher. Then Rose McDuffie, his daughter's school principal. Her usual stern expression had been replaced by an open-mouthed blankness. More people emerged from the dark, each covered in mud and filth and seemingly in shock. Despite their shaken appearance, however, a wave of relief washed over Jacob like a warm blanket. *Survivors.*

"You should help them," Jacob said to the deputy, more an order than a suggestion. "I've got to find Casey and Sarah."

With renewed hope burning in his chest, Jacob ran along the jagged, haphazard debris field. To his left and right, front hoods from half buried vehicles were tilted toward the heavens like black monoliths. Pausing to get his bearings, Jacob felt something crunch beneath his boot. Peering down, he discovered tiny digits peeking out from the earth. *Fingertips.*

Scrambling to pull away the dirt, Jacob revealed enough of the hand and wrist to check for a pulse. He needn't have bothered. The rigid digits didn't move. Whoever it was had already died. Imagining what this poor victim must have endured at the end, Jacob shivered from a mental image of being suddenly sucked up by the very ground at his feet. Lingering no longer, Jacob bolted through the dark, searching for Noelle's home.

Hold on, Case and Sarah, I'm coming!

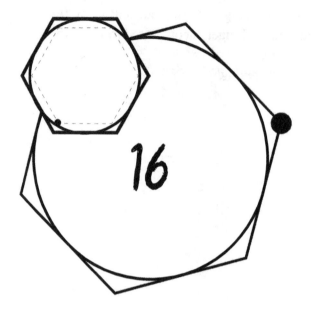

16

The rising water all but forgotten, Casey sat on the staircase, clutching Sarah. "What are you talking about?" she shouted. "How is *any of this* my fault?"

Noelle chewed the inside of her cheek. She hadn't meant to voice her anger, or worse, her fear, out loud. But now the damage had been done, and Casey wasn't going to let it go anytime soon. Noelle could tell from the way Casey had been eyeing her ever since they'd returned from their future pop-in that something had changed deep inside her. Noelle had guessed what it was, though the thought of it put her even more on edge than being buried alive in her house. After all, she knew her boss, Burke, would be along shortly. The line had died while they'd been talking on her laptop, so she figured it was just a matter of sitting tight and waiting for the cavalry to arrive. Unfortunately, by her estimation, time wasn't on her side. Something had been different about Casey from the moment she'd awoken on the bedroom floor. A part of her, probably the long-dormant part with too much knowledge and way too much power for her own good, had woken up as well. Noelle had read the old files, dating all the way back to the late 1940s. Doctor Casey Stevens had been one of only two survivors from the Roswell crash. Neither survivor had been alien, of course. If anything, that might have made things a tad simpler. Instead, the visitors had been from the future. Donovan Daley, the other survivor, had been from the mid-1990s. Although his whereabouts remained unknown, he was assumed dead. Casey Stevens, on the other hand, was a vastly more complicated issue. She was alive and well, living *generations* from when she was last seen, in the winter of 1958. Now, of course, she went by a different name: Casey Anderson. A small-town mother and wife who seemed to have no recollection of her past life or, more importantly, her heightened psychic and physical abilities.

Better to keep it that way, Noelle thought as she eyed the rather plain looking woman beside her.

As much as she hoped to unlock Casey's memories and discover what had happened to her father, Major Reese, she wasn't stupid enough to try and do it down there, buried underground and far from help. Better to have such conversations later, in a controlled environment. Feeling the weight of her pistol at her waist, Noelle couldn't prevent a small smile from curling her lips. Sooner or later, she'd get her answers. She just needed to wait a little longer.

Noting Noelle's grin, Casey glared at the agent. They sat on the lower steps while water continued to pour along the floor, inching higher. "Wanna tell me what you could possibly be smiling about?"

Noelle shook her head. "I was just laughing at the ridiculousness of all this. Sorry. Of course none of this is your fault, Casey. House buried, water leaking in . . . I'm just frightened."

That was at least a half truth.

As the water continued to rise, Casey moved up to the second step and placed Sarah on the third. Still, her glare never wavered from Noelle. She wasn't buying it. Something had indeed been triggered within Casey by the yellow light and their brief vision of the future. Something that seemed to be able to read Noelle's emotions, and her lies, far better than the previous, dependably simple Casey Anderson ever could.

Noelle knew she had to proceed cautiously, not only in what she said but also how she felt. If Casey could read her thoughts, then the next few minutes would require all her training. "Never let the asset in," she'd been told in preparation for this mission. Burke had drilled the order into her so often that it had become a cliché. But not anymore. Now she understood exactly what he'd meant. *Don't let her in, both on the outside and the inside.* Noelle blinked, a physical manifestation of a switch clicking at the back of her mind as she poured out feelings of love, respect, and friendship. Above it all, like icing on a cake, she slathered on a strong dose of fear, which, under the circumstances, wasn't difficult to manifest.

Again, she offered a crooked grin. This time it felt much more natural. "Seriously, Casey, I was just wigging out. I'm fine."

Casey paused as if sizing her up, then stood straighter and glanced down at the black water that covered the floor. It was at least three inches deep. And rising.

"Well, you were right about one thing. I doubt that what happened to my house, and now this, can be a coincidence." She glanced at Sarah, who was lying comatose on the staircase, her wide eyes still as black as night. "God, what the hell is wrong with her?"

Noelle put her arms around Casey, trying to slow her trembling. "We're going to get out of here, and Sarah's going to be alright."

Casey pulled away, surprised. "You . . . you really believe that, don't you?"

She's reacting to my emotions, Noelle decided, *not my words. Tread carefully, girl.*

"We need to get as high as we can," Noelle said. "There's an attic door on the second floor. If help is coming, that's where they'll enter."

Casey glanced at the rising water and then nodded in agreement. "Through the roof."

Noelle sighed, relieved that she'd yanked the conversation back from the brink.

Questions and answers later. Noelle smiled at the thought. *Right now, let's go find us some cavalry.* She climbed the steps, heading back upstairs.

Casey, however, didn't follow. Picking up Sarah in one arm, she paused, lingering on the lower steps. Below, a dim yellowness still glimmered through the otherwise black water.

"Come on," Noelle urged. "We need to get Sarah out of here."

Leaning over, Casey studied the water.

Damn. Noelle huffed as Casey's fingers reached down, plunging into the water.

"Don't!" Noelle shouted.

Ignoring her, Casey pulled her arm back, revealing her fingers. They were covered in a strange yellow substance. "It's not paint. Looks organic," she said, studying it. "Like a fungus."

Organic? Fungus? Noelle knew both to be true, but she hadn't expected the small-town housewife to jump to such a conclusion nearly so quickly. Even if she didn't remember her past, Casey's knowledge and abilities seemed to be reigniting on all cylinders, which only made Noelle's job of getting them the hell out of there and back to Watchtower even more urgent.

"You wanna play biologist," Noelle asked with a grin, "or get the fuck out of here?"

That did the trick. Casey relented and followed her upstairs.

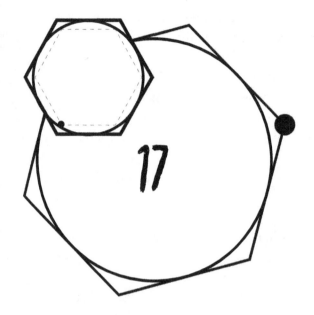

17

Noelle's house lay buried under a blanket of dirt. The only remaining proof of its existence was an angled blue roof, jutting out of the ground like a lopsided dagger. As Jacob crawled over the slanted surface, weathered tiles broke and scattered beneath him. Using his phone's flashlight to guide him, he struggled to find an opening. He needed a way in. So far, all he'd discovered were more and more blue tiles. No windows or hatchways. Pounding his foot against a solid slab of wood, he created a rhythm, using the song "Shave and a Haircut" to keep time.

Punctuating the surrounding darkness, Jacob heard various people shouting for loved ones as they attempted similar rescues amongst the haphazard rooftops dotted about. Occasionally, a triumphant roar burst from the shadows, announcing another soul had been saved. Jacob desperately wanted to feel that same triumph. Even if he could contact Casey with his foot stomps, however, he had no idea how to get to her. His mind turned to the lumber mill outside town, wondering if perhaps they had bulldozers. Any attempt would have to wait until morning, though, and it wasn't clear how anyone could get such large equipment into the crater. Still, it was an idea he clung to much like a drowning man might cling to a life preserver. Slim chance, perhaps, but better than none.

Abruptly, as if someone had heard his prayers, the night sky blazed with bright lights. They crawled over the rocky earth, stopping over Noelle's roof. Jacob's breath caught in his chest as his eyes blinked toward the heavens. Two helicopters swooped over the valley, kicking up dirt in their wake and announcing the arrival of much needed aid. Jacob shouted and waved his arms, hoping to get the pilots' attention. Across the crater, dozens of neighbors did the same. Scattered cheers rose around him until the thudding noise from the helicopters' blades drowned them out.

While the town's few survivors watched the choppers' slow descent, more lights erupted in the distance along the crater's upper lip. A series of trucks, perhaps a dozen, perched at the edge, further illuminating what little remained of Blackwood. That high up in the Oregon mountains in the middle of the night, no rescue team should have been able to get there so fast, Jacob thought. It didn't matter. Right then he'd have taken aid from the devil himself if it might help save his wife and daughter. When the helicopters landed, though, it wasn't the devil who emerged. It was the military.

At least Jacob *assumed* they were military. The Black Hawk helicopters were filled with men and women in hazmat suits with no insignia or rank to reveal their branch of government. But government, he was sure, was precisely what they were. His thoughts drifted back to the van they'd found in the woods less than twenty-four hours ago. Had it only been a day? It felt like so much longer. The computer equipment had been similar to what he'd seen the military use eighteen years ago. Now, it seemed, they were back. The last time the military came, almost everyone in Blackwood had been saved. But not Jacob's father. As he waved his arms to get their attention, Jacob prayed for a happier outcome this time.

He stopped waving once a team of hazmat-suited figures made a beeline toward him. The man in front, with thinning brown hair and round glasses behind his clear plastic mask, approached with a calm smile. The way he carried himself, Jacob thought it was as if the guy walked into mountainous craters and half-buried towns every day.

Maybe he does, Jacob thought, eyeing his hazmat suit. *Lord knows he's dressed for it.*

"Jacob Anderson?" the man asked, his voice distorted through his mask.

Jacob nodded, shocked to hear his own name. Who the hell was this guy, and what the hell was happening? On any other night, he would have turned this into an interview, probing the man with a thousand and one questions. But not tonight. He needed help, and help had come. Despite all his years of mistrusting the government following the incident, Jacob felt his face glow with a bright smile. Salty tears stung his eyes and tracked down his cheeks. *Goddamn* was he glad to see them. Jacob didn't bother shaking the man's hand; he threw his arms around the wiry man in plastic and gave him a big hug. He felt the man recoil, but Jacob didn't care. Help had come.

"Thanks. Whoever the hell you are, thank you!" Jacob shouted over the helicopter's blades.

"My name's Burke. Joseph, Burke," the man said. "Where's your family?"

Jacob pointed to the blue tiles beneath him. "Down there, I think."

Burke leaned over, studying the half-buried roof. "Any sign of life?"

Jacob shook his head.

"Don't worry, Mr. Anderson," Burke said, waving his people over. "We'll get them out."

Again, the man used his name, and again Jacob chose not to question it. All that mattered was getting into the house and saving Casey and Sarah. In the distance, standing over similarly buried homes, various people shouted for help.

With a sting of guilt gnawing at him, Jacob nodded toward the others. "What about them?"

Burke gestured toward the series of trucks parked along the crater's ledge. "We're going to get as many people out as we can." With that, he knelt over Noelle's roof, fingering the tiles and pulling away whatever was loose to reveal the wood beneath. Then he turned to one of his men. "We'll drill here."

Jacob sighed. The confidence in Burke's voice made his head swim with excitement.

Then the blistering pain in his leg returned, shot up his spine, and Jacob passed out.

A thundering noise blared, and the world shifted beneath him. Jacob awoke, lying on his back. Casey's beautiful green eyes leaned into view, but there was no happiness in them. She didn't smile, and her cheeks were caked with tears. Before he could ask what was wrong, the world did another quick turn, and he felt his stomach lurch. A blurry-eyed glance told him they were in a helicopter, presumably headed to a hospital. His fingers lifted from a gurney, searching for Casey's hand. He found it, caressing the warmth of her skin, as if to make sure she was real.

"And here I thought *I* was the one saving *you*," he said.

"My hero," Casey replied with a forced grin. He noted the pain in her voice.

"What's the matter?"

Without answering, Casey moved aside, revealing Sarah, strapped to a gurney. Her skin was milk pale with thin red lines, like veins, running across her skin. Worse were her eyes. Wide open and pitch black. Like muddy pools. Jacob gasped, rolling onto his side to get closer to her.

"What . . . what happened?"

Casey shook her head, the exhaustion of whatever she'd been through readily apparent. "I don't know. There was this yellow light and . . ." Her words died in her throat. Jacob didn't push. He'd never seen her look so fragile.

Like cracked glass, his mind whispered. *One hard press, and she'll shatter.*

He sat up, eyeing the clean bandage around his leg, before taking in more details around him. Noelle was in front, sitting beside a pilot, a headset over her ears. Odd that they'd want her up front, he thought.

Noelle shifted in her seat and removed the headset. "Welcome back to the land of the living, Jacob. You lost a lot of blood, but you'll be alright."

Jacob peered over at Casey, who met his curiosity with an annoyed frown. Nothing about any of this made sense. Not that being hunted by a long-extinct creature had seemed remotely normal either. If it wasn't for his immediate concern for Sarah, he might have laid back down and hoped things would make more sense in the morning. Instead, he turned to Noelle. "Are we headed to a Portland hospital?" he shouted over the roar of the chopper's engine.

Crawling out of her seat, she squatted beside him. "We have a team prepping close by, ETA two minutes."

Jacob shook his head. "I'm afraid I'm not following."

"She's FBI," Casey said.

"That's awfully convenient," Jacob replied, sarcasm plain in his tone. Then his eyes narrowed as he sized Noelle up. "Did you know this was going to happen?"

"We've got engineering teams working double time in Blackwood to get everyone out," she said. Jacob noted that she hadn't answered the question but decided not to push. Not yet. If these people could help Sarah, then for now at least, he was willing to keep his mouth shut.

Something caught Casey's eye. She stood, bracing herself with a handrail as she stared out the helicopter's windshield.

"What is it?" Jacob asked, struggling to rise.

Casey shrugged. "Nothing. Thought I saw something. Just my imagination. There's nothing out there."

"Wait—shit!" Noelle reached around, grabbing something from a bag. "I forgot." She pulled out two square shapes that looked like nicotine patches. Peeling a plastic cover off each, she handed them over. "Here," she said. "Put these on your neck."

Jacob and Casey exchanged nervous glances. Noelle smiled. "Trust me."

"You must be joking," Casey replied. The two women exchanged a long, silent glare, punctuated only by the helicopter's continuous noise. Hoping to break the tension, Jacob slapped the patch on his neck. Reluctantly, Casey followed suit.

After a prolonged moment of nothing happening, Jacob looked at Noelle. "OK. Now what?"

"Look out the window," Noelle replied, a nervous tremble layering her voice.

Leaning against Casey's shoulder, Jacob wobbled onto his stronger leg and peered out the windshield. His jaw dropped, and he felt the world lurch beneath him. This time it wasn't caused by the helicopter's movement. His stomach twisting, his leg threatened to give out as he stared in disbelief at an enormous metal structure, perhaps one hundred stories tall. Erected beside the mountain, it looked like a blood-covered sword jutting out of the ground and attempting to stab the darkened sky above. Seemingly painted red, its jagged beams and twisting architecture looked more organic than man-made. And yet, he knew it must be man-made. God, after all, didn't build with metal beams and angular lines. It was a spire of some kind, but the longer he looked at it, the more he realized that whatever he was seeing hadn't been created by humans or by God. Both transfixed and horrified by what he was seeing growing larger and larger in the helicopter's window, he couldn't find any words to speak beyond a heavy, soul-draining sigh.

Casey came back to her senses much faster. She spoke softly, just loud enough to be heard over the incessant noise. "I've seen this before. How . . . how could I have forgotten?"

Come to think of it, Jacob had seen it too. Plenty of times. Whenever he'd driven to Portland, he'd done a double take and had had the same thoughts he had now. Only somehow he'd forgotten.

"Basically, it works like peripheral vision," Noelle said. "Every day you see all kinds of shit out of the corner of your eye, but your brain don't bother focusing on it, unless you want it to. Same with the tower. Hell of a defense mechanism, huh? The patches will make it so you remember, even if you look away from it. Neuro-blockers. They halt the tower's effect."

At last, Jacob found his voice. "What the hell is it?"

Noelle's expression hardened. "A piece of the future."

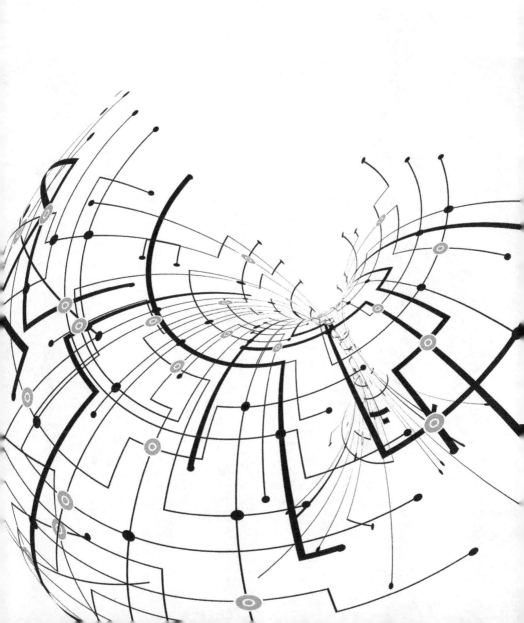

PART II

THE TWO CASEYS

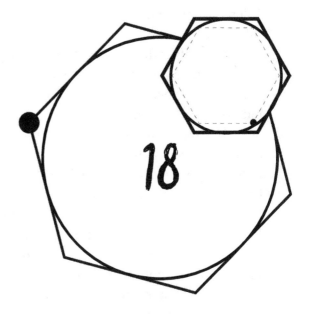

18

Momentarily blinded by a burst of crimson light, Donovan Daley stumbled out of the spinning hypersphere and slowly regained his bearings. Though changed, the underground structure was immediately recognizable. Only a few hours ago he'd been trapped down there in that same place, left to die at the bottom of the seekers' tower. Now he was back. Only this time he knew he wouldn't be trapped for long. The hypersphere, an enormous swirling ball of energy with layers upon layers of spinning spherical lines, floated silently above him. To most, it was considered the engine and the heart of the seekers' technology. While technically both were true, Donovan now knew it was also much, much more. The sphere was alive.

Alien.

Not like the tall gray beings with the black eyes. They were human, in a roundabout evolutionary sense. The spheres, on the other hand, were something else entirely. Not of this earth or even from this universe, at least from what he'd gathered. Somehow the term "alien" seemed entirely too small for whatever the hell those damn things were.

The creature he'd met within the hypersphere—or in another dimension, he wasn't certain—had told him that humanity's descendants had trapped the spheres. Made them into servants to do their bidding. Much like they'd trapped him and Casey all those years ago. Still, Donovan didn't delude himself into thinking these otherworldly beings were any better than the gray things that had abducted him in the first place. After having been abandoned in the 1950s, only to be flung to the far future where he had witnessed the end of humankind, at this point Donovan just wanted to go home. Back to 1996. Back to some semblance of a "normal" life. He almost laughed at the idea, no longer able to even picture what a normal life might be like. Stumbling out of the hypersphere into yet another time period, he prayed this next stop might finally put an end to his seemingly unending nightmare.

All he had to do was find and kill a seven-year-old girl.

Acid burned from his stomach up to his throat at the very notion of what the creature inside the hypersphere had suggested. And it was, Donovan was certain, a creature. Oh, it looked human enough. Pretty damn sexy if he was being honest about it. When she hadn't offered a name, he'd made one up for her, calling her Daphne. But no matter how pretty her figure or sensuous the scent of her perfume, Donovan wasn't fooled. Daphne was an alien. A thing. A creature. If he'd needed any more evidence, her suggestion that to save them both Donovan would have to murder a child was all the proof he needed that the bitch wasn't human. Despite all his many crimes and faults, the idea of killing a little girl ate at his gut something fierce. Still, he lumbered away from the hypersphere's glow, looking for an exit to carry out his mission.

Save humanity, he thought, *lose your soul*. Maybe it was a fair trade. After all, he'd killed before. What was one more notch on the proverbial belt? Better to just get on with it.

Heading through the domed underground structure, Donovan was struck by how much the room had changed since he'd last been there. By his reckoning, only a few hours had passed. But it was clear from the room's multiple additions and subtractions that far more time had passed for the world since he'd left. The additions included rows of fancy computers, powered by snaking cables that ran along the floor like spilled spaghetti. Overhead, large lamps on eight-foot-tall metal poles dotted the room, offering pools of light. What was missing, he noted, were all the dead bodies that had been piled up ten feet high the last time he'd been there. Not human corpses but shriveled gray bony husks. Figures from the future somehow transported to the past.

Like me.

How the whole "retrocausality" thing, as Prewitt had called it, worked was beyond him. The rules Donovan had known, the things that made the universe make sense, had simply gone out the window. Up was down, down was up, and the past and the future worked in the wrong fucking order. Just crossing the room, thinking about how it had changed, made his head scream. A part of him, though, couldn't help but be curious as to *when* he'd arrived. Then another, more primitive and anxious, part of himself cursed his wandering thoughts.

Shut the fuck up and just get going. Time's a-wasting.

As he gained some distance from the swirling hypersphere and its powerful reddish glow, a new light came into view. To his left, a tall, jagged opening in the wall lay before him, illuminated by yellow light. The light didn't flicker or waver. Upon closer inspection, Donovan discovered phosphorescent patches of yellow along the entrance's edge.

Leaning near enough that his nose almost touched the damned stuff, he sniffed, detecting a mildew odor. Whatever this shit was, it sure as hell hadn't been there the last time.

Edging closer, he peeked into the opening, discovering a long cave, its walls aglow with the yellow phosphorescent muck. Hoping it might be an exit, he took a step inside.

Bad idea. Donovan paused, his foot dangling over the rocky earth. Ahead, a crooked shadow blinked past, turning the yellow light to a brownish ochre. Drawing his leg back out of the cave, his eyes narrowed, trying to make out a distant shape. Was it human? A seeker, perhaps?

As if in reply, a guttural roar erupted through the tunnel, causing the hairs on Donovan's neck and arms to stand erect. Spinning around, he decided to find another route. Quickly. Again, he passed the hypersphere, only this time its crimson glow didn't disturb him nearly as much. Compared to the yellowish fungus cave with the loud unearthly animalistic roars, the sphere seemed almost welcoming.

The devil you know, Donovan conceded.

Making his way to the other end of the domed underground structure, something else caught his gaze. Something that obviously didn't belong there, and yet, he couldn't help smiling when he found it. An elevator. Donovan chuckled. They'd built a decidedly human elevator smack dab in the middle of all this weird futuristic crap.

People, God bless 'em. Thrilled to discover technology that didn't set his brain on fire to work out, he felt his muscles relax. Glancing to his right, he found a clothes hanger with several hazmat suits dangling behind a wall of glass. Not bothering to look for a door handle, he smashed the glass with his elbow and grabbed a yellow plastic suit. He doubted the place was radioactive, but he needed a way to blend in, and the suit would do. After having dressed and secured the plastic mask over his face, Donovan returned to the elevator, his finger hovering over the call button.

Go on, dipshit, he told himself, feeling the tension return. *Time to be a child murderer.*

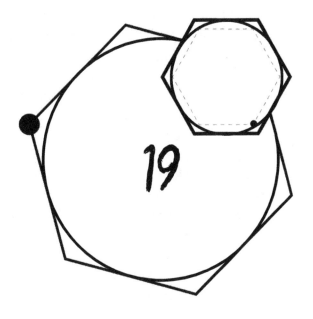

19

No mother should ever have to watch their child die.

Casey stood beside Sarah's bed, separated by a plastic sheet. The stink of disinfectant wafted into her nostrils while, overhead, the air conditioner droned on and on, assaulting Casey's eardrums with its constant whirl. Her vision was blurred by her tears and the plastic sheet. Even the doctors and nurses, floating in from time to time, wore plastic suits and masks. Casey's father had always said that doctors and scientists were no damn good. Now, having watched them poke and prod her little girl over the past two days with the same tests again and again, she was starting to think the bastard might've been right. These doctors had no answers. All Casey could do was stand there helplessly, unable to even hold her baby girl's hand. Another wave of tears flooded her eyes. Casey didn't bother to wipe them away.

Let them come. Some things can't be stopped. Glancing through the open door, she noticed more doctors rushing by. Like scurrying rats. *Why can't any of you people do anything?*

She had wanted to go to Portland, hoping to find an expert in the field of rare diseases, but the government people assured her that Sarah was getting the very best treatment. They told Casey and Jacob that no one on earth knew more about what was happening to Sarah than they did. Still, forty-eight hours later, they seemed to have no answers. Or, as Jacob had suggested before he left, no answers they were willing to provide.

A throbbing flame ran up the back of her calves. Plopping down, she sat in the lone chair beside the plastic-covered bed. Checking her watch, she wondered when Jacob would return. He'd gone back to town under the cover story of helping with the relief effort while secretly hoping to discover the virus's origin. Whatever was wrong with Sarah, the source of it wasn't in this strange biodome they'd placed her in. It was back at Noelle's buried house. More specifically, the strange yellow fungus growing beneath it. Either way, Jacob had left two days ago, and now Casey regretted his decision. She needed him at her side. She wasn't strong enough to bear another day alone. The weight of it was too much. Despite all these doctors and nurses and support staff, Casey had sat utterly alone beside her dying daughter. She wanted to scream and rage and smash something. Instead, she just sat there, waiting.

Have they tried a silicon-based protein injection? a feminine voice asked.

Casey looked up from her lap, expecting to find someone in the room with them, but there was no one. Before she could open her mouth to ask who had spoken, the voice returned.

It may slow the nanites' effect.

It wasn't a voice, Casey realized; it was her imagination.

You know what to do, the voice pressed. *Why are you just sitting there?*

"What?" Casey muttered, her voice barely above a whisper. If this was her imagination, it seemed to have taken on a life of its own. Perhaps she was more tired than she realized.

You passed the virus on to her, the voice snapped. *How could you be so stupid?*

Casey stood, swaying back and forth. Blood rushed to her head as she stumbled from Sarah's bed to the private bathroom. On the walls and toilet were more plastic coverings. Casey leaned on the sink and splashed water over her face. She was just beating herself up; that was it. Blaming herself for whatever was wrong with Sarah. No one knew what had caused the strange infection. It wasn't Casey's fault. Maybe it wasn't anyone's fault. It was a disease, as simple as that. And diseases were caused by nature, not people.

Bullshit! The inner voice screamed so loudly it made her head throb. *You did this!*

Again, Casey splashed water onto her face, hoping the coldness of it would drown out the screams rattling around in her skull. *I'm losing it*, she thought. Peering into the mirror, she felt a sudden inner horror at how much she'd aged. At roughly forty years old (she wasn't certain of her true age, but forty sounded about right), Casey was still a handsome woman. Still, weathered lines had begun to leave their mark. Something inside of her seemed as shocked by what she saw as Casey was by what she had heard. It was as if another version of herself was staring through her eyes at the foggy mirror and didn't like what it saw. Turning off the faucet, she went back into the room, wiped her face, and stared at her sleeping daughter.

Sarah's eyes were open but pitch black, like inky pools. No irises or whites within them. Her skin had turned ashen gray, and red veins crisscrossed her tiny, fragile body.

Why don't you remember? the voice asked, softer in tone. *The virus came from the ship.*

Casey's back straightened, more curious than frightened.

"What ship?"

This time the inner voice didn't reply. Casey felt a sudden vacancy within her mind, as if some vague connection had been abruptly severed. The emptiness, however, didn't slow her curiosity. The voice, which had sounded like her own, had suggested there might be a way to slow the spread of the virus. Even if it had only been a figment of Casey's imagination, she decided to follow its suggestion. But how? Standing, pacing, her pulse quickened as an idea formed at the back of her mind. She needed to find Sarah's blood sample. Casey wasn't quite sure why or even what she would do with it if she found it, but the thought persisted. The bloodwork lab. Before she had time to reconsider or remind herself of how ridiculous it would be to follow advice from an imaginary voice, Casey was out the door.

Her chest burned as she made her way along the white corridor, only this time the burning sensation wasn't from fear or anxiety. Rather, it came from a new emotion, one seemingly lost over the last couple of days.

Hope.

When Casey had first arrived at the strange hidden-in-plain-sight base, she hadn't paid much attention to the structures built around the great crimson spire. Surrounding the tower were three bulbous domed tents lit up from the inside with bright white light, making them glow amongst the flat landscape nestled to the east of the Blackwood mountains. While the tower's architecture felt both otherworldly and yet oddly familiar, the domes were simple, entirely human-built affairs. Though sturdy, they seemed quickly built, like makeshift huts surrounding an enormous, seemingly alien structure. When she'd first entered two days ago, rushing beside Sarah's gurney, Casey couldn't help but be reminded of her now presumably dead fiancé, Arthur. Like so much from Casey's past, Arthur was only a vague memory now, one she carefully avoided. What had happened to him, or what had happened to her, were questions Casey had long ago decided not to fixate upon. The answers might prove scarier than the questions. Still, there had always been the lingering, gnawing questions about where she'd been. Why she hadn't aged. And right then, as they'd been rushed through the bio lab, what had happened to the young science student she'd once planned to marry. Eyeing the various computers and machines, Casey imagined how much Arthur would have loved a place like this. The rooms they raced through, each decked out in high-tech doodads and Star Trek-looking monitors, seemed like just the sort of place Arthur had always dreamed of working someday. Turning down a second hall as they entered what appeared to be the hospital wing, with sterile white walls and a stench of peroxide, the momentary thoughts of her lost lover finally vanished to the back of her mind. Casey had become quite proficient at pushing aside thoughts regarding her past and all the lingering questions that sprang from them. Better to focus on the present. All that mattered was getting Sarah the help she needed. Though, after two days, help hadn't come.

Now as she snuck out of Sarah's room, searching for the blood-work laboratory, she couldn't help thinking she might have gone mad.

Following voices. Really, Case? Is this what it's come to?

Yes, she decided, and she kept moving. In the next hall, a doctor and three nurses, covered head to toe in hazmat suits, blinked into view. Casey ducked behind a supply cart. Their suits' booties squeaked loudly enough for her to track their progress without her having to peek. Whatever those outfits were meant to protect them from, it still wasn't clear. Sarah didn't appear to be contagious. Both Casey and Jacob appeared to be proof of that, as neither had become infected with whatever virus had invaded their daughter. Perhaps the yellow monkey suits were more a matter of protocol rather than protection from any imminent threat.

Hidden behind the cart, she heard the nurses laugh. Casey's fingers dug into her palms, and her face flushed red. Her daughter lay dying a few feet away, and the people charged with saving her were telling jokes. Casey fought against her rising, burning rage, forcing herself to stay put. And quiet. Her body trembled as the squeaking of their booties grew faint and distant.

Suppressing a tight-lipped growl, Casey continued along the hall, keeping her ears perked for the sound of squeaking booties and her eyes sharp for a glimpse of yellow plastic. But no one else came. Following the hall to her right, she found an open door with humming machines and glass cabinets inside. The bloodwork lab. Casey wasn't certain how she knew what it was, but she did. Shrugging the nagging sense of familiarity aside, she entered the laboratory.

Glancing around, she took stock of her tiny surroundings, try-ing to make heads or tails of what she had found. On one side of the narrow lab stood a row of what looked like fancy refrigerators. Rows of vials filled each shelf. Opening the first glass door she came across, Casey noted that the vials all had numeric labels with ab-breviated names written below. What was most shocking, and more than a little concerning, were the names she read printed on each of the countless vials. She recognized each one. "A. Simmons" was Albert Simmons, the town's librarian. "T. Shultz" had been Sarah's kindergarten teacher. Sifting through the rows of blood samples, Casey was stunned to discover she knew every name on every vial. All of them lived in Blackwood. Just how long had these government people been watching them? More importantly, *why* had they been watching them? Studying them? Suppressing a shiver, Casey moved to the next door. Assuming the names must be in alphabetical order, it didn't take long to find her last name. Three vials with three white labels: "C. Anderson," "J. Anderson," and "S. Anderson."

Casey withdrew the vial of Sarah's blood, holding it up to the light. She wasn't sure what she was looking for. Perhaps, she thought, the blood might have turned as black as Sarah's eyes. But it hadn't. The plasma inside appeared no different to the naked eye than any other sample. Turning, she glanced across the various machines with blurry-eyed dullness. She had no idea what any of the devices did or how to use them. Suddenly, the sheer stupidity of what she had considered doing weighed heavily on her shoulders. As if snapping out of a ridiculous dream, Casey opened the glass refrigerator again and put Sarah's blood sample back.

Then she stopped. It wasn't a conscious decision. Her body seemed to have a life of its own. Spinning around, Casey crossed the room and began flipping on machines. Her arms moved in a series of quick motions, placing Sarah's blood vial into one device while reaching over and extracting others, so fast her hands were a blur. Casey felt like a mere observer in her own body, as if her hands were operating under someone else's control.

The vials she grabbed, first from one refrigerator, then from another, and a third from the upper cabinets, each had labels she didn't understand, even if some part of her mind obviously did. Under any other circumstances, Casey would have screamed in horror as her body moved with an instinct she couldn't comprehend. For the moment, though, she merely bit her lip and watched as her body's instincts worked to save Sarah. Whether any of this *would* work, or if she truly was losing her mind, Casey couldn't begin to guess. A chance, any chance no matter how slim, was worth her momentary silence.

Her hands placed the vials into a round device, slammed the lid, and flipped a switch. Then she watched the vials spin with a soft whirl. Watched and waited.

And waited. Her mind drifted; time passed.

Finally, the machine stopped. Again, her hands worked with a life of their own, opening the lid and withdrawing Sarah's plasma sample. Next, she was at a beaker, mixing saline solution with the now-altered blood. She covered the top and gave it a quick shake until the blood-saline mix shimmered with a faint green glow.

So astonished that anything had even come from her body's mad scientist exercises, it took her a long moment and several deep breaths before she held it up to the light and finally wondered what the hell she was supposed to do with the greenish mixture. Was it a cure? A mere stopgap? A potential poison?

Casey lingered, wondering whether she was really willing to turn her daughter into a guinea pig, when the loud squeak of approaching booties urged her out the door. Just before leaving, her hands once again gained a life of their own. They grabbed a syringe.

Working her way back toward Sarah's room, with the vial and needle clutched in her jacket pockets, Casey tried to decide the best course of action. Nothing she had just done could easily be explained, and yet, somehow she felt certain she'd created something that would help Sarah. How she had done it or where she could have possibly learned about blood samples, biology, and science eluded her.

It'll work, her mind whispered. *You know it will.*

And she did. For reasons she couldn't imagine and was hesitant to even attempt to understand, she *knew* the tiny vial in her hand was the very solution all these doctors and nurses had failed to find. Her heart lifted, and her feet bounced along the slick, pristinely white floors, excitement building in her chest as she came around the corner and entered Sarah's room.

Then she stopped dead in her tracks.

A man in a hazmat suit was standing in the room. Having drawn back the plastic curtain, he was holding a pillow over Sarah's head. Casey's stomach twisted and her limbs went numb with shock.

Before she could stop him, the man plunged the pillow on top of her little girl's face.

Smothering her.

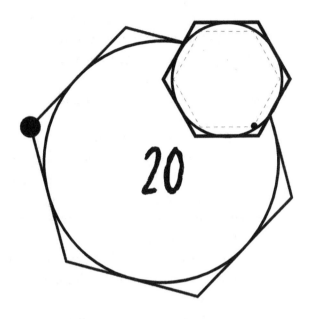

20

For two days, Jacob sifted through mud and dirt, helping to dig out survivors. Secretly, he'd also worked on finding the remains of the sheriff's station and the van that had been parked out behind it for evidence. The mysterious white van, which he hoped and prayed might provide some clue as to what had happened in Blackwood. It wasn't as if the supposed "rescue teams" were offering any answers. Whenever Jacob had pressed, each of them had only shaken their heads or shrugged their shoulders. Playing dumb. Most of them, anyway. Their leader, Burke, hadn't even offered that much. When pressed, he said he wasn't allowed to discuss the matter. "We're here for rescue and cleanup, not twenty questions," he'd said. Over the last forty-eight hours, Jacob had learned to hate Burke most of all. Whether or not Burke and his people were responsible for the disaster, it was clear they'd known about it in advance. They'd shown up too fast and too prepared. When they'd first arrived, Jacob hadn't cared about anything beyond finding his family. Now he wanted to find the truth. And time was running out.

Sarah may not have been his daughter through blood, but in all the ways that mattered, he was her father. He'd been there when she was born. He'd changed her diapers and soothed her crying. He'd loved and cared for her all her life. Now she was lying in a bed, possibly dying, with black eyes and red veins crisscrossing her body. Worse, Sarah was far from the only casualty.

While no one else had reported an infection like the one plaguing Sarah, almost everyone had lost family members, including children. According to the latest figures, the death count had reached 476, with several hundred more still missing. Those who had been found and saved were moved to the Blackwood lumber building at the town's northernmost edge.

Perched just beyond the crater, the two-story structure was so close that the back of the building jutted out over the ledge. Thankfully, it had proven stable enough to house the thousand or more survivors plus the government agencies, who kept the people safe but contained. For whatever reason, no one was able to get a phone signal in or out of the area, and Jacob figured that suited Burke just fine. Whether that was due to the incident or government interference, he didn't know, though he doubted Mother Nature had suddenly put a block on everyone's Internet access and cell phones. In either case, he couldn't imagine what Burke's long-term plan was, if there even *was* a plan.

Jacob maintained his autonomy as best as he could. Still, there always seemed to be a yellow hazmat suit trailing not too far behind him and never too far from view. That they were watching him had never been in doubt, but what precisely they feared he might discover remained an open question that constantly drove him. As the hours turned to days, his need to find answers to what had happened to Sarah grew more and more desperate, as did his search for the mysterious white van.

As the orange sun paled and died at the end of the second day, Jacob wandered back and forth across the crater, mapping out the familiar rooftops in his mind, to make a best guess as to where the police station might be located. After a quick meal at the lumber yard with the hundreds of other survivors, Jacob pretended to go back to his allotted cot, seemingly too exhausted to continue his search.

An hour later, flashlight in hand, he snuck back out and headed toward the crater.

Sliding down from a side window, he made his way along the crater's edge and headed northeast. Sprinkles of work lights showed the way. Even with large groups of yellow-clad agents swarming the area, it proved easy enough in the deep patches of shadow for Jacob to keep out of sight. Although the sheriff's station had yet to be discovered, he'd found the red roof to the doctor's clinic a few hours earlier. As the clinic was located less than a block across the street from the station, making a best guess wasn't overly difficult, even in the dark. Jacob, after all, had one advantage over the agents: he'd grown up there. He may not have been able to map out the entire terrain blind, but he knew it well enough that with the clinic's roof in sight, Jacob had a clear idea of where to dig. As for digging equipment, that was something he was able to find in abundance. Virtually every few feet of caked mud or mound of rippled earth contained shovels and other abandoned equipment from the day's work. Picking up a large spade, he heaved it over his shoulder before passing the clinic's red roof. In the distance, he heard heavy machines chugging, continuing their dig, presumably in a vain hope that further survivors might be discovered. After two days, however, he sorely doubted it.

Perhaps the government was searching for something else, beyond the town's survivors. He doubted they were after the van, as their search seemed focused around his own home and Noelle's place. The places that he and Casey and Sarah had stayed before the world caved in around them.

Keeping a sharp eye on the distant workers and the huge excavators they employed to dig out swaths of earth, Jacob finally stopped at the place he'd marked in his mind's eye as the parking lot to the sheriff's station. Squatting low, he took a hesitant, raspy breath before spitting in his hands, like he'd seen in the movies, and began to dig.

It wasn't long before Jacob began wishing he'd brought some water. Considering that it was just above 50°F, and he was covered in heavy winter wear, it hadn't dawned on him until then that he'd be sweating so hard. Or that his breathing would become so labored. After digging several holes, none of which were more than a few feet deep, he found the sheriff station's roof, right about where he'd expected it to be. Moving roughly ten yards eastward, he spent the next few minutes digging deeper in hopes of finding the van parked behind it. The term "needle in a haystack" bubbled to the top of his thoughts more than once. But Jacob had a good lay of the terrain, so he wasn't surprised when his shovel eventually hit something in the ground with a loud, metallic THUD.

Only it wasn't the van. A little more digging revealed a dull red taillight, its glass cracked from his shovel. Jacob had found the sheriff's SUV, which meant he was close.

A series of shouts over the chugging machines stopped his progress. Jacob lay flat on his stomach, hidden behind several feet of dirt, while flashlight beams combed the ground overhead. It wasn't until then that Jacob realized his own flashlight was still lit, and he fumbled to extinguish it. Above, voices grew closer. Jacob held his breath, trying to come up with possible excuses for why he was out there all alone at night. Part of him simply wanted to stand up and remind these people just who the hell belonged in that area and who did not. This was his home, not theirs. Instead, Jacob held his tongue, and his breath. The townspeople were prisoners. It was never said, but he knew it to be true. No one had been allowed to make outside calls, no one had been able to get online, and no one, outside of himself, had been allowed to leave. Burke and his people had a thousand and one excuses, of course. The roads leading out of town had supposedly caved in. That didn't really wash, though. Burke's trucks had gotten up there just fine. Also, the helicopters refused to take anyone down the mountain no matter how much the townspeople pleaded. The lack of phone service or internet, supposedly caused by the disaster, was at least more plausible. Not that Jacob or anyone else had bought that one either. One way or another, they were all prisoners. And Jacob was out after curfew.

Following another quick sweep of light beams crisscrossing over-head, he heard the agents withdraw. Their voices grew dimmer be-neath the thick noise of the chugging excavators and digging equip-ment. Flopping onto his back, he fidgeted with his flashlight, trying to decide whether to turn it on again or not. Some of the ground could indeed be seen from the large work lights, even at almost thirty yards away. Eventually, though, he knew he would need his own light source. But not yet. Crawling out of the hole, Jacob glanced back at the station's roof before drawing an imaginary line in his mind to the SUV he'd found.

If the sheriff's vehicle was parked here, then the van should be . . .

Scanning the rocky terrain, he pictured the four parking slots behind the station, trying to guess where the deputy's spot would be, then moved beyond that to the next two presumably open parking spots. *The van must have been parked over there*, he decided, moving another five yards, then dropping to his knees. Keeping low, he began to dig again. This time, however, he didn't turn on his flashlight until he'd dug enough to create a mound of dirt between him and the dis-tant machines. The mound wouldn't be enough to hide his flashlight from a wandering agent, but he hoped it might be enough to keep himself hidden from the diggers in the distance.

Scrounging deeper into the damp, cold ground, his body caked in mud, Jacob's shovel once again hit something metallic. Bringing his flashlight to bear, Jacob pushed aside rocks and debris. Beneath the dirt, his beam gleamed across a white surface. At last, he'd found the van. From this angle, it appeared as if the tail end was inverted, lying deep below ground, which meant he'd have to go in through the front. Trapped within the earth, however, it would be impossible for him to simply open the front door and make his way inside. Brush-ing off more debris, his flashlight reflected against the windshield, and he knew what he'd have to do.

Grasping the shovel like a fishing spear, he leaned over the wind-shield and gave it a whack. His attempt hardly had any effect. Too many nights typing and not enough days working out, it seemed, had made him weaker than he realized. He'd seen this kind of thing done in movies plenty of times, but they had had break-away glass, and he had a thick windshield in his way. After hitting it again and again, the effect was only incidental. A barely visible crack splintered and sliced across the glass.

With a tired huff, Jacob stood, his head peeking above the large mound of dirt to his left. Sighing, he considered all that he'd done to reach this point and decided he wasn't going to be stopped by a fucking window.

Standing fully erect, he raised the shovel high above his head, then threw it down at the glass. Over and over he hammered away, no longer concerned with the noise he was making or who might discover him. Finally, the windshield gave way, shattering beneath his shovel.

The suddenness of the breach caused Jacob to tumble forward, cutting his arm along a particularly large piece of fractured glass. Normally, Jacob might have howled and whimpered like a child, but his excitement and adrenaline were so high he barely even registered the wound. Using his boot heel like a jackhammer, he kicked away the few remaining shards.

His flashlight, shining through the opening, revealed a tight, enclosed space below. It looked like a metal coffin.

Without hesitation, Jacob crawled inside.

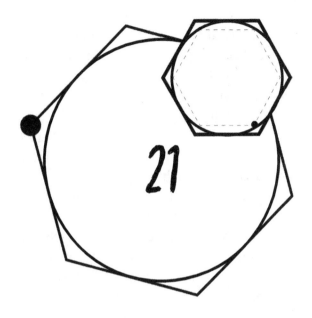

21

The elevator doors opened with a loud DING.

Donovan paused before exiting, chuckling to himself at the sheer hubris of people building a modern elevator inside a structure from the distant future. Someone, it seemed, had thought they could improve upon the seekers' technology. Or, more probably, they simply couldn't get the tower's existing lift to work. In either case, the elevator had not taken him back inside the higher levels of the tower, as he assumed it would. When the doors opened, Donovan found himself standing outside the tower, surrounded by three glowing domes that looked like beehives. Craning his neck, he peered through the hazmat suit's visor at the looming tower above. Though not nearly as enormous as it had been in the distant future, it was still much taller than when he and Prewitt had found it back in the 1950s. The tower was growing, slowly but surely, until it would eventually reach the immense height he'd seen in the future. While Donovan didn't pretend to understand precisely how it had happened, he knew it had something to do with what Prewitt had called "retrocausality", an effect where the tower's debris moved backwards in time instead of forwards. All of it was enough to give anyone a headache, and he didn't care as much about the details as he did the result. There he was, back at the tower once again, trapped in another time. No closer to home than he had been in ages.

Glancing around, he saw the familiar Oregon mountains, and presumed Blackwood lay somewhere beyond. Turning, he noticed three large domed structures, glowing from a white light within, like overturned car headlights. On twin towers to his right and left, armed guards stood at the ready. Again, Donovan was reminded of the last time he was there, staring up at another group of armed guards. They hadn't been enough to stop the ship then, and he doubted they would be now. The hubris of humankind, it seemed, hadn't improved during his absence. Nor had their security. The latter at least made his job that much easier.

Donovan headed toward the glowing beehive structures.

Drawing closer, he noted the domes were not actually smooth but had ripples, like scales, running along their nylon surface. Through an open door he saw various soldiers in black uniforms milling about. Quickening his step, Donovan passed the first dome and continued to the second. A group of yellow-suited men exited the next structure. They looked a bit nerdy, like scientists or doctors. He figured that if Sarah was there, she'd be with the eggheads, not the soldiers. It made sense. Besides, he wasn't about to storm a building filled with armed guards. Eggheads, on the other hand, he could handle. Hesitating between the glowing beehives, he glanced around, taking in more of his surroundings. Several black helicopters and rows of transport trucks ran along the western barrier, positioned between two more guard posts. But no tanks and no armed battalions. He didn't even see any machine guns.

Jesus, these guys really have no fucking clue what they're dealing with.

Fortunately, it wasn't his problem. All he needed to do was find the little girl, do what had to be done, and then get back to the hypersphere and his own time. After all, Donovan had been sent to save humanity. That thought gave him a surge of energy. Marching toward the second beehive's front door, he swung it open and entered.

Finding Sarah's room wasn't difficult. While there were dozens of rooms, she appeared to be the only patient. Donovan noted the security cameras in the hall outside her room but no doctors. Peeking inside, he was glad to discover Casey wasn't there either. The last thing he wanted was to try to fight a mother who could move too fast to see. The seekers' nanites in her bloodstream had given her incredible abilities that had thwarted him on more than one occasion. Abilities that had been wasted on her. Donovan could well imagine what he would have done with enhanced speed and strength. Not to mention her IQ, which seemed to have jumped sky high, earning her three doctorates in less than ten years. During those same ten years, back when they were stranded in the 1950s, Donovan hadn't gained any new knowledge, let alone any sort of superpowers. Instead, he'd been forced into the role of government lacky. The irony that he was once again following someone else's order, this time an alien creature named Daphne, wasn't lost on him.

As he entered the room, his anger toward Casey helped him gather the strength for what he knew had to be done. Donovan had seen the awful future, made even worse, he'd been told, because of this little girl lying behind drapes of plastic. Peeling the curtain aside, Donovan was sickened by what he saw.

This was no mere child; it was a thing from a nightmare. Her eyes were open and filled with black. Her skin was covered in crisscrossing red markings, like veins, covering her face and arms and, he presumed, the rest of her, hidden beneath the sheets. He wasn't inclined to check. Still, the sight of the monstrous little thing lying before him made his job a hell of a lot easier. His resolve hardened. Donovan slid a pillow from beneath the sleeping girl's head. So revolted by her black, seemingly lifeless eyes, he winced just from having his fingers near her head, as if some of the black goo that filled her eye sockets might shoot out and spill all over him. Cradling the pillow, Donovan hesitated. Eyeing the plastic curtain around her, he was suddenly thankful for the hazmat suit. If she was indeed infectious, then what had originally been meant to be merely a disguise might prove to be a saving grace.

Donovan leaned closer, holding the pillow over her face. He was glad to block out the blank stare from those awful black eyes. And yet, his arms grew heavy, and he wavered. No matter what disease this little girl might be carrying, she was, nonetheless, a mere child. Donovan's resolve wavered. He'd killed before. He'd even attempted to kill this girl's mother more than once. But killing a child? No, not even he had sunk so low. Now that the moment had arrived, Donovan didn't think he could do it. His arms slackened, pulling the pillow away from the tiny comatose figure.

Behind him, the door opened.

Hearing its soft squeak, Donovan spun around and found himself facing the girl's enraged mother. Casey glared at him. Her eyes shot to the pillow in his hands, then back to his covered face. With no time left for waffling or indecision or any of the human reserve that had stayed his hand before, Donovan plunged the pillow onto the little girl's face, blocking those black, utterly inhuman eyes from view. Pressing with all his weight, he tried to snuff out Sarah's breath before her mother could stop him.

In a rush, Casey was at his throat. Her fingernails dug at his larynx while she screamed in his ear. Donovan's head swooned from the sudden onslaught, but he still kept all his weight on the pillow, suffocating the little girl.

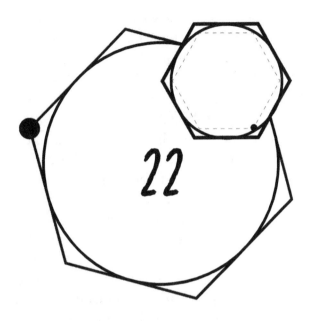

22

Following several thundering heartbeats, Casey's mind caught up with what her eyes were witnessing. The details came slowly, in fractured chunks. A tall man, his features hidden within a hazmat suit, stood over Sarah, pillow in hand. Even when he pressed the pillow over her daughter's face, Casey struggled to comprehend it. Why would these people have gone through all the trouble to bring Sarah to a medical facility, run countless tests, only to abandon it all by smothering her? It made no sense, and even after the third heartbeat pounded in her ears and chest, Casey still doubted her eyes. By the fourth or fifth heartbeat, however, Casey's body finally shook off the initial shock, allowing her to act.

Racing over, she wrapped her arms around the man's neck, clutching his throat while he continued his assault. Casey's nails clawed at the plastic suit. With a wrench, the mask tore away in her grasp, revealing the man's face. Sandy-brown hair, pale skin dimpled with pockmarks, his lips drawn up in a seemingly permanent curl. There was something immediately familiar about him, though at the moment, how she might have known him was the least of her concerns. With the mask gone, her fingers found his cheeks, inching up to his eyeballs. Beneath her nails, skin peeled back, creating long bloody gashes on either side of his face.

This time it was the man who screamed. At last, his grip on the pillow weakened. Stumbling backwards, the pillow fell to the floor, and he shoved himself backwards, slamming her against the wall. Casey saw stars, and the breath went out of her. Still, she refused to let go of the man's face. Pulling her hands aside, he spun around and kicked her in the ribs.

Casey fell to the floor, clattering against the visitor's chair she'd spent so many long hours occupying. It flipped over, sending Casey's skull crashing onto the floor. The stars blurring her vision became more pronounced as the man and the room faded from view.

Struggling to stay conscious, Casey flopped to her side. A second kick to the gut sent her tumbling while the remaining oxygen in her lungs burst from her lips, along with drops of blood. Was she bleeding internally? It didn't matter. Nothing mattered. Not the pain or her blurred vision, not even the silhouette looming over her. All that mattered was getting to Sarah.

Clutching her aching ribs, her hand dropped to her coat pocket, searching for the syringe. When she confirmed the plastic casing was intact, along with its precious contents, a wave of brief relief washed over her. Shielding it with her body, her left ribs suffered several more kicks and blows as the man's onslaught continued.

Where's Noelle? Casey wondered. *And where are all the guards?*

Even as the man yanked her off the floor, bringing his blood-covered face close to hers, Casey still couldn't understand what was happening. His fist rose into view. Arching back, as if for a killing blow, the raging man swung—but the blow never landed.

Casey observed the clenched fist, knuckles white in the air, hovering inches from her. Behind it, the man's flushed red face glared, frozen. Everything halted around her, as if time itself needed a breather. Surprised by the sudden reprieve, it took her a moment to realize that nothing had truly stopped. The fist continued to inch forward.

Nearly imperceptibly, but it *was* moving. Taking a breath through clenched teeth, Casey peeled the man's fingers away from her neck. Stepping aside, she waited expectantly for time to resume its normal course and for his fist to come crashing down with lightning speed. Instead, the man's movements remained slow to the point of being almost comical. If not for the sheer terror of the situation and the threat to her and Sarah, Casey might have burst out laughing from the absurdity of what was happening. But she didn't laugh. This man, who only a moment ago had tried to smother her daughter, now stood before her like an open target, laid bare to whatever tortures she might wish to inflict. Fists balling at her sides, Casey felt a burning fire erupt through her body. It rushed up her legs to her stomach and then her chest and arms until, at last, the blaze swam through her skull. The fire was uncomfortably hot, as if an electric current had been switched on inside her bones, charging her muscles and reflexes. And her mind.

In a cascade of flashes, a series of long-forgotten memories assailed her. Casey recalled places, voices, faces of those she'd known and then forgot. So strong and overwhelming were the images that Casey staggered under the weight of them. Days, weeks, months, years, an entire decade of her life returned to her in a blink of an eye. She recalled her adventures within the ship, the crash at Roswell in the late 1940s, and her eventual work at Area 51. Finally, she remembered everything that the ship had done to her body, including its injection of advanced nanites, which offered incredible abilities on the one hand and an inhuman visage, if not contained, on the other.

Her gaze fell down to the small figure lying in the bed. The girl's black eyes stared blankly upwards. *This is my daughter,* her mind whispered. *Sarah.* The weight of that thought swept all the other rushing memories aside. How she had become pregnant remained a mystery, though she had no doubt the ship was somehow responsible.

Turning her attention back toward the angry man with the slowly descending fist, she finally recognized her attacker. Donovan. His name inside her mind only angered her further as the details of what was happening finally slipped into place. Without another thought, she grabbed him by the collar, wrenched him over her shoulder, and threw him across the room, where he crashed through the thin makeshift wall, spilling into the hallway.

Time resumed.

Donovan screamed. Then his body shuddered, and he collapsed.

Hearing his heartbeat from across the room, Casey knew he was still alive. For now, anyway. Later, she would need to correct that. She remembered a time long ago when she'd spared his life. It was a mistake she didn't plan to repeat.

With the threat neutralized, the nanites inside her continued to blaze like liquid fire. Her head pounding from the rush, she fell to her knees, struggling to slow her breathing. As her body convulsed from the raging adrenaline, her mind whirled. One moment, she appeared to be back in the underground hanger, being chased by a figure with red eyes. The next, she was taking a step forward in the sterile white hospital room. Her memories of the past, and her grip on the present, seemed to be battling for control.

She knew she needed to attend to her daughter, but once again, the world shifted.

Now she was running through gray hallways, panting and frightened. Casey glanced around, recognizing the ship's horrid, seemingly breathing corridors.

SNAP!

She was back in the hospital, wobbling to the bed.

SNAP! SNAP!

Casey was sitting at a desk, writing a report to President Eisenhower. She placed Major Reese's pink necklace in the envelope, then licked the seal shut.

SNAP! SNAP! SNAP!

Blinding white lights above disoriented her. She was in the hospital room. Casey lurched closer to Sarah's bedside. If left unchecked, the nanites and the memories they offered would consume her, eventually transforming her flesh to gray scales. Inches from the bed, Casey paused. Inhaling slow, deep breaths, she forced her hands to unclench and her heartbeat to slow until finally, the nanites went dormant.

Her body went limp. Casey felt the dragging weight of exhaustion consume her. Forcing herself not to stop, she wobbled closer to Sarah, sliding against the wall for support, until she reached the edge of the bed. Leaning over, she bent her ear to Sarah's mouth. When she felt her daughter's breath against her cheek, Casey sighed, and the last of her strength left her.

Tumbling into the chair, she reached into her coat pocket and pulled out the syringe. Now she knew what it was. A simple cocktail she'd used on herself back at Area 51 during those rare times when the nanites had threatened to overtake her. Though she still wasn't quite sure what was wrong with Sarah, she imagined that a mixture of saline along with an injection of iron should steady Sarah's bloodstream enough for the nanites inside her to go dormant. As Casey jabbed the needle into Sarah's arm, she glanced up at her black eyes and cursed herself for inflicting such a disease on her own child. Casey had long ago sworn never to have children, so that she would never have to face such a moment. But the ship, it seemed, had nonetheless found a way. Now Casey could only pray that she wasn't too late to save Sarah.

"What the hell happened here?" a feminine voice snapped behind her. Dazed and only half interested, Casey turned. Noelle was standing in the hall, peering through the shattered wall.

Casey sighed, dropping the spent needle. "Took you long enough."

As Noelle ran over, Casey crumpled in her arms.

The world faded to black.

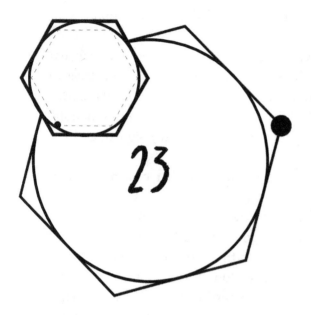

23

Muted moonlight glimmered through the shattered windshield. At the back of the van, several feet below ground, Jacob half stood and half sat behind a crooked computer bank. The screen's light illuminated his face and pieces of the cramped environment as he sifted through files. Turning the machines on had been easy enough, though wi-fi was not available. He'd expected as much. The Internet wasn't working above ground, so it seemed a stretch to imagine it would be working eight feet below ground. Thankfully, the hard drive contained more than enough emails, reports, and desktop folders to keep him busy. There was such an abundance of information that, at first, Jacob doubted he'd find anything useful before he was discovered. Or claustrophobia set in.

When he squirmed to find a comfortable position in which to work, the vehicle lurched around him, sending his stomach rolling and his mind whirring. Jacob couldn't help but feel as if he were huddled within a metal coffin. It was only the burning hope of discovering some secret to help save his daughter's life that kept him firmly planted behind the computer rather than fleeing the entombed vehicle.

He started with the desktop files. The first batch were budgetary reports for what appeared to be research equipment, though what the driver of the van had been researching still eluded Jacob. Closing the file, he scrolled down to a new one, marked "Anomaly." Opening the file, however, offered more questions than answers. Half the words didn't make any sense, and the ones that did sounded like something out of an advanced mathematics class. Jacob had gotten a D in Algebra back in high school, so the equations looked more like hieroglyphics than math problems. Near the bottom he found notations regarding something called the "spherical object," along with a diagram. The image showed a circle drawn within another circle drawn within another, ad nauseam. Surrounding the multi-layered sphere was a series of numbers, which he guessed must be the dimensions of each layer. It looked as if someone had peeled an onion and then decided to measure every layer inside. The long list of equations made his head hurt. His interest, however, grew when he moved to the next report.

The file was labeled "Area 51: 1957–1958."

Like everyone else, Jacob was familiar with the infamous base and all the stories that went along with it. Secret government projects, little green men, and flying saucers. His mind flashed to an image of the ship he'd seen as a child. Digging deeper into the report, his anxiety grew. Then he stopped cold.

His breath escaped him, and his fingers quivered so maddingly that he was no longer able to type. On screen was a vintage black-and-white government ID badge, dated March 2, 1957. The name on the badge: Doctor Casey Stevens. Her hair was done up in an odd bun, and her face looked younger than it did now, but the likeness and the name attached beside it mitigated any doubt that this was his wife. While there had been many mysteries surrounding Casey over the years, including how she hadn't aged more than ten years since her vanishing back in the mid-1980s, no mystery could compare to what he'd just discovered. Casey hadn't simply vanished from

Blackwood and then returned. As impossible as it seemed, she'd lived an entirely different life in an entirely different era. According to the report, Casey Stevens, age twenty-two, had traveled back in time and become a scientist, of all things. The woman who could barely balance a checkbook, had, according to this report, three doctorates, including ones in biology and applied sciences. How was any of this possible? There had to be a logical answer, he told himself. Yet, the further he scrolled, the more fantastical the revelations.

Casey Stevens had been one of two survivors inside the infamous Roswell crash back in 1947. Most of the details had been redacted, including the name of the second survivor. Line after line of black bars covered the digital pages. Still, a few details jumped out. Namely, the mention of a spacecraft, which seemed to have vanished along with Casey, around the middle of 1958. Frustratingly, the precise method of their disappearance wasn't accounted for, though Jacob certainly knew what had become of both eventually. The ship had appeared in Blackwood when he was a child. Then Casey showed up nearly ten years later.

While all of this was certainly fascinating, and more than a little terrifying, none of it answered the most important question, the one that had driven him to dig holes in the ground and climb into a buried van in the middle of the night. None of these reports mentioned anything about the strange phenomenon plaguing the town or, more importantly, the virus that was eating away at his little girl. Frustrated, he shut the file and continued his search.

After scanning several more seemingly unrelated reports, a new file caught his attention. It wasn't on the desktop with the others. Instead, he found it buried in a sub report attached to an invoice for ultrasonic field equipment. The file, dated two weeks prior, was labeled, "Geological Data." That caught his attention. Pages of schematics revealed a computer-generated image that detailed a series of tunnels hidden beneath Blackwood. They looked like the roots of a tree, originating from beneath the mysterious tower, then spreading up through the mountain, climbing toward the town. Scrolling down to the last page, he found a notation, suggesting the tunnels might be burrowing their way toward Casey. "As if drawn to her," the hypothesis stated.

Jacob, though, doubted this conclusion. After having seen the effect on Sarah and not Casey or anyone else, it seemed more likely that the tunnels, whatever they were, had not been stretching up through the mountain for his wife but rather for his daughter. He couldn't be certain why, though an idea began to form in his mind. Along the ground where the holes had first opened, Jacob had discovered multiple examples of a yellow phosphorescent fungus. His mind flashed back to the last time he'd seen Sarah, lying on the hospital bed, her flesh covered in a map of red lines and her eyes inhumanly black. Could the yellow shit he'd seen growing all over town be the cause? If so, could it also offer a cure? Jacob was no scientist, but he doubted these same thoughts hadn't already occurred to the doctors at the tower. And yet, they hadn't found a cure.

Or had they?

Was it possible the government already knew what was wrong with Sarah and simply didn't wish to cure her? Perhaps she was simply another test, just as Blackwood had been. After all, these were the same fuckers who had known these tunnels were rising up through the mountain and hadn't warned anybody. Recalling all the destruction and loss of life that the tunnels had caused, Jacob knew that if anyone was going to find a cure for Sarah, it sure as hell wouldn't be the bastards behind the town's destruction.

Jacob needed a sample of the glowing yellow fungus. What he would do with it once he got it, he didn't know. But for the moment, at least he had a direction. A goal. Hopefully, a plan would soon follow. One that included saving his little girl before it was too late.

Luckily, the yellow fungus was the one thing in ready supply. It caked the buried town and the ground around it. The stuff was literally everywhere. Fueled by a renewed purpose, and the first inkling of a plan, Jacob switched off the monitor and climbed toward the front of the van.

Before he could escape, however, a glowing pulse of light erupted at his back.

The light grew brilliant and blinding, flooding the small van in yellowish ochres. Glancing down, he found its source. The entire rear of the van was overcome by a shimmering luminance, as if the yellow light was eating away at the bottom of the vehicle, consuming metal and machinery. The light threatened to overtake him. Jacob scrambled, clutching at the passenger and driver's seats for purchase, while he pulled himself upward. He didn't need to guess what was happening; he already knew. Under foot, a new portal had opened. Jacob had no intention of waiting around to discover into which new land the opening might lead.

Below, the light grew brighter, closer.

Through the corner of his eye the brilliant radiance threatened to overtake him. He was almost at the shattered windshield, inches from freedom, when the light closed in around him.

He wasn't going to make it.

Suddenly, a gloved hand jutted through the broken windshield, reaching for him. He didn't pause to worry about who it was or how they'd found him. Grasping the hand with his right hand, he used his left to push himself up and out. Biting night air slapped Jacob's face, welcoming him out from the vehicle's wreckage. Above, Burke smirked at him from behind his suit's visor.

Jacob didn't stop to catch his breath. Pulling Burke along with him, he clambered out of the ditch and away from the buried vehicle. Behind them, the yellow glow burned brighter and brighter, consuming the earth with jagged ripples of pale, sickly light. Jacob cursed, knowing what would come next. He dragged Burke behind him, trying to gain as much distance from the wreckage as possible. As they stumbled along the uneven earth, Jacob ignored Burke's loud protests. All that mattered was getting away. Far away. Too late—

The ground erupted at their feet.

It didn't sink. Instead, Jacob and Burke were thrown forwards by an earth-shattering shockwave. Landing on the ground, Jacob flipped onto his back. To his left, the van was spit out of the ground, tossed high into the night sky. Then it crashed, rolling end over end several feet away. The impact sent debris everywhere, kicking up chunks of dirt. When it finally stopped, the van stood like a broken white tooth poking out from a gummy earth.

As strange as that sight was, it became immediately overtaken by an enormous shape bursting out of the spot Jacob had vacated only seconds earlier. From the ground's open wound sprang a huge black monolith. Rocks rained down with bone-crushing speed. Erupting from the earth, the black shape climbed higher and higher. Huddled below, Jacob and Burke cowered inside the thing's stretching shadow, dodging left, then right to avoid the falling debris.

When the violence eventually subsided, they turned in unison toward the hulking mass looming overhead like a sword. Only, it wasn't a sword.

It was a *submarine.*

The vessel's metal body lurched, swaying with a deafening crunch of grinding metal. Eventually, the sub settled comfortably in place. Stunned into silence, Jacob and Burke stood quietly beneath its long shadow. When Burke's people rushed over, weapons in hand, shouting frantically, Jacob finally found his voice. He spun on Burke, his fists shaking.

"You *knew* this would happen. I saw the geographical data. You could have warned us!"

Burke didn't bother to protest or offer another halfhearted lie. Instead, his eyes widened. "We never imagined anything like this. A submarine . . . here?"

Above, a hatch opened, and several dark figures crawled out near the top of the slanted vessel. Noting the shape of the ship and the dress of its crew, Jacob groaned inwardly.

"Not just a submarine," he replied. "It's a Nazi U-boat."

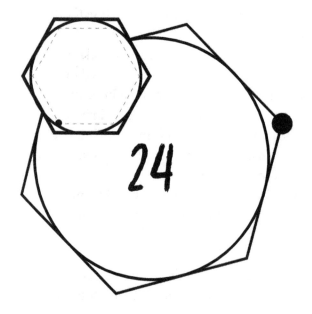

24

Perched on a metal chair, Donovan fidgeted in handcuffs. His face was a mishmash of purple bruises, and his eyes darted around the small room like a rat searching for a hole in which to hide. A door opened, revealing a young woman in her mid-twenties. *Attractive,* he thought, eyeing her black hair and equally dark eyes. Under other circumstances, Donovan would have enjoyed a chance to get to know her more intimately. Now he just wanted to skip the chit-chat and make a beeline out of there. As the door shut behind her, he glimpsed two armed guards outside and realized he wouldn't be leaving anytime soon.

The woman sat calmly across from him and took out a strange device. It lit up in her hands as her fingers scrolled across it. She was reading something on the small screen. Curious, Donovan leaned closer to get a better look.

"It's a phone," the woman said, holding it up.

Donovan had owned a mobile phone back in the 1990s, but it

looked nothing like the Star Trek-type device that looked so small and compact in the woman's thin fingers.

"Remarkable," he exclaimed. "Any chance I could get one?"

The woman started to smile, then frowned.

"Not likely, Mr. Daley."

"You know me?" he asked, more than a little surprised.

She spun the phone around, showing him a picture of himself from back during his time in the 1950s. "Gotta say," she continued, "you look rather spry for a man of your age."

Now it was Donovan's turn to grin. "If that's a proposition—"

"It's not. Care to tell me how you got here? Our last report has you in 1958, and yet, here you are in the twenty-first century. Quite the magic trick."

"We could say the same about your friend, Casey Stevens."

"She's not my friend," the woman replied. At the sound of that, Donovan's back straightened, and his ears perked up. Perhaps he might find a way out of his situation yet.

"She's dangerous, you know, Miss . . .?"

"Reese," she replied. "Special Agent Noelle Reese."

Donovan cocked his head. "Funny. I used to know a *Major* Reese."

Noelle leaned closer. "He was my father."

Encouraged by this bit of news, Donovan began formulating a plan on how to get her on his side. And, more importantly, how to get the hell out of there. In this instance, he decided the truth might be the best approach. As the saying goes, *the truth will set you free.* He certainly hoped so.

"He was a brave man. You should be very proud."

"Sooo," she said, "he *is* dead?"

Donovan worked his facial muscles to convey the appearance of sorrowful regret. "I'm afraid so." He didn't elaborate. He wanted her to work for every single morsel.

She leaned in even closer, inches away. Donovan wondered if he could simply overpower the young woman and make a run for it. But he recalled the two guards outside the door and thought better of it. Still, he didn't shrink back into his seat; he met her gaze head on. After a long pause, the woman relented and asked the next inevitable question.

"How did my father die?"

Again, Donovan tried to convey the proper level of sympathy in his eyes and in his voice. "We were flung into the distant future. A horrible future that I'm here trying to prevent. Just like your father would if he were still alive. He died trying to stop those things Casey calls 'seekers,' though I don't know if they actually have a name." Donovan shuddered at the remembrance of the gray beings. That part wasn't an act. "I've seen . . ." He paused, trying to form the words to describe all the horror he'd witnessed in the past and the future. "I've seen what becomes of us. Of humanity."

"And you think that by killing Casey and her daughter you can somehow prevent it?"

Donovan nodded. "I've been told as much."

"By whom?"

He hesitated, not out of any concern about the truth but more from uncertainty on how best to describe it. "Other beings."

Noelle's eyebrows shot up. "You mean aliens?"

Donovan nodded. "I call her Daphne."

Noelle thrust herself back into her chair, and her face turned sour. "Is this some kind of joke to you?"

"No, no, no—I'm being serious," he protested, waving his hand-cuffed arms. "That's just what I called her. At least, *it* appeared to me as a woman, though I know it wasn't." He lowered his voice. "I don't know how to describe what I saw. Like I said, it was something . . . other."

"And where did you meet this 'other'?"

"Inside the sphere." He cocked a thumb toward the door. "You know, that red shiny thing you've got hidden in the basement? The seekers use it to travel through time, but they didn't create it." His eyes narrowed, and his tone grew conspiratorial. "The damn thing's alive."

Noelle shook her head in frustration. Donovan couldn't decide if she didn't believe him or she was simply too overwhelmed by the new information. "Let's get back to my dad for a moment. How *precisely* did he die?"

And there it was. Donovan saw this as the moment to turn her to his side. Once again, all he needed to use was the simple truth. He shrugged. "He died saving Casey."

The young woman's face flushed beet red. It was as if she'd long suspected this, and now he'd confirmed her worst fears. *Oh good*, he thought, *she hates Casey as much as I do. Now there's something I can use.* He tried to make his eyes water, but the best he could do was twitch his lip and make his back shiver. It wasn't a great performance, but it didn't need to be. He already had her. Hook, line, and sinker.

"He would have made it back, just like I did, but instead he decided to save Casey's life, at the cost of his own." He sniffed back tears that never came. "I wish I could say I was as brave as he was. But if I was, I wouldn't be here to warn you, would I?"

She took that in, her knuckles whitening on the table. "Warn me about what?"

"Casey and her daughter carry a disease. A terrible virus meant to wipe us all out and replace us with those gray beings, the seekers." Donovan held up his bound hands. "You need to let me finish my mission. For everyone's sake."

Noelle didn't reply. She simply sat across from him, studying his face. Behind those eyes, however, Donovan could see the wheels turning.

Yep, he thought, grinning inwardly. *Hook, line, and sinker.*

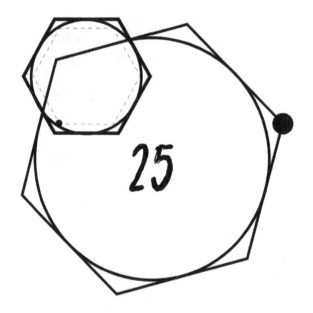

25

Mommy..."
Casey Anderson awoke a new woman. Or, rather, she
awoke as a new version of herself. A version she'd long suppressed,
which now clawed its way back to the surface with all the memories
of her missing years fully intact. Opening her eyes, she found herself
sitting beside the hospital bed with Sarah peering at her through a
sheet of plastic. Casey tore the curtain aside and revealed her daughter's tired but seemingly healthy face staring back at her. Sarah's eyes
had returned to their emerald green, and her skin was no longer
crisscrossed with red veins. Casey's gamble, it seemed, had paid off.
She hugged her daughter, feeling Sarah's tiny body tremble in her
arms.

"What happened?" Sarah asked, looking around. "Is this a
hospital?"

"Not quite," Casey replied. After a sustained embrace and a tight
squeeze, Casey released her. When she did, the emptiness in her arms

made her heart sink from the momentary loss. After two days of hoping and praying, Casey's relief was tainted by the knowledge that although Sarah's infection had been quieted, the disease in her blood was permanent. It would never go away. Casey Anderson might not have known that, but Doctor Casey Stevens certainly did.

Unless . . . she thought, the wheels turning in her mind, *unless I can find the ship.*

The idea was a slim hope at best. Casey had no way of locating the ship. As soon as it had dropped her off, naked and pregnant eight years ago, the damned thing had probably flown back to the future. Careful to keep her bubbling rage in check, she pushed the absurd idea aside. Glancing around the sterile environment, with the broken wall on one side and the bathroom on the other, the two versions of Casey fought inwardly for control. Half of her, the logical and intelligent scientist who had helped create Area 51, wanted to leave that room and find out precisely what had caused the tunnels beneath Blackwood. The other half, Mrs. Anderson, the loving mother and wife, pleaded to stay right where she was, beside her precious daughter, who only hours ago seemed to be on the verge of death.

Sarah noted the conflict written across Casey's face. "What is it, Mom?"

Casey eyed the guards standing outside their clear plastic door. Then she put on her best version of a warm smile. "Nothing. Everything's fine, honey."

Of course, it wasn't. At least not until she had more information. Casey needed to find Noelle Reese and get some answers. Pausing, Doctor Stevens finally understood who Noelle really was. Major Reese had mentioned his little girl long ago. His grown daughter, it seemed, had followed in his footsteps, all the way back to Blackwood. Though, unlike the man who had sacrificed so much for Casey, including his life, Casey doubted she could trust his daughter nearly as much. The major had never lied, never kept her in the dark, and she doubted he would now if he were still alive. Whatever Noelle's motives, she couldn't be trusted. Not yet. Perhaps, not ever. A pang of guilt shot up from her gut and made her throat tighten with nausea. She shoved the memory of Major Reese away. She had a far more immediate problem: the frightened little girl trembling beside her.

While Mrs. Anderson had been a devoted wife and loving mother these past eight years, Doctor Stevens realized there was a much bigger picture at play. Mrs. Anderson had known nothing about the threat she faced, even when the world itself had swallowed her up, burying her in the earth. Doctor Stevens, on the other hand, knew there must be a connection between the little girl and the tunnels that had swallowed the entire town. Her mind leaped to the hypersphere buried beneath the spire. Had Noelle and these people done something to cause it to create the tunnels? Or had the hypersphere simply been seeking out Casey or Sarah, or both, of its own accord? Whatever the cause, she had to put an end to whatever it was doing. If she didn't, the base and the very earth beneath them might suck them down into the ground. And this time no one would be left to dig them out.

Casey glanced past Sarah, eyeing two guards standing outside the clear plastic door. Covered head to toe in yellow hazmat suits, it seemed clear that whoever was in charge knew at least a little something about what was contained in her blood. The living machines. The nanites. Not that those silly costumes would help the guards stop her.

Turning her gaze back to the little girl who called her "Mommy," Doctor Stevens had to assume that if they knew about her, they must also realize Sarah was just as potentially dangerous. Perhaps more so. Doctor Stevens had sworn long ago never to have children because if she did, the virus within her would eventually spread, just as she'd seen in a vision long ago. An image came bubbling back in her mind, one of countless hospital beds filling an entire Portland football stadium, with giant ships looming in the sky above. It had been a glimpse of a future she'd sworn would never happen. But now, having given birth to a child, that future might become a reality. Neither Mrs. Anderson, nor her alter ego, Doctor Stevens, was quite certain who the father was, though Doctor Stevens could certainly guess.

Her former assistant at Area 51, Harold. The ship had fueled his mind with sexual desires and lurid images. Could the ship have manipulated Harold to the point that he had forced himself upon her? She couldn't believe he would have gone so far even under the sway of the ship's control. Still, it was the only theory that made sense. Not that it really mattered. Whoever might have been the biological father, it was clear now that the ship had manipulated Casey's impregnation for the very result that was now staring back at her with wide, teary eyes. The ship and its masters, the ones she called "seekers," had finally accomplished their goal.

Inching away from the little girl, Doctor Stevens eyed the closed doorway. She needed to get out of that room and find some answers. Only then would she have any chance of stopping whatever might happen next. Standing, Doctor Stevens busied herself with forming a plan until small fingers wrapped themselves around her arm, urging her to pause.

"Don't go, Mommy," Sarah pleaded. "Please don't leave me here."

Doctor Stevens felt an ache, like an invisible knife piercing her rib cage. Despite what she knew must be done, the mother inside her refused to walk away. A surge of frustration bubbled inside. Mrs. Anderson, it seemed, was fighting for control. Except she wasn't real, Doctor Stevens assured herself. The small-town wife and mother had simply been a façade, created by Casey's lack of memory. Like a fill-in-the-blank picture, she'd been used to paint over a void. Now that the picture was complete, the façade wasn't eager to relinquish control. Even after having discovered that her child was a biproduct of rape, Mrs. Anderson refused to abandon her daughter. With no time to argue, Doctor Stevens acquiesced. Huffing, she pulled Sarah off the bed and wrapped her in a blanket.

Then the lights went out.

In the pitch darkness, Sarah trembled in Casey's arms. "What's happening?"

"Shh," Casey hissed. Stretching out with her senses, she felt pulsing agitation emanating from the two men outside. Stretching out farther, a wave of confusion smashed into her. It didn't come from the guards. They were curious about the blackout but not concerned, and they certainly were not frightened. But someone was. Trying to make sense of the sudden onslaught of anxiety and confusion from somewhere outside, Casey closed off her other senses. Sound, smell, and even the feel of her daughter's shaking fingers withered away until, at last, there was nothing but the onslaught of voices in her mind.

"*What the hell is that?*" She heard a feminine voice scream.

"*Not possible. Not possible,*" a masculine voice said. "*Run! We have to get out of here!*" Then the din grew to a cacophony of noise, and Casey lost the connection.

Yanking her mind back, she heard Sarah's voice in her ear. "What are we going to do?"

"Leave," Casey replied. Her icy tone silenced any further questions. She placed Sarah on the floor and prepared herself for what she knew was about to happen. She didn't need light to see the exit or those blocking it. With half the wall broken open, the guards hadn't bothered to lock the door. Not that it would have mattered. Igniting the nanites, Casey felt the familiar inner warmth as they activated throughout her bloodstream. With a wrench, she pulled the door so hard it broke from its hinges. The masked guards swung toward her, their headlamps peering backwards with blinding luminance. Even so, a blur of movement accosted them, faster than their eyes, or their lamps, could register.

Casey gripped the man to her right, lifting his arms before he could raise his rifle, then flung him head over heels until his back smacked into the floor.

Watching the violence illuminated by the guards' headlamps, Sarah's eyes bulged.

Casey spun to the guard to her left, knocking his weapon aside and kicking him so hard, he tumbled six feet across the floor. The entire attack lasted mere seconds. When it was over, the guards lay sprawled about like broken dolls.

Sarah's voice turned from concern to horror. "Mommy!"

Casey reached back into the room, grabbing Sarah with one hand and a rifle with the other. "Don't worry, honey. They're just sleeping."

Casey left the guards' flashlights behind. She didn't need a lamp to make her way in the dark. And besides, it would be best if Sarah didn't see more than necessary. Pulling her daughter along, they ran down the hall.

Outside, alarms blared. They seemed too faint and distant to have been caused by her escape. Whatever was happening, for now at least, Casey welcomed the diversion.

As they turned a corner, she continued to stretch out with her senses, trying to keep her awareness limited to the halls in front of her. But the dome appeared to be empty. Where had all the nurses and doctors gone?

As if in reply, the curved wall to their left began to sway inward, its metal bones shattering to the floor. Something had crashed into the structure. Something big. Worried that the dome might collapse on them, Casey tossed the rifle aside and pulled Sarah into her arms.

Above, the roof sank. Sarah couldn't see what was happening, but she could hear it. Her screams rose above the noise of bending metal and blaring alarms. Clutching Sarah close to her chest, Casey tapped a little deeper into her nanites, activating them just enough to give her some speed.

In a whirl, Casey bolted down the hall, rushing around corners in search of an exit. Overhead, the dome buckled and swayed, tilting farther and farther downward. In moments they would be crushed. Casey ran faster. Ducking her head protectively over Sarah, they crashed through the closed front door. It shattered like metal confetti.

Casey lunged outside just as the dome came tumbling down behind them. Reeling, she knelt on the ground, gasping for breath. As soon as her mouth opened, however, she quickly shut it. The air tasted wrong. Like spoiled milk. The stench of it made her throat tighten and her stomach convulse. Casey stood amidst a congealed fog, tinged with an eerie yellow. It reminded her of the fungus in the ground. Only now the stuff, whatever it was, had seeped into the air. It hung around them with a soggy wetness, entering Casey and Sarah's lungs before they had time to realize what they were breathing.

Adding to Casey's growing concern, something clambered behind them, smashing over the dome's wreckage. She spun as weirdly
shaped silhouettes emerged through the yellow fog, bearing down on
them. Reeling from the noxious air, she stumbled backwards, pulling
Sarah into the mud. Overhead, the weird shapes took form.

Slithering into view.

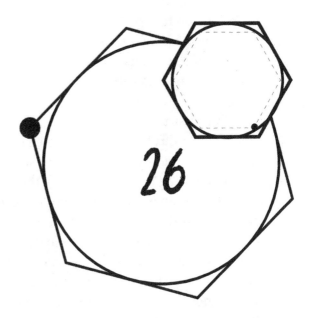

26

W hat are you waiting for?" Burke shouted over the helicopter's thumping rotors. "Land!"

The pilot turned, his eyes wide and his face sour. "Land *where,* sir?"

Peering over the side, Jacob understood what the pilot meant. The entire makeshift base was drenched in a fog. The mist, glowing pale yellow as if lit from within, drifted about unlike any fog he'd ever seen before. It didn't seem to melt into the landscape; rather, it smothered the earth with a densely globular shape. Thick and soupy, it engulfed the camp and the lowest portion of the tower. The helicopter banked, lurching violently. At that height, Jacob would have expected the helicopter's rotors to dissipate the fog directly beneath. Instead, it lay billowing below, seemingly unaffected by the chopper's presence. Somewhere down there were his wife and daughter. Desperate to find them, Jacob inched his head farther out the open doorway, trying to see how far of a drop it would be.

As if reading his thoughts, Burke pulled him back inside.

"We're too far up," he said. "You'll kill yourself."

Relenting, Jacob's brow furrowed as he tried to imagine where such a vaporous blanket might have originated. Over the course of two days, Jacob had witnessed so many strange scenes that mere fog shouldn't have concerned him to the degree that it did. Yet, what lay below wasn't simply an evening mist; that much seemed certain. Normal fog didn't have clearly defined borders. But from his vantage point, it was plain to see how the mist encompassed only the tower and surrounding base. Beyond that the mist was completely absent, as if cut off by an invisible border. Whatever the fog was, it had to be connected to the tower and the tunnels and all the strange occurrences. His mind flashed to the sabertooth tiger tearing through the hunters while he hid at the cave's entrance. Before he could linger on that horror show, however, he turned his thoughts to the most recent, and perhaps oddest, event so far: a submarine rising out of the ground like a monolith . . .

The giant cylinder, covered in rivets and bolts, swayed uneasily, perched halfway out of the earth. It seemed to Jacob that it wasn't a matter of *if* the U-boat would come crashing down on all their heads but *when*. Though, admittedly, that hadn't been his first concern. Burke's men had quickly raised their sidearms, pointing them at the sub's commander. He and his officers watched them with astonishment. Taking in the scene around them, they probably wondered if this was all an elaborate trick or illusion. And by the look of Burke's unhinged jaw behind his plastic visor, it appeared that he was having the same concern. Never had anyone seen such a sight. The fact that those who had emerged from the underwater vessel were part of the most hated army in human history certainly didn't help the situation. Seemingly more out of a resigned duty than any real hope for survival, the U-boat commander drew his sidearm, pointing it at the yellow dots below. As surreal as the image of the submarine may have been to those on the ground, Jacob could only imagine what the sight of yellow hazmat-clad men raising weapons must have seemed like to the U-boat crew. It must have been as if they'd landed on an alien planet. Considering how different the world was from their own time, Jacob decided they wouldn't be completely wrong.

With that thought, he stepped forward, gesticulating wildly.

"Damn it!" Burke barked. "What do you think you're doing?"

Ignoring him, Jacob slowly approached the vessel. *We come in peace*, was the first thing that came to mind. Then, realizing just how awful these adversaries might be, his thoughts hardened toward a more somber response.

"You're in Oregon!" Jacob shouted. "It's alright! The war is over!"

The commander peered down at him, frowning. Either he didn't understand English, or he assumed this was all some sort of elaborate trick. Perhaps both. Pointing his weapon at Jacob, he shouted something in German.

Careful not to do anything to startle the commander, who was already on edge, Jacob turned slowly toward Burke and his team. "Anyone here speak German?"

No one replied. *Oh, good. As if things weren't difficult and weird enough.*

After a pregnant pause, one of the yellow-clad figures stumbled forward, a woman, and raised her hand like a schoolgirl. "I do."

She was a nurse, Jacob assumed, noting her medical bag. Her legs stumbled and quivered as she lumbered over. Stopping beside Jacob, she craned her head all the way back, finding the sub commander through her restrictive visor. As if trying to balance speaking loudly while simultaneously hoping to keep her tone non-threatening, the nervous woman addressed the commander in German. When she finished, he didn't respond. Turning to his men and then back toward the yellow-clad woman, he offered nothing more than a quizzical glare.

Breaking the silence, Burke approached. "What'd you say to him, Monica?"

"I told him he was in the twenty-first century, it was peacetime, and asked him to please not shoot us."

"Doesn't look like he understood you," Jacob said.

"Oh, he got the message, alright." Burke said. "He's just trying to decide if *we're* all crazy or *he* is." With broad, slow gestures, he raised his weapon for all to see and then placed it in the watery mud. When the commander still didn't respond, Burke took several steps back, away from the gun. Behind him, his team did the same. Not under orders but rather because no one seemed eager for a fight. The Nazis had been the evilest regime in recent memory, but that's all they were to Jacob and his generation now, a memory. The fight was long over, and the Nazis had lost. There didn't seem any reason to start it all up again on top of the Oregon mountains nearly a hundred years later. At least, Jacob hoped not. As he turned his gaze up to the commander, they all held a collective breath and awaited his reply.

Even though the commander and his men were lost and out-numbered, fear, Jacob knew, could make a person do just about anything. If backed into a corner, a soldier—or sailor, in this case— would always fight. Jacob only prayed that Burke's gesture would carry enough weight to stop what might have seemed inevitable moments earlier.

After a long, cautious pause, the commander's weapon dropped from his gloved hand, tumbling and clanging down the side of the submarine until it landed in the mud. When his officers did the same, everyone seemed to exhale at once. The crisis had been averted.

Or so Jacob thought.

Less than an hour after the Germans had been brought down from the submarine and secured in the lumber yard, Burke received a panicked call. Stunned to see a working phone, Jacob followed as Burke rushed from the lumber yard toward the crater. He heard Burke shout into the phone, panic rising in his throat. "What are you talking about? What the hell is happening?"

Something was wrong back at the Watchtower base, although ap-parently, what it was remained as much a mystery to Burke as it did to Jacob. Unable to get an appropriate answer, Burke rushed toward one of the black helicopters, its blades already spinning and ready for takeoff.

Not bothering to wait for an invitation, Jacob jumped on board. When the pilot started to rise from his seat, presumably to remove him, Burke waved him back.

"It's alright; let him come."

Jacob nodded a silent thank-you, though he didn't really have anything to thank Burke for. Jacob had seen the files in the van. These people had known about the tunnels for months and had done nothing except watch and wait.

An experiment, Jacob thought with a frown. *And we were the lab rats.* Only the experiment was no longer contained to Blackwood.

As the helicopter descended along the side of the mountain, swinging about and heading toward the hundred-story mystery tower, they soon found their way blocked by a blanket of fog.

If it *was* a fog, it certainly didn't behave like any natural occurrence Jacob had ever seen. Whatever the smoky yellow substance was, it refused to give way, even under the helicopter's swirling blades. Somewhere down there, Jacob's family needed him. Burke had said it was a hundred-foot drop at least. Eyeing the white domes, he noted only two out of the three remained standing.

Jacob turned to the pilot. "Can you get me over one of those?"

The pilot nodded. Burke's jaw fell open. "You can't be serious . . ."

Recalling the hunters who had died while he cowered in the cave, Jacob leaned out of the helicopter and prepared to jump. A wave of nausea hit him as they drew closer to the vaporous mist. The air stank of spoiled milk. His throat tightened, and his stomach lifted as it threatened to lurch its contents. Eyeing Burke's blank reaction through his visor, Jacob wished he had one of those hazmat suits himself. When one of the dome's structures filled his view, Jacob pushed away the fear and nausea and focused on his wife and child.

Then he jumped.

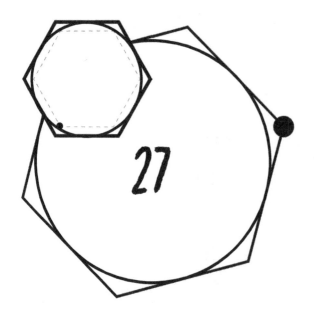

27

One moment, Donovan Daley had been hoping to sway the pretty FBI lady into helping in his macabre quest; the next, the world had come crashing down around him. Literally.

It began with flickering lights, the bulbs pulsing, dimming. Then total darkness.

His mind racing, Donovan once again urged Agent Reese to unlock his handcuffs, and once again she refused. Next, the walls and the ceiling came crashing down around their heads. Noelle was quicker to react, diving beneath the table for protection. Donovan wasn't as fast. His upper back took the brunt of it as thin support beams bent and twisted, tumbling over him like a batch of matchsticks. More a glorified tent than an actual building, the structure collapsed in a mixture of nylon fabric and strips of metal. The impact hadn't been enough to kill him, but it was more than enough to make Donovan see stars and his lungs to burst, coughing up dust and bits of debris. Preoccupied with checking his body for broken limbs, he didn't have the time or the inclination to wonder what had caused the world to come crashing down in the first place. Once he was sure no bones were broken and that the pain shooting along his spine wasn't anything too serious, he struggled to roll over and find his bearings. Above, a dark blanket of plastic cloth and thin beams covered his view.

"You still alive?" Noelle asked from somewhere behind him.

"Yeah. No thanks to you."

Noelle crawled over, guided by a flashlight. Only, he noted, it wasn't really a flashlight. She was holding that same odd rectangular telephone he'd seen before. An electrical Swiss Army knife of sorts, it certainly seemed handy in a pinch. Eyeing the device as it swung about, Donovan couldn't help wishing he had one. If given the opportunity, he'd probably have taken it from her. But right then, still cuffed and buried under a mountain of debris, he needed this woman a lot more than she needed him. That, he decided, had to be rectified. If he'd learned one thing from Prewitt during the 1950s, it was how to insinuate himself so that everyone around him thought they needed him. That tactic had kept Prewitt in power until he died. Donovan wanted to seem just as invaluable now to make sure he lived. Turning onto his side, he glanced around, finding a patch of darkness about ten feet to his left. He pointed toward the spot. "I think I found a way out."

Noelle's phone light turned left, illuminating the black patch. A haphazard pile of beams had punched an opening in the cloth ceiling, making it appear like a tiny cave. Not big enough to walk through, but if they stayed low and crawled . . .

Without waiting for her reply, Donovan led the way. "Stay behind me," he said, trying his best to sound protective. As if to say, *We're in this together, sweetheart, so don't leave me down here.* Whether or not the thought had even entered the young FBI lady's mind, he didn't know, and he wasn't about to ask. By the time Noelle had crawled over to the tiny opening, Donovan had lifted the beams higher, creating a larger exit for her.

Still, she lingered beside him, hesitating to turn her back on him. Holding the phone's light in one hand and her sidearm in the other, Noelle searched his face, as if looking for any signs of deception.

"Thanks," she said with a cautious tone.

"Like I told you, lady, we're on the same side." Donovan paused, struggling under the weight. "Although this would be a hell of a lot easier if I weren't handcuffed."

"Nice try," she replied with a coy grin before heading through the opening.

Donovan had overplayed his hand, and he knew it. Without further comment, he followed her out. Even under distress, though, he couldn't help admiring the curve of her ass inches from his face. Usually, he'd have sneered, offering a poignant quip, but right then the young woman's attractive anatomy was the last thing on his mind.

Another woman consumed his thoughts. *Casey.*

Four times now he'd tried and failed to kill the blonde bitch. Perhaps it might be easier to get the FBI lady to do it for him. That was another lesson he'd learned from the little shit, Prewitt. *Why dirty your hands when you can find someone who's already playing in the mud?* It didn't take a telepath to know this lady loathed Casey, blaming her for her father's death. With the correct amount of pressure, Noelle might just finish the job for him. Then he could deal with the little girl. Not that he was overly eager for that part either. Whatever his faults, Donovan had never been eager to hunt down and murder a child. But having seen the disastrous future that awaited if he faltered, he'd finally come to terms with the dirty business at hand.

Like mother, like daughter, he thought. *They're both dangerous.*

And, like a dangerous animal, they needed to be put down. Just as soon as Donovan got out from under this damnable collapsed dome. Maybe Casey and the girl had been crushed to death by whatever had knocked the dome down. He doubted he was that lucky. Not with all those nanite abilities Casey possessed. When she'd first stumbled upon him in the hospital room, he thought for sure he was a goner. Only, Casey didn't seem to have her heightened abilities.

That is, until the moment he thought he might finally choke the life out of her. Then, of course, the nanite thingies came back on, tossing him clear across the room.

Whatever else Casey might have been, she was certainly resilient. Then again, Donovan reminded himself, so was he. After all the years and his travels through time and space and everything they'd been through, he knew it had to come to an end. One way or another.

"Keep up," Noelle urged.

Shaking off his lingering thoughts, Donovan crawled faster.

When they eventually found a way out of the crumpled dome, Donovan wished they hadn't.

A din of screaming alarms assaulted his eardrums, and nauseating stenches assaulted his nose and mouth, turning his insides to a rumbling thunderstorm. Worse still, his eyes were blinded by a hazy yellow fog that drenched him like a damp blanket. Falling to his knees, gagging, Donovan wished he were still trapped inside the debris.

"Dear God," he said, plugging his nose, which turned his voice into a nasal whine. "What's that awful stench?"

Noelle didn't bother opening her mouth to answer. She clamped both hands over her face and shook her head, though whether she was silently saying that she didn't know what the smell was or was trying to repel the stink, Donovan couldn't tell. Before he had time to worry about it, however, he heard an awful sliding sound beside him, loud enough to be heard above the blaring alarm.

Noelle's eyes narrowed in the gloom. She'd heard it too. Reluctant to follow her gaze, Donovan forced his shoulders to turn until, with great effort, his neck pulled his head around, searching the soupy atmosphere. The sliding sound returned. Thick, moist, and close.

Stumbling backwards, Donovan tumbled into Noelle as a curved shape arched into view, rising far above, veiled in the haze. He felt the FBI lady's fingers tighten around his arm, pulling him away. Behind the curved obstacle, a second thing, just as large, slid into view. Even at close range, however, Donovan couldn't make out what the shapes were.

Then a loud hissing snapped the last piece of the puzzle into place. Donovan opened his mouth to scream, only to be stifled by the sickly aroma. Coughing, he keeled over and crumpled to the ground. The curved things turned in his direction. Hissing.

Through the damp ochre fog, two giant snakes lurched forward. So large in size and scope that Donovan couldn't make out their faces or darting tongues. Only their underbellies and scaled sides were visible. But it was more than enough to cause Donovan's head to swim and his legs to give out. He would have fallen in the dirt, lying prostrate before the serpentine creatures, if not for hands reaching out through the muck and pulling him away.

With a surprisingly firm grip, Noelle pulled him backwards toward one of the two still-standing domes. With each lumbering step through the heavy, squishy mud, the snakes' forms grew more and more distinct. They were huge beyond belief. After all these years of running from gray creatures, oily monsters with black tentacles, and flying ships that fucked with his mind, Donovan didn't believe anything could frighten him anymore. But as he took in the enormity of the twin snakes' bodies, forty feet long at least, he realized he had been dead wrong. Unlike the other horrors he'd faced over the years, this fear was primal. Everything about the creatures seemed wrong to him, and his mind protested at what his eyes saw and his ears heard. So consumed by a fit of trembling, Donovan no longer noticed the sickly stench invading his mouth and nostrils.

It wasn't until he heard a series of distant shouts that his eyes turned away, only to find another serpent blocking their path. This one's pointed head was clearly visible. Between its jaws a man screamed and screamed until he vanished in the beast's mouth and screamed no more.

"What are you waiting for?" Agent Reese whispered in his ear. "Move your ass, or I'm leaving you here." The warmth of her breath against his skin momentarily snapped him out of his horrified daze. Noelle yanked him into one of the remaining dome's arched entrances. Though what good that would do, Donovan couldn't imagine. Now that he knew the source of what had destroyed the first dome they'd been inside, he doubted the second or third would offer much protection. And besides, did snakes even use their eyes to hunt? He didn't know, and he didn't want to find out.

As if in answer to his many questions, Noelle's whispered voice returned. "They're called Titanoboa," she said. "Prehistoric snakes from South America. I learned about them in school."

Donovan's first question was: "What kind of school taught such stuff?" But he pushed it aside and moved straight to his second: "Wh-what the fuck are they doing here?"

While Noelle had had the good sense to whisper, Donovan's voice carried loudly. Thrusting her fingers over his mouth, her face tightened as they silently waited to see if he'd drawn the serpents' attention. When the hissing drifted away, her grip slackened. Then she raised her sidearm, seemingly hoping to drive home the point: *Keep quiet or else.* But at that moment, guns didn't frighten him. Nor did FBI ladies. Hell, he'd have taken a whole damn army of bug-eyed seekers over the enormous reptiles slithering past. Donovan shivered.

In the distance, a mixture of human screams, presumably as people were being eaten, punctuated the dire situation. His head slowly clearing, Donovan decided it was time to cut and run. Casey and her mutant daughter were no longer a concern. Let humanity die from whatever plague those two carried. He no longer cared. Not even a little. All he was worried about was getting the hell out of Dodge.

He needed to get back to the hypersphere.

Noting Noelle's haggard, raspy breath, a plan began to formulate in his mind. After all, if he was going to get past the giant prehistoric snakes, he'd need a diversion.

Bait.

His gaze swiveling around, he considered how best to use the young female agent to aid in his escape. First, he would have to re-move the firearm she clutched at her side. Second, he'd have to get the key to his handcuffs. And third, Donovan thought as his lips curled into a grin, he needed to push her into the snakes' path.

But as quickly as the idea had come, it vanished. His smile turned to a frown. If he hoped to get back to the hypersphere, he would need someone with clearance to enter the tower. Without his hazmat suit for disguise, he doubted he'd be able to simply stroll in. Especially now, with the alarms blaring and the base in lockdown.

Before his rambling thoughts could progress any further, two figures bolted along the dome's curved wall and stumbled into view. One was draped in a hazmat suit, a machine gun in his gloved arms. The other, dressed in jeans and a plaid shirt, looked even more frightened than Donovan, if that was possible.

"Where's my wife?" the man whispered through gritted teeth. "Where's my daughter?"

Wife? Donovan thought. *Daughter?* His expression turned to stone. *Shit.*

He could well imagine what would happen once Mr. Casey and his armed companion learned about what Donovan had done. Attempted murder of one's family wasn't the sort of thing someone quickly forgave. Now more than ever, he wanted to crawl into a hole and hide. Edging away from the men's questioning gaze, something poked between his shoulder blades. Noelle's gun.

He was trapped.

"Who's this?" the man in the hazmat suit asked. His tone made it clear that he was the FBI lady's boss. Holding his breath, Donovan fidgeted, waiting for the bitch to tell the men everything.

"Burke, meet Donovan Daley," Noelle said, nudging him forward with the barrel of her gun.

The man behind the plastic visor, Burke, smiled broadly. "Reeaaally?" When Donovan didn't answer, Burke took it as silent confirmation. "I thought you were dead. Our reports say as much. But I guess if Casey's still running around after all these years, why not you?"

"I do seem to get around," Donovan said, hoping to keep the nervousness out of his tone.

Burke noted the handcuffs and tilted his head toward Noelle. She shrugged. Thankfully, it was a silent conversation. Whether this was evidence that she might help him kill Casey and her daughter or she simply didn't wish to elaborate in front of Casey's husband, he couldn't be certain.

"Where's my family?" Casey's husband asked, peering into the soggy mist.

When neither Burke nor Noelle responded, Donovan decided it might be a good time to turn their attention away from himself and back toward the woman who'd caused all this in the first place. Offering up his best smile, his fingers spread open like spidery legs.

"I know where they are," Donovan said, and for once he wasn't lying. He knew precisely where Casey would go. The same place he would, if not for the giant snakes and the gun at his back. Everyone waited for him to finish his thought. Instead, Donovan lifted his cuffed wrists. "I must admit, I find it hard to think clearly in these things."

The two men exchanged a curious look, as if trying to decide how to respond. Before either of them did, Noelle shoved Donovan out of the archway and into the fog.

"No problem," she said. "You're free to go,"

Donovan stumbled through the soggy mist. His first instinct was to run, though his knees refused to stop shaking. A loud hissing came from behind—no, from his left. He turned just in time to see something enormous slither past. Rough scales grazed against him. The smell of the creature was even worse than the yellow mist. Its stench caused his head to float and his stomach to spin. He was so sickened by the sensory overload, it took him a moment before he noticed Burke had hauled him back into the archway.

When Donovan finally regained his composure, he stood there, trembling, and nodded. "She's headed for the hypersphere," he said through chattering teeth. What he didn't add was what awaited her once she got there. The sphere wanted her daughter dead.

Good, Donovan decided. *Let the goddamned thing do its own fucking dirty work.*

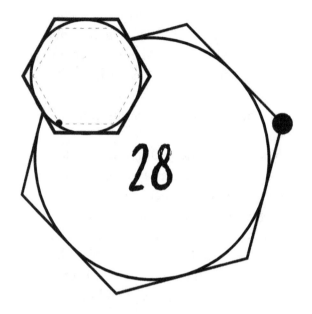

28

Hidden beneath a jeep, Casey cradled Sarah in the wet mud while impossible monsters, seemingly drawn from myth, slithered past. Unable to see the creatures' entire form, she decided she'd already seen more than enough to give her nightmares for the rest of her life. Then she felt a small arm wrap around her neck and heard a soft "Shhh" in her ear. Was this seven-year-old seriously trying to protect *her*? The idea seemed preposterous to Mrs. Anderson, who wanted—needed—to steal her daughter away from all of this. Only, Sarah didn't seem frightened. At least, not as frightened as her mother. The girl's gaze narrowed, and a deep frown set in as she watched the monsters slide out of view. Sarah wasn't cowering, and she didn't cry. If anything, she looked, for lack of a better word, determined.

"We can't stay here, Mom." Her voice had a steely hardness that hadn't been there before.

Brave girl, Doctor Stevens thought admiringly.

Mrs. Anderson interjected, reminding Doctor Stevens that Sarah was her daughter too. It was difficult for either version of Casey to fully reconcile the two completely different mindsets fighting for control. It wasn't simply that Casey had lived two lives; she had created two different personalities to inhabit their two very different worlds. One, the brilliant and brave scientist who had conquered her fears of both fantastical monsters and her own father long ago. The other, having never defeated either, took over now, huddled in the mud, hiding from the impossible creatures lurking about. Mrs. Anderson had no desire to confront the monsters of her past any more than she did those lurking outside. She'd spent the last eight years not wanting to know where she'd been or what had happened to her. And now that she did, Mrs. Anderson found no comfort in any of the answers she'd discovered. She just wanted this to all be a bad dream. But she knew it wasn't.

As if to punctuate the direness of their situation, loud hissing and bloodcurdling screams erupted from behind the blinding fog. Casey clutched Sarah tighter while both sides of her mind struggled to figure out how to survive. Doctor Stevens wanted to run for the hypersphere. She knew it must be the epicenter to the gateways that had unleashed so many horrors. Mrs. Anderson, on the other hand, wanted to hide and protect Sarah.

Let someone else handle it! Mrs. Anderson screamed inwardly. *We have to protect Sarah. Nothing else matters!*

That's what I'm trying to do, you sniveling coward, Doctor Stevens snapped. *Hiding in the mud and hoping someone else will save her isn't a goddamn plan. I—we—can save her. No one else can!*

Mrs. Anderson shook her head so hard, Sarah nudged slightly aside. *If we go out there, we'll get eaten by those . . . those things.*

And if we stay here, Doctor Stevens protested, *we'll be crushed. Neither of your choices are gonna save your daughter.* After a brief pause, she corrected herself. *Our daughter.*

As if reading her thoughts, Sarah nudged her. "Mom, come on! We need to keep moving."

Again, a hardness had crept into Sarah's voice. Somewhere between the little girl who had whined about her part in a school play and the one who was now lying in dirt, studying the mist with a steely gaze, something had indeed changed. Maybe, Doctor Stevens thought, it had been caused by the vision of the old woman tied up in tubes. The child's future self. Had young Sarah gained something from that encounter? Or had the vision of her future simply terrified her far more than a bunch of overgrown snakes ever could? Either way, it was clear that Sarah had changed. If so, Mrs. Anderson doubted it was for the better.

Doctor Stevens grinned inwardly. *She sounds like me.*

A giant, scaly form slithered past, knocking the jeep above them with a thud. The vehicle shook, rattling overhead, while the sound of crunching metal set their teeth on edge.

We've faced monsters before, Doctor Stevens reminded Mrs. Anderson before an image of their father entering their bedroom bubbled to the surface. Even after all these years, Mrs. Anderson could still smell the mixture of cigarettes and whisky on his breath. Still felt the awful weight of his body pressed—

"No!" Mrs. Anderson screamed.

Sarah covered her mother's mouth. "Mom! They'll hear us."

Before Mrs. Anderson could respond, another image followed. On the ship, years ago, Casey had faced and destroyed her father. It hadn't been real, only an imagined threat, but it had terrified her just as much as the real flesh-and-blood monster she'd known as a child.

I beat him, Doctor Stevens said. *We beat him. And we can beat these things too.*

Beside them, Sarah propped herself up on her knees, ready to make a run for it. Mrs. Anderson couldn't help wishing she had that same strength. She sighed inwardly. *How?*

By getting the fuck off our ass, Doctor Stevens replied.

With a solemn nod, both sides of herself agreed. She turned to Sarah.

"Alright, hon," Casey whispered. "You ready?"

Sarah nodded.

Casey rolled out from beneath the jeep, pulling Sarah along. Even before they'd stood, the sickening fog hit them like a thick blanket, oppressively pushing down. Not wishing to linger, Casey drew the girl up into her arms and made her way toward the giant tower looming ahead. Although it stood only fifty yards away, getting to it was anything but a straight path.

Ahead, serpentine shapes blinked in and out of view, devouring everything in their wake.

Though unable to see more than a few feet ahead, her mind sensed a mixture of emotions, fear and disbelief, emanating from behind the sickening veil of fog. The noise thundered through her skull so loudly that Casey was forced to turn the volume down, dimming her perception of what lay ahead. She took each step forward with a gingerly sluggishness. Her feet squished in the mud. With each step, another slithering cloud of vapor erupted beneath her. The mist, whatever it was, poured up and through the ground like a constantly bleeding wound. Each step forward seemed to open the wounded earth, causing the soggy air to grow even denser. The farther she drew into the billowing curtains, the louder the serpentine hisses became.

It wasn't until a huge, scaly surface brushed her left shoulder that she realized how close the snakes were. Casey stopped, holding her breath behind grinding teeth. Without looking, she could sense Sarah's rising scream just before her mouth opened to release it. No matter the child's newfound resolve, she was still a little girl surrounded by monsters. Clutching her daughter, Casey hoped a comforting squeeze might—

HHHIIIIIISSSSSSSSSSSSSSSSSSS!

The sound reached their ears just before a giant serpentine head burst through the foggy curtain. The thing loomed above, swaying from side to side, its split tongue darting in and out of its gaping mouth. Twin fangs, each larger and longer than Casey, sprang from its mouth. Yellow venom dripped from the fangs, falling to the ground in front of them in wet splashes.

At last, Sarah screamed.

The thing darted forward, lunging at them. Its blood-red mouth consumed Casey's vision. Needle fangs jutted downward, plunging toward them.

Instinctively, she activated the nanites within her bloodstream. Time slowed.

The serpentine head stopped mid-lunge. Rushing beneath its gaping mouth, Casey carried Sarah as they twisted left, then right, bolting around the thing's enormous body. She didn't stop running until the tower's entrance rose out of the frozen stench. What greeted her, though, wasn't the same entrance Casey remembered from the 1950s. Erected on the tower's side stood a modern and altogether man-made entrance. An elevator, of all things. Unsure of where it might lead, she hit the call button.

Time resumed. Then everything happened all at once.

Sarah's screams returned to her ringing ear. The snake behind them twisted around, its coiled shape searching the mist for them. The doors opened. Casey pulled Sarah inside and pounded on the lowest button. Wherever the elevator led had to be better than where they were.

The snake's head lunged just as the twin doors shut. The serpentine head smashed against the metal doors, caving them in. Pushing themselves against the back wall, Casey and Sarah held their breath until the elevator, at long last, began its descent.

Exhausted, Casey crumpled to the floor, holding Sarah in her arms. She wanted to comfort Sarah, to tell her everything was alright now, that it was all over, but she couldn't. Casey let Sarah scream and scream until her lungs choked. Better to let it out. Inwardly, Mrs. Anderson joined in, screaming in terror and confusion at all that had happened. Doctor Stevens, though, didn't need to scream. She wasn't afraid.

She was angry.

The elevator stopped, and the doors opened, revealing moving shadows. In the distance a bright crimson glow greeted them. The room was warm, and the air didn't stink of spoiled milk. She took that as a good sign. Nudging Sarah out of the elevator, they approached the swirling red light. After so many years, Casey had finally found her way back to the hypersphere.

Only this chamber was different than she remembered. The stacks of deformed gray bodies were long gone, replaced by clean floors and walls that reflected the sphere's pulsing light, washing the room in bloody crimson. Rows of computer screens lined the red walls, running from one end of the room to the other. In the center, spinning with a crimson glow, the hypersphere waited silently.

Casey felt its invisible touch growing stronger and tighter around her with each step. Tightening like a vise. She could sense the thing's growing urgency. Its eagerness as the sphere watched her hesitant approach. The thing wanted her there. It wanted her to reach out and touch it. The longing was so loud and clear in Casey's mind that it rang like a fire alarm. Or a scream.

"Wait here," she said, halting Sarah twenty yards in front of the swirling sphere.

"Don't leave me," Sarah pleaded.

"Never."

With a half-hearted smile, Casey squeezed Sarah's tiny hand, then let it fall to her side. Holding her breath, Casey spun around, staring at the layer upon layer of interwoven circles that created the hypersphere. It was not of this earth. Not even from this dimension. The hypersphere was a three-dimensional representation of a fourth-dimensional entity. She used to assume it was an engine of some type, but now she understood it was so much more. Like herself and so many others, the seekers had used the spheres for their own plans. To manipulate the past so that the future, *their future*, could survive. But too many had died to fulfill the seekers' desire to live. Stepping toward the sphere, she hoped this time they might finally find a way to stop the seekers. Or, at the very least, put an end to whatever was happening outside.

"Long time," Casey said, her voice ringing with newfound hope. "Miss me?"

The sphere spun silently, but the urgency it projected pulled at Casey's gut like an invisible string. The sphere had attempted to save her once before. She hoped it would do so again. Only this time, she added inwardly, with a bit more success.

Spreading her fingers, she reached out toward the crimson surface.

"Wait!" a familiar voice shouted from across the room. It was Jacob. She didn't know how he'd gotten down there, but the fear in his tone stopped her cold. Casey turned—

Too late. With an audible SNAP, the sphere grew larger, engulfing her outstretched hand in a burning embrace. The air left her lungs as her body was yanked into the sphere.

Engulfed, Casey's vision turned blood red.

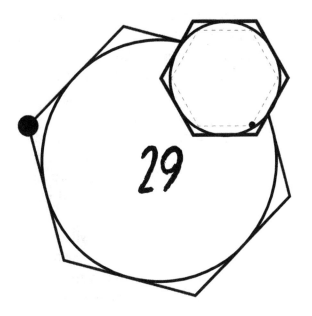

29

Casey's face, arms, and torso vanished within the strange, swirl-ing sphere. Jacob lunged across the room. He grabbed his wife's legs before they too could disappear. Her jeans slipped through his fingers, as if someone or something was pulling her with incredible strength from inside the sphere.

"Help me!" he shouted. Noelle and Burke rushed to either side, each grabbing a leg. Sarah approached, but Burke waved her off. Donovan, meanwhile, kept his distance, choosing instead to linger by the child's side while the others worked in unison, arching their backs and pulling at Casey's flailing legs.

With a great wrench and a loud pop, something gave way within the red orb, loosening its grip on his wife. Casey's stomach slid into view, her shirt bunched up beneath her breasts. Then her shoulders appeared.

"One more pull should do it!" Jacob shouted, urging the others on. "Three, two, one—"

The last pull brought Casey clear out of the sphere and sent her saviors sprawling. Casey gasped for breath, writhing on the floor. Jacob rushed over to her.

"Can you breathe?" he asked. Casey rolled to her side and grabbed his arm for purchase, attempting to stand. "Wait, hon," Jacob said. "Get your bearings first."

Reluctantly nodding her assent, Casey's breathing slowed to shallow gulps. Her body stopped trembling, and her muscles relaxed. Then her gaze moved past him toward something over his left shoulder. The color drained from her face, and her eyes narrowed to slits.

Before Jacob could ask what was wrong, she sprang to her feet and dove past him. Momentarily stunned by his wife's newfound strength and speed, he spun around, dumbstruck.

Casey leaped across the room, landing on the man at Sarah's side. The prisoner, Donovan. She straddled his chest, her fingers at his throat, strangling the life out of him. Jacob seemed unable to process what he was seeing. In eight years he'd never seen Casey so much as kill a bug. Now her hands were tightening around a man's neck, cutting off his oxygen. Donovan's face flushed, his body twitching beneath her. In a matter of moments, he'd be dead.

Everything had happened too fast. Burke and Noelle were just as slow to act as Jacob. Noelle was the first to clamber over, attempting to push Casey off the man. Burke followed. Jacob, meanwhile, struggled to catch his breath. None of it made any sense.

"Honey—stop!" he shouted from across the chamber.

The pile of wrestling bodies stilled, pausing in their various attacks. Casey's head lifted above Noelle's shoulder, her cold gaze turning in Jacob's direction. For the first time, he found himself afraid of the woman he loved. Then she spoke, and everything changed.

"He tried to murder our daughter!"

A hushed silence seemed to draw across the room. A sudden ringing in Jacob's ears blocked all other sounds, narrowing his other senses. Slowly, the weight of his wife's words settled in his mind. Like marking things off a checklist, his thoughts turned over all that he'd seen but hadn't considered. Not until now. Donovan's handcuffs. His eagerness to find Casey. That they had somehow known each other was obvious from the start. But that he'd wished her, or even worse, their daughter, any harm had never occurred to him. His chest tightened, burning,

Stumbling over to Donovan, Jacob recalled the cold fear and burning rage he'd felt the moment when he'd been forced to kill his own father. This was different. This time he knew he was going to kill this man, and all he felt was a growing numbness.

Before he could act on his impulse, however, the prisoner spoke, his voice raspy and haggard. "Y-you . . . need me . . . Casey."

Jacob prayed she wouldn't listen. She didn't. With a hard shove, Casey kept Donovan planted firmly on the floor. Her fingers still lingered along his jugular, ready for the kill. If need be, Jacob stood ready to pull the others off her, so she could finish the job.

"The only thing I need is for you to die," she said. "Here, now. Once and for all—"

Before she could finish, the underground chamber shook violently, tossing them all to the floor. Pieces of rock and dirt cascaded down. Jacob crawled over to Sarah, hunching over her protectively as chunks of dirt smacked his neck and spine. Gritting his teeth, he counted to himself, waiting for the trembling to halt. It wasn't until he'd hit thirty-two that the shaking ceased. A few more painful seconds later, the debris finally stopped raining down.

Glancing over, he found Casey and the others still leaning over their prisoner. Donovan coughed, trying to clear his throat enough from the constant pressure crushing it. Even as the world had come tumbling down, Casey hadn't released her grip. Loosened it, perhaps, but her fingers were still clamped tightly enough around his neck to leave red marks from his collarbone to his chin.

"The sphere," Donavan said, pushing out the words. "The sphere sent me."

"It tried to save me once before," she said. "Why would the sphere send you to kill me now?"

"I'm not here for you."

Casey's fingers opened, releasing Donovan. Silently, she turned and scanned the room. Following her ashen expression, Jacob found Sarah standing beside him, her tiny hands clutching his legs. Meeting Casey's watery gaze, his jaw tightened, and his stomach turned.

"No," Jacob said. "No . . . No . . . No . . ."

He felt icicles grow along his spine, curl up his skull, and stab him behind his eyelids. The implication was clear. The sphere, whatever the hell it was, wanted Sarah dead. The reasons didn't matter. All that did was to make sure Donovan was never able to touch his little girl again. Jacob rushed over, his fist swinging down at the man's face.

The blow never landed. Jacob blinked in disbelief, staring at his wife's delicate fingers wrapped about his wrist. Somehow she'd caught his blow with ease.

"We can't kill him," Casey said with a resigned sigh that seemed to reverberate through her shoulders and down her body. Husband and wife locked eyes, a mixture of rage and fear shared between them. Below, Donovan lay perfectly still, waiting for his fate to be decided.

Again, the room shook. Jacob widened his stance, bracing himself as the ground shifted beneath him. Along the walls, computers and monitors spilled in a shower of sparks.

The violence didn't cease; it intensified.

"The roof's coming down!" Burke screamed. Glancing up, Jacob was forced to agree with him. Thick wedges of rock and dirt tore loose from the ceiling, crashing down around them. A single blow from any of them would seriously injure, even kill. Jacob tried to clamber to his feet, hoping to reach Sarah, but every step he took was met with another upheaval, sending him sprawling. Then he saw Casey clutching their daughter.

How did she cross the room so quickly?

Before his mind had time to dwell on that question, the shaking ceased. Everyone stood, catching their breath. Casey brought Sarah over to Jacob, then approached the sphere. Holding his daughter close, Jacob wanted to shout to Casey to stay away from the damned thing. Instead, his attention moved to the swirling orb in front of her. Sometime between when they'd entered the room and now, the sphere's color had seemed to diminish. It was as if someone had poured ink inside, turning the once-bright crimson to a thick blood red.

"It's damaged," Casey said. She glanced at the various computers about the room, then turned to Burke. "What the hell were you doing down here?"

Burke waved his arms. "We had *nothing* to do with the seismic activity."

"Seismic activity? Are you fucking kidding me?" Casey said. "Did you see the giant snakes outside? Or how about the entire town that sank into the goddamn earth?"

"I can assure you," Burke said, "our tests have been harmless."

"What sort of tests?" Casey raised an eyebrow.

"You wouldn't understand."

"Try me."

He huffed loudly, as if pausing for dramatic effect. "We've been observing how ion particles reflect and refract in and out of the sphere."

Casey's stony glare burrowed into him. "You mean you've been poking and prodding the sphere to see what makes it tick?" Burke didn't bother to respond, though it was obvious to everyone in the room that she'd hit the proverbial nail on the head. "Didn't it ever occur to you that *zapping* foreign elements through a fourth-dimensional object of unknown origin might—oh, I don't know—go badly?"

As Jacob listened, it wasn't what she said that most piqued his interest. It was the way she said it. The inflection in her voice had changed. It sounded sharper, more clinical. Then, as if to punctuate her point, the chamber shivered with a series of quakes. Jacob braced Sarah, waiting until the shudders stopped. Even when they did, no one seemed to relax.

"I'm telling you," Burke shouted, "we didn't cause this!"

Casey ignored his plea and turned to Noelle. "That's what you meant earlier," she said. "You think this is happening because of me?"

"Not you," Donovan interjected, struggling to pick himself up off the floor. "Like I said, your kid is *dangerous*."

At the mention of Sarah, Jacob's fists clenched, and blood rushed to his cheeks. Casey, however, didn't react emotionally. If anything, she seemed more curious than upset.

"Did the sphere actually tell you that?" she asked. "Or are you just guessing?"

"Why even listen to him?" Jacob shouted, incredulous. "He tried to kill our child!"

"But that's just the thing," Donovan said with a smirk. "She ain't your kid. Is she?"

Jacob froze. He felt his insides harden as all the blood rushed from his face.

"What does he mean, Daddy?" a soft, small voice asked from behind. Jacob was slow to turn and face her. He'd always known that someday he and Casey would have to tell Sarah the truth, at least what little of it they knew. But he hadn't planned on doing it that night. Certainly not under such horrible conditions. Craning his neck, he forced his head around to meet his daughter's waiting gaze.

"You're my little girl, hon," he assured her. "Always have been, always will be."

"But that man said—"

"It's a long story, honey, and I'm sorry you had to hear it this way." Pulling her closer, Jacob felt her heart pounding through her chest, reverberating against him. "When I found your mother, she was already pregnant, without any memory of who your birth father might be."

Casey knelt beside her. "Jacob is your daddy, Sarah, in all the ways that matter. From the moment you were born, he was your daddy." She turned to meet Jacob's gaze. "And my husband."

Sarah's tear-covered face bobbed from her mother to her father, then back again, seemingly too stunned to speak. When she did, her voice was hoarse, and her body trembled. "So, nobody knows who my real father is?"

Real father. The words stung worse than anything Donovan could have said. Jacob wanted to protest, to scream that he was her one and only father. Instead, he simply shrugged and looked at Casey. She sighed but offered no other clues.

When Sarah didn't receive the answer she wanted, she turned to the most unlikely source. The human monster, Donovan. "Do you know?"

The bastard appeared just as shocked as everyone else that she was asking him, of all people. His smug demeanor vanished, and he shrugged. "No idea, kid. That's the truth."

Jacob felt a new rush of anger flood his senses. Why was his daughter even speaking to the man who'd tried to kill her? Why wasn't she rushing into Jacob's arms and saying how much she loved him and that he was her only daddy? Instead, she'd turned to a monster for the truth. And that thought, more than any other, ate at his insides.

"Don't speak to him," Casey said to Sarah. "You can't trust him. Not now, not ever."

"He's not any worse than the rest of them," Sarah replied with a coldness in her voice that hadn't been there before. "At least he didn't lie. Not like you." She turned to Burke and Noelle. "And not like them."

Casey shook her head. "It's not the same," she said. "Your daddy and I would have told you eventually. And these government people aren't dangerous. Not like *him*."

"She is," Sarah replied, pointing a tiny finger at Noelle. "She hates you. She wants you dead." Pausing, her voice broke, as if from a realization. "All of them do."

Whether Sarah was simply guessing or if she knew something he didn't, Jacob couldn't be certain. But as his gaze drifted from Burke to Donovan to Noelle, he felt the truth in her words. Donovan sighed, as if glad to have the attention taken off himself for a change. Burke looked nonplussed. Noelle, though, squirmed. Her fingers inched toward her sidearm. Sarah was right. They were surrounded by enemies.

Casey and Jacob stood, flanking their daughter, as the other three stared back.

Suddenly, a loud CRACK stole everyone's attention. Above, the ceiling collapsed in a shower of boulders and debris, the entire place crashing down upon their heads.

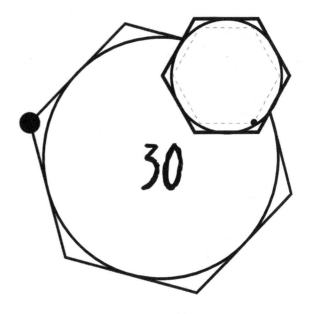

They're all morons, Donovan thought, moments before the ceiling came raining down on them. One minute, the little girl was pointing fingers at the FBI lady, suggesting she was an even bigger threat than he was. The next, the surrounding structure collapsed in a shower of rocks and broken debris. While the others had been arguing about who posed the most danger, the greatest threat had seemingly been ignored—at least by everyone except Donovan. He'd kept his focus locked on the swirling sphere the entire time. So, when the next quake came, he was ready.

Ducking low, he made a run for it.

Agent Reese was right on his heels. He couldn't tell if she wanted to try and stop him or follow him into the sphere. Either way, he didn't plan to look back long enough to figure it out. Ahead, the sphere blinked in and out of view. Wedges of metallic beams dropped from above, threatening to skewer him. In all the chaos, Donovan didn't bother worrying about where Casey and her family were. That proved to be a mistake.

As he ran toward the pulsing red sphere, it grew larger and brighter, as if extending itself to embrace him. Donovan welcomed it. Leaning forward, he tried to grind out a bit more speed, rushing through a shower of deadly debris. Either he would make it to the sphere, or he'd be crushed in the attempt. He hadn't counted on a third option.

Just as Donovan reached out his arms, mere inches from the sphere and the safety it would secure, Casey's dimwitted husband came crashing into him. This wasn't a mistake or an accident. Jacob had leapt in his way, blocking his exit and knocking him back to the ground.

Having come so close to escaping, the disappointment that ate at Donovan's gut was even worse than the prospect that they were about to be crushed by falling boulders. Jacob was on top of him, screaming about something or other. Then he started punching him—in the face, the stomach, a shoulder here, a nick of his collarbone there. None of it hurt, and none of it mattered. Donovan kept his eyes on the prize. Over Jacob's shoulder, he could see the giant sphere. He had to get to it. Now.

Along the walls, banks of computers were shattered, extinguishing all light in the room, save for the sphere's bloody red glow. Scrambling to his feet, Donovan finally unleashed an attack of his own. A quick kick to Jacob's sternum sent him sprawling, leaving the way open for Donovan's escape. Stealing a glance over his shoulder, he looked to see if any more surprises were headed his way. But neither the FBI lady nor Casey were in sight. Only the sphere. Donovan ran for it.

But before he reached the spinning sphere, the world around him *changed*.

His primal, lizard-like instinct seemed to sense the shift right before it happened. Just before the world transformed from tumbling black boulders into slick, cool gray walls, he felt a strange, ominous, cold touch at the base of his skull, like an itch he couldn't scratch.

He'd felt it before. Donovan stumbled to a halt as flickers of light and shadow erected gray tunnels all around him. The images were moving, as if sliding into place. In fact, he knew that was precisely what was happening. *It* had come back. For whatever reason, it had returned. Phasing through the ground, it was now solidifying all around him. Donovan's stomach twisted, and his knees buckled.

No. He cursed inwardly, recognizing the strange architecture. *Not this. Anything but this.*

Once the walls were solid and the chamber with the sphere was gone, Donovan found himself in an all-too-familiar environment. A place that had filled his nightmares as far back as he could remember. Worse than giant snakes and crushing boulders, worse than any other place he'd ever been. And now he was back. Trapped.

The ship had returned.

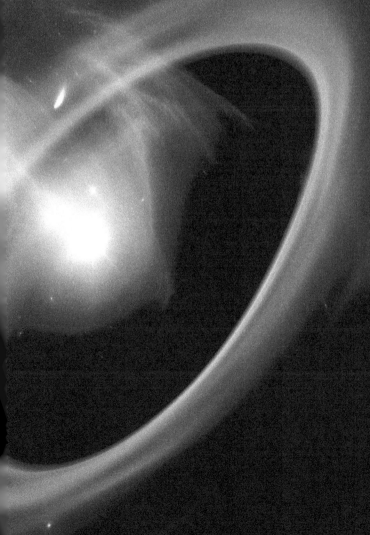

PART III

THE PILOT

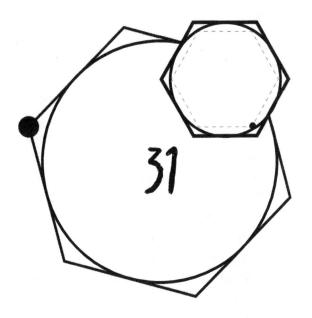

31

A din of confusion flooded Noelle's senses. Pulsing red light blinded her while a strange, echoing noise assaulted her eardrums. When the thundering subsided and her focus finally settled, forms and shapes slid into view, revealing an alien world.

The sheer size and scope of her new surroundings made her head spin and her legs buckle. Having grown accustomed to a reality built upon a relatively small scale, with mountains being the largest structures she'd ever known, what she saw made her eyes water. It was too much for her mind to process. Too much size. Too much scope. Too much of everything.

Peering over a metallic ledge, she stared down at a seemingly bottomless pit. Her fingers found a handrail and gripped it tightly. She was standing on a long catwalk. Trying to calculate the distance from end to end, she guessed it to be roughly ten miles across. Giving it an estimated length helped reduce the enormity of the place into something more manageable. Instead of trying to take everything in all at once, her mind broke it down into bite-sized chunks. If the walkway was ten miles across, then how deep might—

Noelle looked down again, and immediately regretted her decision.

Nope. She shut her eyes. *Terrible idea.*

Clutching the handrail, Noelle tried to piece together what she'd seen. Countless similar catwalks crisscrossed the pit, extending farther and farther into a seemingly endless void. Still, her mind assured her, it couldn't be endless. *There must be a bottom.*

Forcing her eyes open, she regained her balance, if not her composure. Studying the smaller details of the meticulously fabricated structure, it seemed like a cathedral without end. Noelle began to grasp just where she was standing, though the structure's familiarity offered no relief. She was still inside the tower. But whereas before it had been a comparably miniscule hundred stories tall, this was a thousand, perhaps tens of thousands of sizes greater. Noelle stood in the heart of the now fully built tower. Despite the tremendous height, however, no violent winds accosted her, nor did the air feel any thinner than at ground level. If her instincts were correct, she wasn't standing on an alien world. She was precisely where she'd been moments ago, only now she was far above ground and in a completely different time.

The future.

Searching for the others, she looked around the catwalk, then spun around and stopped cold. A huge gray shape loomed over her, casting a shadow that sent a shiver along her spine. The thing's surface was blanked by a vast network of thick cables, like enclosed tentacles. Even though its shape was too large to take in, she already knew its dimensions. A mile wide from end to end. It had been in Doctor Stevens's reports.

The ship.

It seemed to be watching her. Noelle felt a weight press upon her shoulders, as if an invisible force were holding her in place, frozen before the enormous gray vessel. Even after having read all the reports and seen multiple photographs, none of her studies had prepared her for how the thing made her feel. Nausea rose in her stomach, bubbling up her throat. Worse, the cold, invisible touch upon her shoulders and skull pressed her downward, as if it wished her to bow before it in supplication. The sheer force of will emanating from the ship was potent. It made her skin crawl and her feet stumble backwards, only to be stopped by the railing behind her.

The cool, crisp touch of the metal against her lower back caused her spine to rocket straight and her legs to jump. *No more*, she thought, replaying the words over in her mind. *No more. No more.* Hoping to silence the overload of sights and sensations, Noelle clung to the railing. She needed time to breathe, to center herself.

Then, as her heart slowly ceased its pounding, a distant voice prickled her ears.

Although the words were too soft to make out, she instantly recognized the husky voice. The sound of it pushed all the air from her lungs as she stumbled to her knees. The voice grew louder. Clearer. There was no mistaking it. Though she hadn't heard it in almost two decades, not since she was a child, Noelle was certain about its source.

At the end of the catwalk stood Major John Reese. Her father.

Although he hadn't turned in her direction, she knew it was him. At long last. But when she tried to stand, her legs refused to budge. After years of hoping and praying she might see him again, she suddenly found herself unable to move. Her head swam, and her vision blurred. Reaching for the handrail, Noelle pulled herself up. One foot in front of the other, she slid forward. Slowly and hesitantly at first, then faster, and more desperate. The ship's consciousness continued to press down upon her head and shoulders while the floor wobbled beneath her. Still, she pressed on. Her father was only fifty yards away now, perhaps less. As she approached, his words grew less garbled.

"Let me in!" Major Reese cried as he pounded against the ship's hull. "Casey! Let me in!"

Prying her fingers from the handrail, Noelle's walk turned to a limping run, her legs seeming to grow stronger with each step. Ahead, a green light poured out from the ship, bathing her father in an emerald glow. A round door appeared, opening like an iris. Casey Stevens, a younger version of the woman Noelle knew, stepped out of the ship.

Noelle inched closer. "Dad! Daddy! It's me! It's Noelle! Dad!"

Her father never turned. Then something happened, so fast and unexpected that it took seconds for her mind to grasp what her eyes had witnessed. Casey shoved Noelle's father over the railing!

He fell into the void.

Noelle screamed as she watched him vanish from view. Ahead, Casey turned to her and smiled. Triumphant. Clutched in her hand, a necklace dangled. At its end was a familiar pink heart shape. Noelle recognized it; she'd made it for her father as a child. Now his murderer was holding it up to her like a trophy.

Unable to work her vocal cords into a scream, let alone find the will to charge after her father's murderer, Noelle crumpled to the metal floor. So engulfed in grief, it took a moment before she noticed the crimson tower darken, fading from existence all around her. Her stomach turning, she felt the world pitch end over end. Flung from the walkway, Noelle fell into the void. Trailing her father's faint screams, farther and farther down into the pit.

Noelle awoke on a cool gray surface.

Vomit rose from her gut and spilled across the floor. Once the heaving ceased, she found herself lying in a curved tunnel with walls glowing in a faint rhythm. Like a heartbeat. She stood, relieved to find her body strong and unaffected by the dream or vision or whatever the hell it had been. And yet, even as she glanced around the oddly shaped corridor, feeling renewed strength in her legs, Noelle couldn't shake the effect of what she'd experienced. Had Casey truly killed her father? It contradicted Donovan's account. While he was certainly an untrustworthy source, his hatred of Casey was real enough that she doubted he would leave out such a vital piece of information. Especially when he'd obviously hoped to enlist Noelle's help in killing both Casey and Sarah. That meant either Donovan didn't know the truth, or the vision Noelle had experienced had been an elaborate lie, though for what purpose she could not tell.

Pushing her questions aside, Noelle made her way along the curving corridor. She needed to find the others, including Casey. The answers would have to wait. But they would come, of that she was certain. And if Casey had indeed murdered her father, well, then Donovan just might get his wish after all.

Turning a corner, Noelle noticed the sound of her feet against the floor seemed louder than they should have been. It was as if she were clomping about, even though her footsteps were slow and careful. Whether or not this strange environment proved any more real than the last, she at least had a pretty good idea of where she was. The hallway matched Doctor Stevens' earlier reports in every detail. Glowing walls, curved gray tunnels, right down to the hollow sounds her feet made along the floor. It appeared she was now inside Casey's infamous ship. How or why didn't matter. What mattered, she decided as her pace quickened, was figuring out how to escape. After having heard so many nightmarish stories, she half expected a bug-eyed monster to pop out at every turn. So, when she heard a commotion coming from around the next corner, Noelle's footsteps slowed, and her heartbeat raced.

Peeking around the bend, she found two figures arguing.

Jacob shoved Donovan against the wall and kneed him in the gut.

"Stop it! Both of you!" Noelle yelled as she rushed over to them.

Jacob had every reason to wish Donovan dead, but now wasn't the time. Besides, if Casey truly had been responsible for her father's death, Noelle would need an ally. While Donovan was far from a perfect choice, he was all she had.

Drawing her sidearm, she cocked it behind Jacob's ear. "Let him go."

"Sarah was right," Jacob snapped. "You're on *his* side."

She lowered the gun and pulled Donovan away. He smirked at Jacob. Noelle ignored it.

"I'm not on anyone's side," she said, wondering whether she was lying or not. "Look around you! Look where we are." They paused, glancing around the dimly glowing corridor. "This shithead is the least of our concerns right now."

Jacob studied his surroundings, then shrugged. "It's a tunnel of some kind. So what?"

"No, you idiot. We're inside the ship."

Jacob stopped; she could practically see the wheels spinning in his mind as he turned this way and that, eyeing the strange walls and moving shadows with renewed interest. When he finally spoke, the life had drained from his voice. "The ship? The one I saw when I was a kid?"

Noelle nodded. Though she couldn't be certain it was the same ship, it seemed the most reasonable answer. Jacob turned about, his jaw hanging, as if he'd been awaiting such a moment his entire life. Donovan, on the other hand, didn't appear nearly as excited. He was sweating, and his eyes darted around like a frightened animal. Noelle sighed. She knew she would need an ally. Someone who owed her. *God help me, he's my best bet.*

She lowered her gun and dug out a set of keys. "Raise your hands."

Donovan didn't bother to ask why as he raised his wrists. Noelle uncuffed him. When his smarmy smirk crept back across his face, she grabbed him by the collar.

"For now we're in this together," Noelle said. "But one wrong move and I'll kill you myself. That's a promise."

"And if she doesn't," Jacob added, "I sure as hell will."

Donovan lost his smirk as he peered down the winding tunnel. "Trust me, guys. Like the woman said, this *shithead* is the least of your concerns."

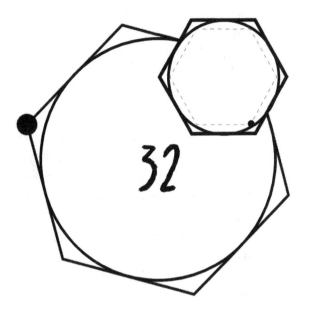

32

After what had felt like a lifetime, Casey was back aboard the ship. Years of marriage, family vacations, working at the diner, raising a beautiful daughter, all of it suddenly vanished from her thoughts. It was as if she'd awoken from a wonderful dream, only to find a nightmare awaiting her.

Despite the familiarity of her surroundings, something about the ship felt altogether different. Or perhaps she was the one who was different. Like an adult returning to her childhood home. The winding hallways seemed the same, though smaller than she remembered. Less ominous. The high ceiling was just as tall as before, as if made for giants, and yet the sense of dread was gone. Whether the effect was a difference in her surroundings or within herself, she couldn't be certain. Consumed by the odd sensations whirling in her mind, it wasn't until she felt a small pressure against her pant leg that she even realized she wasn't alone.

Sarah stood beside her.

The girl didn't say a word. She appeared more curious than

concerned, more interested than reprehensive. If anything, Sarah seemed excited to be there. That thought didn't offer Casey much comfort. Still, she supposed it was better than screaming and crying. Or was it?

"You OK to walk for a bit?" Casey asked.

Sarah nodded. "This place, it looks like where we saw . . ."

Her voice trailed, then died. Casey knew what she meant. The tunnels were similar to the place they'd seen in the future. The place with the old lady suspended by cables. The ancient one, the future Sarah. Casey shook her head as Doctor Stevens bubbled to the top of her mind.

"That was one *possible* future," she said. "Let's go see if we can make a new one."

Forcing a smile, Casey offered her hand. Sarah took it and followed.

They headed down the tunnel, following a path of glowing, pulsing walls.

After so many years, Casey was back. And this time, she promised herself, she wouldn't fail. Too much depended upon it. Not just humanity in some abstract form or even her own life. This time she had a daughter to protect. Casey only hoped that her newfound resolve might give her some previously unknown or untapped strength. In reply, an inner voice, detached and calculating, emerged above her swirling thoughts. Doctor Stevens.

By now the Prime must know we're here. He'll be coming for us.

Mrs. Anderson tried to remember who or what the Prime was. Then a nightmarish image of the red-and-black figure with blank white eyes emerged from the back of her mind, and she quickly smothered it. A shiver ran up her back, and her neck muscles spasmed when she swallowed.

The Prime.

Casey had forgotten about the hideous thing Doctor Stevens had cooked up in the lab all those years ago. *No,* she chided herself, *the thing I cooked up. My very own Frankenstein monster.* It took an effort to remind herself that there weren't two Caseys. She was Doctor

Stevens *and* Mrs. Anderson. Two lives with two different personalities, but they were still one and the same. She knew that if she hoped to protect Sarah, she would need both.

Pulling Sarah along, Casey followed the winding tunnels. She kept to the outer rings of the ship, hoping to keep her distance from the bridge, where she assumed the Prime was waiting. Casey would have to go there eventually but not until she found the others. Even with her enhanced abilities, the Prime had defeated her the last time. Now she hoped strength in numbers might offer her a slight advantage. It was, she conceded, a slim hope.

As they continued along the winding corridor, the structure changed. Walls viewed from a distance were no longer there when they approached, while other, newer passageways opened. Sarah commented on the strangeness of the ship. She thought it was funny how everything shifted in front of them. "Like whack-a-mole," she said. Hoping to keep the child engaged rather than afraid, Casey offered Doctor's Stevens's observations from over the years. After a decade of studying the ship at Area 51, she understood how the ever-changing layout worked. There was a pattern. While at first it appeared random, with walls and hallways springing up haphazardly, the phenomenon was neither random nor haphazard. The ship's tunnels changed from left to right, creating new passageways that grew from the center outward, circulating oxygen throughout the vessel, much like a giant metal lung.

"The ship breathes," Casey told her. "It's alive."

Sarah shrugged. "Yeah, I know."

Casey grew silent. She didn't bother to ask Sarah *how* she knew, though she could guess the answer. Sarah was connected to this place somehow. That, Casey assumed, was why the ship had come back. It had saved her. Or had it? Her mind drifted back to the vision of the future, one in which an elderly Sarah was strung up, feeding her life's blood to the seekers. That's all she was to them, a cure for some future disease. It was, as Doctor Stevens had once thought, like a scientist traveling back in time to reverse engineer a specific ancestral ape in hopes of curing cancer. Only her daughter wasn't an ape. She wasn't some experiment to be used. Casey fumed. She wouldn't allow the seekers to do to Sarah what they had done to her.

"Mom, look!" Sarah tugged at her arm.

Ahead, a lump of yellow plastic lay sprawled along the curved floor. Burke's hazmat suit. Casey stopped, leaning over it. Seeing no signs of rips or blood, she assumed Burke had simply stripped off the garment. She turned, then rushed around the next corner, pulling Sarah with her. They stopped again, spotting a figure standing perfectly still, awash in the ship's pulsing light. It was Burke, his back to them.

Releasing Sarah's hand, Casey approached. "Burke, you alright?"

He didn't answer.

Casey hesitated. She knew what that place could do to people. So many of her research assistants at Area 51 had come in whole and healthy, only to leave insane. Or, in some cases, dead. Prolonged exposure to the ship often had a mind-breaking effect on those who entered. It wasn't that the vessel attacked its occupants. Rather, it communicated through emotion, often by digging into one's primal fears and anxieties to elicit an emotional response. Those emotions overwhelmed all who felt them. It usually began with a physical sensation of weight pressing down on their heads and shoulders. Then the outward weight dissipated, and the sensation grew inside the person's mind, offering visions of their greatest desire or worst fear. In either case the eventual effect was often the same: insanity or death. But not for her. And not for Sarah. The nanites in their blood would protect them, at least enough to keep their sanity intact. Still, Sarah was young, and if the ship wanted to, it could easily overcome her mind and break it, though Casey doubted that was its plan. If anything, Casey surmised the ship would be cautious around her, perhaps even block her completely. But that was only a hope.

Casey stopped behind the frozen figure, then reached out and touched his shoulder. "Burke?"

He turned to face her, his eyes wide and his mouth agape. "Isn't it amazing?"

Casey felt Sarah's hand return to hers, gripping it tightly. "What's wrong with him?" Sarah whispered.

Burke smiled widely. "Nothing's wrong, my dear. Look at where we are!" He glanced at the gray walls with pulsing lights as if he were staring at the most beautiful of cathedrals. "We're inside the ship! I've dreamed of this moment my entire life. And now, to be standing inside it . . ."

"Yeah, quite a thrill," Casey said dryly. "You sure you're OK? This place can have . . . an effect on people."

Burke's feverish gaze turned away from the hallway and fell full upon her. It took an act of will for Casey not to step back and withdraw from his crazed grin. Strings of spittle dripped from his mouth as he spoke. "Do you have any idea how long I've waited for this? My grandmother, Ruthie, used to tell me all kinds of stories about this ship. How it could phase in and out of solid rock and even move through time. And yet, she never made it this far. Did she? You never let her go inside."

"Because it wasn't safe," Casey replied. "Not then, and not now."

"But you brought us here."

"I had nothing to do with it, Burke. The ship came back for us. It saved us. I don't know why." That, of course, was a lie. Not that it mattered. Burke continued to look around with open astonishment, lost in his own private paradise.

"This is what I wanted," he said, sounding as giddy as a schoolboy. "It's why I dedicated so many years to studying the tower, in hopes of one day finishing what my grandparents started."

"Your grandfather died."

"And whose fault was that?" he asked.

Casey didn't shrink from the question. "I saved Ruthie and her unborn child. I did what I could."

"Is that what you tell yourself?" he asked, still smiling, as if the conversation were amusing to him. "Grandma Ruthie told me all about how you would study the ship but never let anyone else inside. Only *you* could go in. I've always wondered how many secrets you kept to yourself." He leaned closer, as if awaiting an answer. Casey reflexively nudged Sarah behind her. Before she could reply, Burke continued. "Tell me, *Doctor*, did the seekers kill my grandfather, or did your secrets do it?"

Sarah pulled herself free from her mother's grip and stood protectively in front of her, glaring up at the man. "Don't you talk to my mother like that," she said with an icy calmness that unnerved Casey. "You could have stopped this. You could have warned us! You . . . you . . ." The strength in her voice gave out, and the frightened little girl finally reemerged. Tears welled in her eyes, momentarily silencing Burke and Casey.

Tightening her grip around Sarah's shoulders, Casey's cheeks flushed, and her heart thundered. She fought to keep her tone in check, not wishing to further alarm Sarah. After all, Casey reminded herself, she wasn't as blameless as Sarah might have hoped.

"I was trying to find a cure for what the seekers had done to me," she said. "And what about you? The guy who poked and prodded the hypersphere until it ruptured. Tearing holes in time and creating tunnels that consumed an entire town."

He shook his head so hard she thought it might fly off like a bottle cap. "No! No! I had no way of knowing anything like that would happen. I was simply trying to find the ship."

"Congratulations. Enjoy." She threw her arms up. "Let's see how long you last in here."

Burke's smile finally soured, and his complexion paled.

"Daddy!" Sarah shouted. Casey turned and saw Jacob run over and hug their daughter. Behind him, Noelle appeared. And after her, Donovan. Someone had removed his handcuffs. Watching his approach, like a protective lioness guarding her cub, Casey reached inward, preparing to activate the nanites within her bloodstream.

But nothing happened. Curious, she stretched out her consciousness to probe Donovan's thoughts. Once again, she felt only a dull silence in response. Something was wrong. When he stopped mere feet in front of her, she didn't want to admit she was suddenly powerless. Casey bit her lower lip until it bled.

"Wait, wait!" Noelle shouted, stepping between them. "As long as we're trapped in here, we need all the help we can get."

Casey steadied herself, but she kept her emerald gaze locked on the man who had tried to murder her multiple times. "Not from him."

Donovan spread his empty palms. "Bygones?"

Casey's face flushed, and her skin grew hot. God, how she wanted to smash that smug smirk off his face once and for all. She wanted to punch and kick and bite until there was nothing left for her to break or tear apart. She stepped forward, ready to pounce.

"Wait, Mom," Sarah said, tugging her mother's arm. "You saw what happens to me. In the future," Sarah added, her voice trembling. "Maybe he's right to be afraid of me."

"That won't happen, honey," Casey assured her. "I won't let it."

While mother and daughter argued over Donovan's fate, his face took on an odd expression. He seemed confused. Not by Sarah's words but rather that she would offer her support for the second time. Twice now Sarah had stood up for the man who had tried to kill her. Whether that was simply youthful ignorance or something more, Casey couldn't be certain. Not that it mattered. She still wanted him dead.

"Noelle's right," Sarah said, continuing her argument. "We need all the help we can get."

"*We* don't," Casey replied coolly. "*I* don't."

That was another lie. Without her abilities, she and Sarah and everyone else were vulnerable. The last time she'd fought against the ship, it had stripped her of her ability to tap into the nanites, and she'd lost. Casey paused, rocking back and forth on the balls of her feet.

Last time it took my powers . . . right before it attacked.

Peering over her shoulder, Casey stared down the hall, searching for moving shadows. Without her additional senses, she felt partially blind and completely exposed. *Naked.* Behind her, Sarah said something, but Casey was too involved in her own concerns to hear it. She assumed it was about Donovan. One more problem she would have to deal with. But not now.

"We should get moving," Casey said, hoping to keep the nervousness out of her voice.

"And go where?" Noelle asked. "How the hell did we even get here?"

"We need to get to the bridge," Casey replied, ignoring the second question. "The ship can only have one pilot. If I can take control of the ship, I might be able to—"

"Oh no, no, no," Donovan interjected. "The last time you took control you crashed the fucking ship and left me for dead." He stepped closer, his eyes burrowing into her skull. "If anyone is going to take control of this thing, it's me."

"You're welcome to try."

"I will," he said. "You're not so special. If you can do it, anyone can."

Casey imagined the ship tearing Donovan's mind apart, and a smile broadened her lips. "Be my guest."

She turned away from him and looked in either direction, trying to decide which way down the tunnel they should go. Without her connection to the nanites or the ship, the best she could do was make an estimated guess. "The bridge is at the center of the ship. That way, I think."

Donovan rolled his eyes. "That's my Casey. The girl with all the answers. After all these years, you haven't changed a bit. You say do this, do that, and everybody follows."

Before Casey could reply, Sarah grabbed her hand. "Mommy! Something's coming!"

Everyone turned this way and that, searching wedged shadows. But no movement was detected. After a tense pause, the group relaxed. Everyone except Casey.

"Wow," Donovan quipped, "like mother, like daughter."

Jacob shoved him. "Here's an idea, why don't you keep that mouth shut for a while?"

"And if I don't?"

Noelle revealed the gun at her side. "I could still shoot you."

"It's down there!" Sarah shouted, pointing down the tunnel. "It's coming!"

Suddenly, shadows broke apart as the sound of heavy footfalls erupted along the hall.

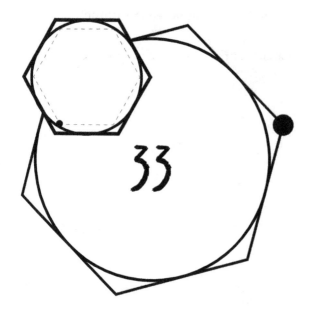

33

Once again, Jacob found himself running from monsters. Racing through the winding tunnels, Sarah clutched against his chest, he struggled to keep up with Casey. His feet slipped and slid as if the floor were caked in ice. On either side, Noelle and Burke followed, arguing about how best to make a stand. Both were armed, Noelle with a handgun and Burke with a rifle. Whether or not such weapons would be of any use against whatever was chasing them remained to be seen. *Let them fight the monsters*, Jacob decided. All he cared about was keeping Sarah safe. If that was even an option inside a giant flying saucer.

Still, he couldn't fully wrap his mind around the notion that he was inside the very ship he'd spent nearly eighteen years trying to forget. If it hadn't been for his father's death, Jacob might have been able to chalk the spaceship up to an overactive imagination, much as the town had tried to do all these years. They'd hoped to brush it aside, like a nightmare that could soon be forgotten. However, some nightmares couldn't be ignored or didn't vanish once the sun rose. Some nightmares kept coming. Blackwood had already learned that lesson. Now, it seemed, it was Jacob's turn. Hearing the thundering footsteps grow closer, his legs pumped faster.

"Here," Noelle said as they crossed a four-way intersection. "We can create crossfire from either side."

She and Burke slowed as Donovan ran past, not stopping for anything.

Casey hesitated, glancing back, which caused Jacob to reluctantly do the same.

"It would help if we knew what was chasing us," Burke replied, holding his rifle up and watching the pulsing hallway behind them.

"I called it the Prime," Casey said, her voice steady despite the run. "It's an augmented gray clone, strengthened with neurotoxins."

Jacob had no clue what any of that meant, but the others seemed to understand.

"You made it *stronger*?" Burke asked.

"I was trying to find answers," Casey snapped. "Much like you were hoping to do with the tower."

"Who cares who did what or why?" Jacob interjected. "All that matters right now is, can it be killed or not?"

Casey glanced at Burke and Noelle's raised weapons. "By those? Doubtful. They might be able to slow it, but . . ." Her voice trailed off as a figure raced into view. She gestured for Jacob to hide behind the two government agents as the creature lumbered closer. It was tall, at least seven feet, with skin covered in red and black blotches that seemed to dance about its body. Worse were its blank white eyes. They seemed to stare directly at Jacob and Sarah.

"I don't get it," Noelle said. "Why go through all the trouble to come back and save us, only to try and kill us?"

Burke nodded toward Sarah. "I don't think it came back for *us*."

Jacob heard them but was too frightened to react. He watched as Burke raised his rifle. Across from him, Noelle positioned herself to his right, holding her sidearm with both hands. Standing at the ready. If the creature recognized or understood what their weapons were, it didn't seem concerned. Focusing only on Sarah, it clambered forward without hesitation.

When the agents opened fire, Jacob covered Sarah's ears to block out the loud gunfire. Keeping his own head low, he didn't bother to look up and see what, if any, impact the rounds might be having. Instead, he backed away until Casey stopped him and tried to pull Sarah away. Jacob kept a firm grip around her, not wanting to let go. He needed to keep her close, to keep her safe.

"Give her to me!" Casey shouted over the ear-piercing noise. Then Sarah pulled away from both of them, peeking down the hall as the Prime advanced. Feeling his daughter's absence, Jacob reached for her, but Sarah shook him off.

"No," she said with an unnerving calmness, "I want to see it."

Suddenly, the gunfire ceased. "Empty!" Noelle shouted.

Burke checked his rifle's magazine, then slapped it back into place. "Six rounds left."

They peered down the smoke-filled hallway behind them, waiting for the mist to clear. The stench of gunpowder overwhelmed Jacob, reminding him all too clearly of the night he'd shot and killed his father. Shoving the memory aside, he kept his eyes glued to the dissipating smoke, waiting to see if the thing was dead.

"Can you hear its voice in your head?" Casey asked Sarah.

The girl nodded, then turned away. Her expression reminded Jacob of their last Christmas, when she'd been caught searching the closet for gifts. It was the look of someone who felt guilty for seeing—or in this case hearing—something she shouldn't have.

"What's it saying?" Jacob asked.

Sarah turned toward him, then spoke with a detached calmness that set Jacob's nerves on edge. "That I'm special . . . and you're not."

Noelle and Burke exchanged nervous glances. Jacob couldn't blame them. Sarah's words and the way she'd spoken them were hardly comforting.

Casey, however, had a different reaction. Her emerald eyes sparkled, and her lips curled into a grin. She had an idea.

"It's right, honey, you are special," Casey said, her voice rising with excitement.

Behind them, the smoke began to clear. Burke snapped his rifle back into position. Down the tunnel, something moved. Rising from the floor. Casey ignored it, concentrating solely on Sarah. "Do you remember that movie Daddy showed you? King Kong?"

Jacob spun. Had he heard her correctly? Was she really bringing that up *now*? Sarah seemed equally perplexed. She paused, as if trying to recall anything before the last couple of days.

"Remember when the villagers had those giant doors to keep him out?" Casey asked.

"It didn't keep Kong out though," Sarah protested. "He still got through."

"That's because the doors were made of wood," Casey replied. "I want you to imagine those same giant doors made from *steel*. Thick and heavy. Lots and lots of them, filling up the entire tunnel behind us. One after the other."

Jacob couldn't believe what he was hearing. Too dumbfounded to speak, he kept his mouth shut and waited to see what the hell Casey was playing at. He didn't have to wait long.

"Close your eyes, honey," Casey continued. "It'll be alright. I want you to create a picture in your mind. Pretend you're drawing those giant doors, made of hard, thick steel, all down the tunnel. Something so thick and strong that not even King Kong himself could break through them."

"I . . . I don't understand," Sarah stammered.

Casey smiled, seemingly unconcerned about the creature behind them. Jacob heard its stomping footsteps crunch along the metal floor, drawing closer.

Burke raised his rifle, but Casey waved for him to lower it. "Wait!"

Burke didn't bother to turn toward her. "Are you out of your mind? It's still coming!" He fired two more rounds, hitting the creature in the legs and chest. It wobbled, grasping the curved walls for support, but this time it didn't fall. The Prime continued to stomp forward.

"Run!" Noelle shouted.

Burke, meanwhile, readied himself to fire his four remaining rounds.

"No," Casey urged. "Wait!"

"Wait for what?" Burke cried.

Beside him, Noelle abandoned her position, making a run for it. Jacob didn't budge. He stayed beside his wife and daughter, watching in horror as the Prime wobbled toward them. Burke raised his weapon, preparing to fire a final, desperate volley.

Then . . . WHOOSH! Something slammed down behind it.

THUNK!

Suddenly, a series of enormous doors pounded shut behind the Prime.

THUNK! THUNK!

The creature's white eyes swiveled as the doors came crashing down behind it.

THUNK! THUNK! THUNK!

At last comprehending what was happening, the Prime spun back toward Sarah. Drawing up whatever reserves of strength it still possessed, the creature lunged at her.

Jacob thrust his body in front of his daughter, ready to give his life for hers without a second's hesitation. But that proved unnecessary, as the Prime vanished from view. In its place stood an enormous steel door that had fallen in front of the Prime just before it could reach them. Unable to believe what he'd just seen, Jacob scrambled to his feet, speechless. Noelle and Burke approached, gawking at Sarah.

"How . . ." Noelle began to ask, then stopped, unable to find the words.

Out of the shadows, Donovan appeared, having not fled nearly as far as Jacob had surmised. Unlike Burke or Noelle, though, he didn't appear particularly surprised.

His smirk returned. "See? Told you. Like mother, like daughter."

The group seemed too stunned to reply. Even Jacob couldn't find the will to argue. Shuddering, he felt the mad rush of adrenaline throughout his body slowly begin to dissipate. The shakes, however, remained.

"You did good, honey." Casey brushed hair away from Sarah's eyes. "Really good."

"Can I do it again?" Sarah asked eagerly.

"What precisely did she do?" Burke asked.

"She took control away from the Prime," Casey replied as if her words made any sense to the others. They didn't. For once, everyone else seemed just as confused as Jacob.

"Control of what?" he asked.

Casey studied the thick door. "The ship is like an animal. It needs a master, and it will follow the strongest and healthiest one it can find."

"So," Noelle said, trying to catch up, "when we injured the Prime . . ."

"Sarah became the dominant voice that the ship could hear," Casey finished.

"What about you?" Burke asked. "I thought only *you* could talk to the ship."

"It blocked me."

Hearing that, Jacob's stomach turned. "But the ship didn't block Sarah?"

"It won't," Casey said, shaking her head. "It needs her."

Silence overcame the chamber. Jacob noted Donovan and Noelle exchanging worried glances. Burke, for his part, still appeared in awe of what Sarah had done. Jacob didn't know how he felt. His limbs grew numb, and his mouth struggled to work.

Then a distant pounding punctuated the silence.

The group turned, staring at the giant steel door that Sarah had erected. Behind it the Prime could be heard, thrashing and smashing against it, trying to get out. Sarah's momentary enthusiasm seemed to vanish.

"Why, Mommy?" she asked, her voice trembling. "Why am I so special?"

Casey took her hand. "Because you're my daughter."

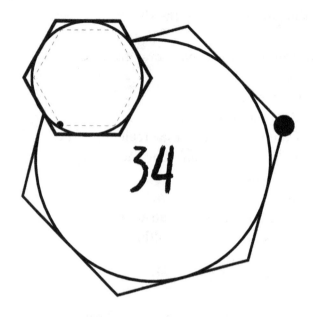

34

Just before it happened, Casey had whispered something in Sarah's ear. Noelle wasn't able to make out the words, but shortly after that, the ship began to change. Passageways closed, and walls crinkled, shifting about like mercurial Lego bricks. Everyone stood back to back, watching as the labyrinth around them was reduced, piece by piece, to a single narrow tunnel.

Behind them was a solid wall, a monster on the other side. Ahead, an archway stood, waiting.

"What's down there?" Noelle asked.

"The bridge," Casey replied without so much as a backward glance.

That wasn't a comforting thought. Noelle wanted another option. *Any* other option. She felt she'd lost all sense of agency. From the moment she'd signed up with Burke, Noelle had simply followed someone else's orders. Now she found herself following, of all people, Casey.

Noelle's feet grew heavier with each step.

To her left, Burke fidgeted with his rifle, checking, and rechecking his remaining ammo. Somewhere along the way, it seemed, the theoretical scientist had turned into more of a "shoot first, ask questions later" type. Except he *wanted* to be there. He had wanted to find the ship and learn all its secrets. What had been his plan for when he actually *found* the damned thing? If he'd ever had one, he seemed to have abandoned it sometime after seeing that red-and-black creature. Part of her couldn't blame him. The rest of her sure did.

To Noelle's right, Donovan appeared eerily calm. If anything, that made her even more nervous. When he caught her watching him, he grinned, then nodded toward Casey and Sarah as if to say, *See? I told you she was dangerous.*

As hard as it was to admit, he was probably right. Noelle felt the empty gun in her hand and wished she'd saved a few rounds. Not that she could ever harm a child. Still, the more she considered it, the heavier the empty weapon felt. *Like dead weight.* She dropped it.

Finally, they reached the end of the hall, where they stopped and peered up at a giant archway.

Casey and Sarah went in first, followed closely by Jacob. The others weren't nearly as quick to enter. They lingered outside, peering through the dimness. Beyond the arch, light and shadow twisted and turned, as if alive. The effect reminded Noelle of the giant snakes, slithering about, only this time there was no hissing noise. There was, however, a smell. Not wretched and sulfuric as the mist had been. This was something more familiar, perhaps even inviting under other circumstances. Yet, the smell was out of place. Noelle's nostrils flared. *Chlorine?* It couldn't be. She turned to Donovan.

"What's that smell?"

"Exactly what you think it is," he said with a defeated shrug, then stepped inside.

Burke rocked back and forth on the balls of his feet, inching toward the doorway. It was as if his scientific curiosity and his abject terror were fighting for control. Eventually, curiosity won out. Clutching his rifle to his chest, Burke entered.

Noelle lingered alone in the hall, feeling no desire to enter and yet having nowhere else to run. As if seeking confirmation, she glanced back the way they'd come. Behind her, the straight, empty hallway stared back. Noelle sighed and then stepped through the doorway.

The air on the other side was humid. It made her clothes stick to her skin almost as soon as she entered. The ship's bridge didn't appear to be a bridge at all. Shadows brightened, revealing a domed structure with a large, almost Olympic-size pool stretching across the floor. Beside it, three empty chairs with tall backs stood like silent statues. Donovan and Burke stopped at the water's edge. Noelle approached.

Light reflecting off the pool created moving shadows throughout the domed structure. At the center, Casey pressed Sarah backwards, laying her horizontally against the gentle current. If not for the uncanny surrealness of the scene, Noelle might have considered the image of the mother and daughter at play in the pool to be beautiful, even loving. But not this. Watching Casey as she lay beside Sarah, all she felt was a nagging sense of dread. *What next?*

As if in reply, lights flickered and pulsed overhead. Slowly at first, then faster. The ship, it seemed, was responding to their presence.

If those two make nice with the ship, what's that going to mean for the rest of us?

Jacob sat at the pool's distant edge, watching his wife and daughter with a hollow, detached gaze. He appeared small and helpless. Alone. Noelle figured she should feel sorry for him, but she couldn't muster the emotion. Instead, her gaze dropped toward Burke's rifle. She wondered how many bullets he had remaining.

He'll need at least two. She glanced back at Jacob. *Possibly three.*

As soon as the horrid idea entered her mind, a second thought followed. She *should* feel guilty. She *should* be disgusted with herself. What crime could be worse than gunning down a mother and her little girl? And yet, it was her sudden lack of guilt that bothered her the most. Peering at the two feminine figures drifting in the pool while the ship began to shudder and shake, Noelle felt no remorse for wanting them dead.

They're not human. Not anymore.

Her gut drove home the point with a boulder-size knot that worked its way up from her stomach to her throat. Consumed by her own tumultuous thoughts, she didn't pay much notice when a noise, distant and shapeless, drew closer. It was a constant clanging. There was a rhythm to it. She should have turned to find the sound's source, but instead Noelle continued to ruminate on the humanity of mercy killings. Her mind was slow to switch gears. The pool, its water sloshing and swaying about, seemed almost hypnotic.

Behind her, the thundering solidified into an echo of footsteps. Noelle finally forced her head to turn away from the pool, back toward the entrance, just as the Prime clambered into view. She froze. Donovan ran, but Burke raised his rifle. Instinctively, Noelle reached for her own weapon, only to find it missing. The creature filled the doorway.

Burke fired, point blank.

Noelle's pounding heart throbbed so loudly in her eardrums that she barely registered the sound of gunfire. Then she felt something wet splash her face. Blood. Not her own. With a single swipe of its elongated talons, the Prime had torn Burke in two, drenching her in his blood. One half of Burke's body spasmed, twitching on the floor. The other half sank into the pool. The blue water turned dark purple. Blinded by the blood covering her face, Noelle lost sight of the creature.

By the time she wiped the gore from her face, her thoughts began to reassemble. Her eyes blinked once, twice, then found their focus. The Prime had ignored her and was already halfway across the pool, wading through the blood-stained water in long strides, heading straight toward its seemingly dormant targets: Casey and Sarah.

Despites all of Noelle's training, preparing for a moment just like this one, she found herself unable to act. Instead of fighting or causing a diversion or doing *anything*, Special Agent Noelle Reese simply stood there, watching. Gore continued to drip down her eyelids. She couldn't find the strength to wipe it away.

At the other end of the pool, Jacob jumped into the water, a small, frightened speck of a figure compared to the seven-foot monstrosity

wading toward him. With a single backhand swat, it sent him sprawling, tumbling beneath the water's surface.

Having lost track of Donovan, Noelle spotted him hidden behind
the three large chairs. He peeked out, waving to her to join him. She
didn't see the point. If, or when, that thing wanted them dead, they'd
be dead. For now it only wanted Casey and Sarah.

As it approached, neither of them opened their eyes.

Then the creature lunged, heading straight for the little girl.

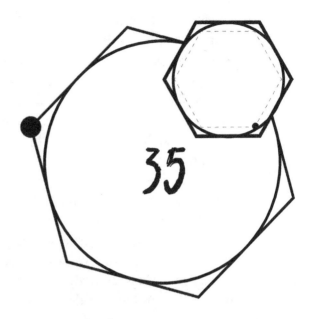

35

Lying in the tank of water, the sense of floating extended past Casey's limbs to her mind. Her thoughts drifted upwards, out of her body, as if carried across an invisible ocean. Casey's consciousness continued beyond the domed bridge, through metallic walls and wiring, out into the vacuum of space. She could sense Sarah's presence beside her, emanating a calmness she hadn't seen or felt in her daughter since this nightmare began. Although Casey couldn't see or hold or even communicate with Sarah, just knowing she was there, touching her mind, made what Casey had to do next that much easier. Pushing her thoughts back down into the ship's steel hull, she spoke not with words but with feelings. She was now tapped directly into the ship, and within that connection, the only way to communicate was through emotion. She picked a single word and pushed the feeling of it outward into the ship's consciousness.

Danger!

At first, there was no reply, only silence. Then a soft tickle at the back of her awareness began to grow. The black, endless void of space was replaced by marble columns. A floor rushed up to meet her imaginary feet, and a projection of her body was surrounded by rows of shelves. Leather-bound books, each one ablaze with long numeric lines of text on their spines, stood on either side of her, stretching farther than she could see. As she walked naked across the cold floor, the illusion grew solid and familiar, sending tingles up her toes and through her legs, though she knew the sensations were no more real than that place or the nude form she inhabited.

The cosmic library was the ship's, or perhaps the hypersphere's, way of making the abstract tangible. The ship had used this place to communicate with her before, but she doubted it had created the library. Casey assumed the hypersphere projected the environment but that the ship, like with everything else within its hull, remained in control. Along the seemingly endless rows of books lay countless coordinates to countless worlds. The last time she'd raced down that corridor of books, she'd been afraid, chased by the visage of her father, which the ship had used in hopes of controlling her. That time she'd won. The last time she faced the ship, however, Casey had lost. This time she didn't care about winners or losers. She needed help. Despite all that the ship and its creators had put her through, she knew there was no other way.

Time worked differently in the library. A second in the "real" world might seem like hours there. So, when Casey finally found an end to the row of shelves and stepped into an open area, she had no sense of how long it had taken. She didn't feel tired or even anxious. If anything, a wave of calm seemed to settle over her naked form, causing her to stroll about with little fear or concern as to what might be happening to her actual body outside that place.

Ahead, a small figure stood beneath a swirling projection of the universe. Sarah ran over, hugging her. Casey felt the imaginary warmth of her daughter's embrace, then stopped cold.

Another figure emerged through the swirling, projected universe. Her father, or at least the ship's pale reflection of the man who had tormented her for so many years. But he was dead, and Casey had conquered her fear of him long ago. He, or rather *it*, still stank of cigarette smoke and booze. The smell of it through her imaginary nostrils made her woozy. Straightening her back, Casey pulled Sarah behind her, trying not to project any cause for concern. Sarah didn't know anything about her grandfather, and Casey intended to keep it that way. When she spoke, Casey addressed the ship directly, ignoring the mocking image it had chosen.

"We're in terrible danger," she said, a slight tremble in her voice. Despite her knowledge that this was all a grand illusion, she couldn't help absently covering her breasts with folded arms. The ship's visage made her more uncomfortable than she was willing to admit, even to herself. Gritting her imaginary teeth, she continued. "The hypersphere at the base of the tower is damaged. It appears to be leaking time, opening portals from the past and future. It destroyed Blackwood. If it continues, it will consume *everything*, both my world and yours."

"Possibly," the ship admitted "But this is *not* your world. Nor is it mine."

Casey paused, reeling. If her body had lungs, she'd have held her breath.

"Even after everything you've seen, your understanding of the universe remains so . . . pedestrian," it said with a disappointed frown. "When one such as yourself travels back and forth through time, your destination is never from the same timeline you began in."

Casey shook her head. "I was taken in 1985. We went to the future and then the past. *My past.* Roswell, 1947. I knew that place from history."

"You arrived in *a* 1947," the ship replied, "but not *your* 1947."

Noting the confusion on her face, he stepped in front of the holographic universe, causing it to split into multiple layers, like thin sheets of paper, one on top of the other. "An infinite number of Caseys traveled in an infinite number of ships."

"Then why come back?" she asked. "You saved us."

"My pilot saved the child," the figure replied. "We don't require the rest of you."

"You didn't answer my question," Casey said. "If there's *so many* Caseys, then there must be just as many Sarahs. So, why come back?"

"Because the spheres want her. She's more vulnerable to them in this timeline. Unlike the other versions, *this* Sarah wasn't conceived at Area 51. She wasn't even conceived on Earth. This Sarah was created *here*. On the ship."

Casey trembled as fractured thoughts solidified in her mind. "When Harold raped me."

"You should have been lovers. You were supposed to be. In all the others you were. But when I was unable to instigate such an affair, another avenue was created." The figure of her father leaned closer. "In either case, *your* Sarah is not, strictly speaking, of this timeline."

Casey felt her imaginary stomach turn. That was it; the spheres wanted Sarah. But did they want her dead? She was about to ask when a new, more concerning question rose to the surface:

If I'm so expendable, why bother telling me all this?

Reading her thoughts, her father's visage laughed. "That's my clever girl."

Eyes widening in recognition, she spun around. Sarah was gone.

The conversation had been a distraction. Casey opened her mouth to scream, but she had no mouth. Glancing down, she watched her body evaporate, piece by piece. Her legs dissipated first, then her hands, chest, and arms. Before her face vanished, the library melted away like smeared paint.

Casey awoke to the sensation of her lungs burning. Water poured down her mouth, engulfed her throat. She flipped over in the pool, found purchase, and tried to stand. She coughed liquid from her lungs while her eyes saw stars. It took her mere seconds to realize she was back on the bridge, in her body, drowning in a pool, but she worried those precious seconds might cost her dearly.

When her senses returned in full, she had to blink to make sure that what she was seeing was real and not just another illusion. The Prime was in mid-lunge, its talons aimed for her throat.

But they never hit their mark. The creature stood frozen, as if time itself had ceased to exist. It took another moment for Casey's thoughts to clear themselves enough for her to drop her gaze, finding the source of the disturbance.

Sarah was lying in the pool, half of her face covered in gray flesh. On one side, a large black oval eye stared back; on the other, a natural green. The black eye and the scaly skin around it were misshapen and horrific. Casey had changed before. She'd been able to activate the nanites in her own body, and when enough were triggered, her flesh had changed, and she too had been able to slow down time. It had been like standing in a bubble, one that she knew would eventually burst, but in that bubble, she'd been able to save her own life on more than one occasion. Now, it seemed, Sarah had tapped into a similar ability. It was one thing for Casey to experience it herself; it was another to see her seven-year-old daughter so horrifically changed. For the first time, Casey could well imagine why Donovan had been so frightened of her. Still, she reminded herself as she activated her own nanites in a flood of anxiety, this was her daughter. No amount of deformities would ever change that.

She knew the time bubble would soon burst. Casey had to act fast.

The change happened so immediately that Casey didn't even realize the right side of her body and her arm were covered in a thick layer of gray skin until she'd struck the Prime's chest. She aimed for the bullet holes along its hideous red-and-black ribcage, using them like targets as the memories of what this thing had done to her years before came rushing back, though even those horrors were a mere blip compared to the flood of rage she felt at seeing her daughter so close to this thing's taloned clutches. Casey showed no mercy.

Her fist plunged into its chest wound, breaking through flesh and cartilage and bone until her fingers wrapped around its beating heart. *Not so different from us after all*, she thought. With a violent wrench, she yanked her gore-covered hand out, pulling the Prime's heart along with it.

Time resumed. The Prime's blank white eyes rolled back. A wet gurgle escaped its needle-teeth-filled mouth before the thing, at last, collapsed into the pool with a dull splash.

It was over. The monster she'd dreamed up in a lab all those years ago was now dead.

Without a moment's reprieve, Casey felt something break apart inside her. It started along her left side, burning through her stomach and rising to her throat. She tasted acid on her tongue. It was as if her organs were being burned from the inside.

When she collapsed, trembling, in the pool, Casey couldn't find the strength to scream.

Darkness overtook her. Then small hands dove into the water, pulling her mouth back to the surface. Casey coughed and noted drops of blood pouring from her mouth and nose. As Sarah's face came into view, Casey wiped the blood away.

"Are you OK, Mommy?"

Casey forced herself to stand. The burning in her gut subsided, though the taste of acid remained. She knew something was terribly wrong. Still, she smiled. "I'm fine, honey," she said, hugging her daughter. "You saved me."

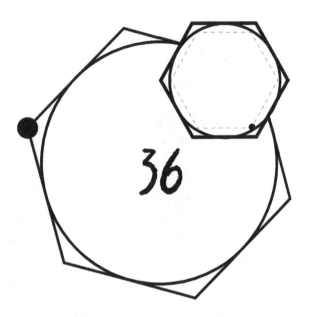

36

Pulsing pain shot up Jacob's right side and forced his eyes to open. As his mind swam through a disoriented fog, he used the pain as a focal point. Like a tether, he pulled at the pain, bringing the world back into focus. When his vision cleared, a little girl with gray flesh, one green eye, and one enlarged black eye stared unblinkingly back at him. Not until she said "Daddy?" did his mind process that it was Sarah. Instead of relief at finding his daughter alive and safe, nausea crawled up his belly. Jacob struggled with his facial muscles, hoping not to reveal the revulsion he felt inside.

As if sensing his disgust, Sarah's misshapen face twisted into a terrifying scowl. Before Jacob had time to process what was happening, she lunged. Her tiny fingers, stretched to tiny talons, swiped the air. Her mouth opened, revealing rows of sharp teeth. Jacob's mind whirled as his daughter's words returned: "I ate him, Mommy! I ate him alive."

Jacob flinched backwards as Sarah's claws lunged for his throat.

Suddenly, another gray scaly arm came into view, pulling Sarah away. It was Casey. Like her daughter, half of her body was covered in scales, crowned with a single bulbous black eye glaring from the right side of her face. Jacob flopped in the water, terrified, and splashed through the water to the pool's ledge. Heaving himself out of the water, his stomach's contents spilled across the floor.

Wiping his mouth, he noted the hurt and pain written across Sarah's misshapen face. And his wife's. A gnawing doubt ate at him. Had Sarah *really* tried to attack him? Or had she simply tried to leap into her father's arms? Uncertain, Jacob couldn't bear to look at her.

"I'm sorry, Daddy," Sarah said. "I didn't mean to scare you."

Hearing the pleading in her voice, Jacob's heart sank, and his fear dissipated. He flung himself back into the pool and pulled both of them into a tight embrace. "Sorry," he muttered, but anything else he might have wished to say was drowned beneath his sobs. His wife and child were alive. That was all that mattered.

When Casey finally pulled away, Jacob was startled to find that her skin and eye had reverted to normal. "Your face . . ." he began, then caught himself.

Casey glanced at Noelle and Donovan, noting their expressions of horror as they continued to watch her child. Sarah also noticed. Her body trembled as she glared at them. Jacob felt anger pouring out of her like a physical wave. He worried what might happen next.

"What are you staring at?" she screamed. Neither Donovan nor Noelle answered. They both lingered, fidgeting nervously at the far end of the pool. It didn't take any sort of clairvoyance for Jacob to know what they were thinking. They were terrified of her.

Hushing Sarah, Casey bent low, shoulder height in the shallow water, and whispered something to her. Jacob stood in the pool, exchanging nervous glances with Donovan and Noelle. He worried what they might do next. Then he noticed something else.

"Where's Burke?"

Noelle didn't answer. Donovan did, but only with a wave toward the back of the pool. Jacob turned slowly, not in any rush to see any more horrors, and then instantly regretted his curiosity. An arm and half a chest bobbed in the dark, blood-soaked water. Beyond it, perched on the floor, lay a clump of meat and flesh. Burke's remains. Jacob didn't look for long. He turned away, letting his imagination fill in the gaps, which proved even worse.

The thing that had killed Burke, the thing that Casey had called the Prime, was floating face down at the other end of the pool. Jacob didn't bother to ask how it had died. The blood along Casey's right arm and the breast of her shirt told him more than he needed to know. She was still whispering to Sarah. He watched as their daughter closed her remaining human eye and took deep breaths, presumably in hopes of slowing her heart rate. At first, Jacob wasn't sure what they were doing. But when Sarah's flesh turned pink, reverting to its human form, he understood. Casey had been able to help her change back to normal, at least on the outside. Her right eye was the last to change, morphing from a large black oval into a small white eye with an emerald-green iris.

The little girl smiled. First at her mother, then at her father. If she noticed the distance between them, with Jacob lingering near the water's edge, closer to Noelle and Donovan than to her or Casey, she didn't show it. Her face glowed with warmth.

Jacob struggled to match it, offering her a faint smile.

Then something else caught his eye. A red mist, like vaporous blood, curled off the water, turned upwards, and slithered past Sarah's face. Jacob bolted forward, terrified that the unknown substance might touch her. It didn't. The mist swirled around her and Casey, as if searching with clear intent, then darted straight toward Jacob. He didn't have time to dodge or even dunk himself beneath the water. The vapor was on him at once, clutching him with misty fingers, drawing his face to it. The stuff filtered up his nose and down his throat. It moved so fast that he couldn't process what was happening. The more the mist poured down his throat, the dimmer his vision grew. Jacob saw stars, then nothing at all.

"No!" he heard Sarah scream, though the world had turned black. "Daddy!"

He felt the vaporous tendrils slithering down into his lungs before spreading out into the rest of his body. His mind was first. Images flashed like an old movie, the film flickering and everything moving double time, though what the images were attempting to reveal, he had no idea. He was too focused on the numbness crawling up his legs to his chest and snaking toward his neck. Jacob was being consumed by something *alive*. Invisible fingers clutched his chest and strangled his throat while a secondary personality bubbled to the surface, as if hoping to take over his body.

Then, suddenly, it was gone.

Fresh air burst through his lungs, and the world returned. Blinking through tears, he watched the red mist spill from his nose and mouth before it flew up toward the roof. A thundering noise, like a vacuum or a giant fan, reverberated through the chamber. It was deafening, causing Jacob and the others to cover their ears. The red devil vanished from the bridge. When it was gone, the noise stopped, and the chamber seemed to grow brighter. Warmer. While Jacob would never consider such an environment safe, with the Prime gone, the shadows seemed to recede. Sarah waded through the water and clutched his waist.

Jacob wished he could share in her relief, but he knew their nightmare was far from over.

"What the hell just happened?" Noelle asked, pacing back and forth along the water's edge. Her face was ashen, and her hands fidgeted at her sides. She looked like someone who hadn't quite decided whether to curl up in a ball and cry or just start screaming.

"The ship protected me," Jacob replied, as surprised as anyone.

"It wasn't the ship," Casey said. "It was Sarah."

Her expression soured, not looking nearly as relieved as Jacob would have imagined. Glancing around the room, he watched as each member of their party silently turned their gaze toward the little girl still clutching her daddy.

"I thought *you* were going to take control of the ship," Noelle said, nervousness bubbling through her voice.

"That was the plan," Casey admitted. "Unfortunately, it chose a different pilot."

Jacob tightened his grip around Sarah. "What do you mean? She's only a child."

"Yeah, pal," Donovan said with a nervous laugh, "you keep telling yourself that."

Noelle and Donovan exchanged fevered glances. Jacob certainly understood their fears, but that didn't give them license to harm a child. Not his daughter. And she was *his*, he reminded himself. Whoever her biological father might have been, whether a human or a bug-eyed monster, Sarah was still his baby girl. He'd been there when she was born, raised her, loved her, and would protect her. No matter the cost. His own sudden resolve pushed away any lingering hesitation he'd had, and it felt good, powerful even, to be reassured of his love for his family. Without thinking about it, he wrapped his arms around them.

As they climbed out of the pool, it became clear that there were now two groups: the Andersons and the others. Perhaps there always had been. Donovan and Noelle lingered at a distance, as if trying to decide what to say or do next.

It was Casey who finally spoke.

"We need to go to the hypersphere at the heart of the ship," she said. "It's what the ship uses to communicate and travel through time. Hopefully, we can convince it to help us—and itself—by closing the ruptured sphere back home."

"And if we can't convince it to help us?" Noelle asked, her voice rising higher than normal.

Before Casey could respond, the world changed. The pool vanished, and Jacob found himself standing in a giant chamber filled with bright crimson light. Still holding on to Sarah and Casey, he looked around the strange room. "What happened?"

Sarah smiled like a girl with a secret. "Mommy said she wanted to come here."

Casey bent low, a look of alarm washing her face. Even before she spoke, Jacob could tell that it wasn't the new environment that most concerned her.

"Yes, honey," Casey said in an even tone. "But *how* did we get here?"

"I thought you wanted to come," Sarah replied.

Casey stood and met Jacob's gaze with a hesitant flicker of her eyes. "I did, Sarah. I just . . . I just never could do that. Manipulate walls and objects, yes, but leaping from one end of the ship to the other? No."

"They're all the same room," Sarah replied, as if the answer were obvious. It certainly wasn't for Jacob. He was about to ask for clarification when he turned and stopped.

The sheer size of their new environment stole his words.

It reminded him of an empty colosseum, except where the bleachers and roaring crowds should have been, huge pipes snaked along the walls. His eyes followed the pipes to the center of the domed structure. They all fed into a round metal platform. Hovering over it was a familiar swirling red sphere. Brighter than the one at the tower, it offered a warmth that spread throughout the enormous chamber, filling his lungs with hot air. He felt its presence, like invisible tendrils coiling around him. The sensation was so overwhelming that it took him another moment before he realized that only Sarah and Casey were standing beside him. Noelle and Donovan were missing.

"Where are the others?"

"They're dangerous, Daddy," Sarah said. "They want to hurt us."

Jacob had had similar concerns; still, the assuredness in her voice made the truth of it hit home. "You . . . read their minds?"

When Sarah nodded, nervous butterflies danced about in Jacob's belly.

"Where are they?" Casey pressed.

"Still on the bridge." Sarah paused, shut her eyes. "They're talking about you." She turned to her mother. "Donovan says they need to take *you* out first."

Jacob shuddered. They were plotting to kill his wife. Then him. And then Sarah.

"Fine," he said, his face burning. "Just leave them there. Let 'em *rot* on that fucking bridge."

"No," Casey replied, much too calmly. "Bring them here, honey."

Jacob spun on her. "You can't be serious."

"Why, Mommy?"

"Better to keep them close," Casey said. "Where we can keep an eye on them."

Jacob paused, considering her answer. She wasn't wrong per se, though that certainly wasn't the sort of advice the woman he'd known would have ever given. Not for the first time he wondered how much of his wife remained beneath her beautiful shell.

With a sigh and a shrug, Jacob conceded. "Alright. Go ahead, hon. Bring 'em here."

In a blink, Donovan and Noelle appeared beside the hypersphere. Stumbling about, it took them a moment to find Jacob and his family. When they did, though, he found little relief in their expressions. Donovan and Noelle glared at them. No longer afraid, they looked angry.

Sarah's right. They want us dead.

Before anyone could speak, a strange figure emerged from the hypersphere, stealing everyone's attention. An inky blot against the red swirling light. As it drew closer, its features became more defined and more surreal. It looked like a walking Crayola sketch. Jagged lines of purple, green, and yellow. Its face was a mockery of a crooked smile and round eyes.

"Look at all of you together," the figure said. "My children."

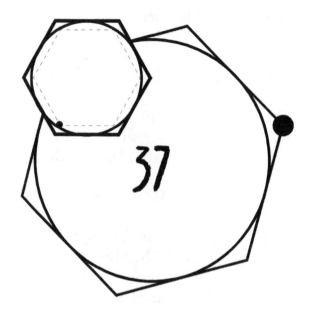

37

The Crayola figure, drawn with a kaleidoscope of bright, ever-changing colors, approached. At first, Casey wondered why the ship had chosen such an odd form. Then she remembered that she was no longer the pilot. The ship had formed its new visage around the mind of a child. Despite its crude form, however, the figure's voice still dripped with all the menace she'd come to expect.

"You," it said, fixing its gaze on Jacob. Casey turned, surprised that it would focus on her husband first. "The boy from the woods," it continued, drawing closer. "Now all grown up."

Jacob hesitated, and when he did speak, his voice was higher than normal. "We've met?"

The figure changed into a black man dressed in heavy military armor. Whoever it was supposed to be, Jacob seemed to recognize him. "Pidgeon?"

Without a response, the figure reverted to its cartoon form, then turned to Noelle.

"The daughter of Major Jonathan Reese," it said, leaning closer, as if to smell her hair. Repulsed, Noelle backed away. "You are like him in many ways," the figure continued. "Less so in others. You have his strength but lack his discipline."

Casey could see Noelle's mouth working, trying to find a retort, but the words never came. The ship's avatar moved to Donovan. "Ah, Donnie, Donnie, Donnie. Back again, I see."

"Don't call me that!"

"Would you prefer *Dipshit Donnie*? That's what they called you back in school." The figure glanced at Jacob and Casey, then returned to Donovan. "I see you aren't any more popular now than you were back then." The figure shrugged. "Must be in your nature."

Finally, the figure approached Casey, but instead of speaking to her, it tilted its oddly shaped Crayola face toward Sarah. Round dots for eyes blinked, and the crudely rendered mouth broadened into a large smile.

"Sarah," it said. It watched as Casey's arms wrapped protectively around her daughter. "She's my pilot now. She has nothing to fear from me."

"I was your pilot once," Casey said. "It didn't go so well."

"You chose to crash us in the past," the figure replied. "I followed your commands."

"You helped the Prime take control of this ship. You helped it murder countless people. And . . . and y-you—" Her voice broke, and she whispered the final words. "You . . . raped me."

"I served my purpose," it replied.

Jacob approached, his face flushed with anger. "What gives you the right to do any of this?" he screamed. "You snatch people from their homes. Use them. You took my father and—"

"*I* didn't kill your father," the thing interjected, holding up a green finger. For a moment, Casey thought Jacob was going to take a swing at it. She saw his shoulders shake, his fists clenched at his sides. "If it makes you feel any better, Jacob Anderson, your father was proud that you protected your sister. His last thought, after you emptied the two barrels from your shotgun into his chest, was one of pride."

The colored shape shrugged. "Even after centuries of study, our simple-minded ancestors still find ways to surprise me. All of you have, each in your own way."

"Good news," Casey said. "I've got one last surprise for you."

The thing paused expectantly.

"You're going to help us set the hyperspheres free," she continued, pointing to the swirling orb behind them. "Starting with that one."

"These beings are trying to kill your daughter," it said, "and you wish to . . . free them?"

"See?" Donovan exclaimed, "I told you they wanted her dead!"

"What happened in Blackwood was not random, nor was it an accident," the ship continued. "The spheres believe that by destroying my creator's cure, they can free themselves. The child must be protected."

"I've seen your idea of 'protection,'" Casey said, her voice dripping with venom. Her eyes stung, and tears dripped down her cheeks. "Strung up to machines, wires pouring out of Sarah's body and—"

"A possible outcome but not the only one," the thing interrupted, offering a twisted smile. "Besides, what choice do you have, Casey? If you leave here, the spheres will find you. They'll find *her*." It gestured toward Sarah. "Isn't a slim chance at life better than no chance at all?"

Before she could reply, Casey felt fire burn along her side, gnawing at her insides. The pain she'd felt before, after stopping the Prime, had returned. Grinding her teeth, she struggled to remain standing. No one seemed to notice except the ship, which continued to study her.

After a pregnant silence, Noelle cleared her throat and approached the ship's visage. "But what would happen?" she asked. "What if we *did* free the spheres?"

The ship seemed to consider her question. When it spoke, its voice was flat. "They originate from outside our universe. Time has no meaning to them. No past, no future. If they were set free, none of this would have occurred."

Noelle gasped. "You mean . . . my father would still be alive?"

The visage didn't reply, but the implications were clear.

Casey noted the growing excitement on Noelle's face. Beside her, Jacob's eyes crawled into their sockets, as if having similar thoughts about his own father. Even Donovan, for once, looked genuinely happy, seemingly mulling over the possibilities on offer.

Still, none of this sat right with Casey.

The ship had rarely divulged any answers. Now, suddenly, it seemed to be telling everyone how to stop its creator's designs. That was impossible. As the thing had said earlier, it served its purpose, and its purpose was saving its people, not offering a solution to their destruction. Where was the catch? Her gaze dropped to Sarah. This all revolved around her. Both the ship and the spheres wanted her. One to use her, the other to kill her. So, why would the ship admit to such an easy solution?

Within her mind's eye, imaginary puzzle pieces snapped into place. When the complete picture of what the ship was telling them came into focus, Casey's arms grew numb, and her chest burned. Finally, she understood. There was no solution.

This is a trap.

"Y-you're s-saying," Casey stuttered, "everything you ever did, across all timelines, would be erased? My abduction? All my friends who died? Arthur, Earl, Colonel McKellen, all of them would be safe except . . ."

"Sarah would never have been born," the ship finished.

The chamber grew quiet, with only the soft whirl of the red sphere breaking the silence.

I should have seen this coming. How could I be so stupid?

Her thoughts raced, trying to find a loophole in the ship's logic, but there wasn't one.

"So," the ship said, "what will it be? Save all those who have died trying to save you over the years, including Noelle's father?" He paused and leaned closer. "Or save your child?"

Casey's eyes watered as she glanced around the room, searching Jacob's face for an answer, then Noelle's. She even looked at Donovan. Unsure what to say or do, Casey remained silent. Inwardly, however, her mind was tearing itself apart.

Think of it, Doctor Stevens urged. *I could save everyone. Not just my friends but all the soldiers who died at Area 51.* Her thoughts drifted back even further, to the giant chamber on the ship where she'd seen thousands, perhaps hundreds of thousands, of people trapped. Frozen in time. They too eventually died. Not because of her actions but due to her inaction. When she'd last seen them, Doctor Stevens, then merely Casey Stevens, had talked Earl into leaving the frozen figures behind. "We'll come back for them, Earl," she'd promised. Only, she never did. Now it seemed, she could keep that promise.

Have you lost your mind? Mrs. Anderson's voice blared so loudly through her skull, Casey stumbled backwards. *She's my daughter!*

Doctor Stevens wondered if there had been children on board the ship when she'd crashed it in the past. She hadn't seen any. *If there were,* she thought, *then what makes them any less important than Sarah?*

How can you even ask that? Mrs. Anderson said. *She's your own flesh and blood.*

Doctor Stevens glanced down at the little girl beside her, studying Sarah's features with clinical detachment. She could indeed see herself in Sarah's green eyes and her pale complexion. But she also saw Harold. The memory of him and the thought of what he had done to conceive Sarah burned her from the inside. As if hearing her thoughts, Sarah turned and met her gaze. There was no fear in her small, round face. Did she understand what was being said? Could she even comprehend what was on offer? As if in reply, Sarah approached the ship's visage.

"How would we free the sphery things?" she asked, her voice so soft, it seemed to drift across the vast chamber like a soft breeze. When the ship didn't reply immediately, Sarah's tone grew harsher. Stronger. "I'm the pilot, right? So, answer me!"

You tell him, Sarah, Doctor Stevens thought.

The ship hesitated, its features squirming. "It . . . can be done . . . I *could* free it."

Over the many years that Doctor Stevens had sparred with the ship, she'd never heard it sound so frightened. The big bad ship was being brought low by a mere child. *By my daughter*, she realized. Mrs. Anderson may have only been a construct, created from the lack of Casey's memory, but the façade had grown its own voice. Now it seized on Doctor Stevens' trepidation.

See? She thinks and acts just like you! Mrs. Anderson prodded. *How could you even consider throwing her to the wolves?*

The simple answer was that Doctor Stevens couldn't. She understood that now. And, just like that, Doctor Stevens and the façade, Mrs. Anderson, no longer felt like separate entities. Their love for Sarah fused the two warring identities into one until only Casey remained.

Watching her little girl stare down the ship, she couldn't help but feel a sense of pride. Like Jacob's father had felt about him, she imagined. Following that trail of thought, Casey glanced at Noelle, thinking about her father, Major Reese, and the sacrifice he'd made years ago. So many had died to help her. If given the chance, how could she not try and save them?

Behind her, Noelle and Jacob were arguing, discussing their fathers' lives versus Sarah's, as if the choice were up to them. Casey ignored them. Drawing in upon herself, she worked the problem just as she would any other scientific theory.

Slowly, an idea began to form in her mind, growing larger, moving forward until she could almost see it. Perhaps there was another answer.

"I have to go back to the tower," she said. When Donovan and Noelle continued their argument, Casey shouted above the din. "I have to go back to the tower!"

Everyone stopped and turned.

"Back to when it began, in the future," Casey continued. "Right before the tower collapsed and the sphere first ruptured."

No one replied. They didn't understand. Neither, it seemed, did the ship.

"Why?" it asked, a look of confusion written across its cartoon mask.

Casey's lips curled into a Cheshire grin. "To make a deal."

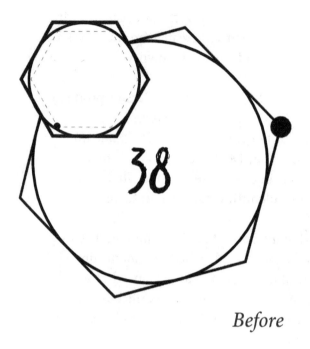

38

Before

Four-year-old Noelle Reese awoke to the sound of a muffled scream. Rising from her bed, she slipped on a pair of pink flip-flops and creeped to the bedroom door. Through the open crack, she heard voices, an unfamiliar man and her mother arguing. Noelle opened the door and made her way to the second-floor banister, which overlooked the front entrance. Her mother was crying. At the door, a man in a military dress uniform wrapped his arm around her shuddering shoulders.

Noelle felt her stomach turn. "Mom?"

The officer and her mother spun toward her, startled. The look in their eyes made Noelle afraid. As soon as she'd spoken, she instantly regretted the decision. Noelle wanted to jump back in her room, close the door, and hide behind the blankets. Before she could flee, however, her mother spoke with a voice like broken glass. "Come down, honey."

Her feet heavy, Noelle lingered at the top step, unable to move.

Her eyes danced in her skull, pointing back toward her open bedroom door. She wanted to go back to her room before it was too late. Instead, she descended the stairs, her mother's gaze following her. The military man's back straightened at her approach.

"Your father," her mother began, then paused. Noelle kept her lips pressed shut while butterflies assaulted her insides. "He's missing, honey."

At first, Noelle didn't think she'd heard her correctly. Then she studied the stoic man, with his tired, sad expression, and she knew that she hadn't. But it made no sense. She'd seen her daddy just a couple of days ago. They'd gone out for ice cream. He bought her two cones because the first had spilled in the backseat. He didn't get angry, though. He just wiped up the mess and turned the car around. They shared the second cone outside before it could melt.

Now her daddy was missing.

"I-I don't u-u-understand," Noelle said. "He works at an office. I've seen his desk."

Her mother and the military man shared a look, and Noelle noted the frustration in her mother's eyes. Although her parents had never married or even lived together, they'd gotten along alright. Better than most of her friends' parents. Even if they hadn't loved each other, she could tell her mother was hurting. And that, more than anything, drove home the reality of their words.

The man leaned close, stinking from a cologne that made her nose itch. "Major Reese was sent on a special secret mission, honey. We haven't heard from him in days."

Noelle started to back away, but the man's arms came up to her shoulders, holding her in place. She twisted her head, trying to get as far from his sorrowful expression as possible, but the man's grip held strong. Noelle couldn't escape, so she lashed out.

"You're lying!" she shouted, smashing her tiny first against his face. After the second, third, and fourth hits, he threw up his arms and blocked the blows. Noelle kept hitting him.

"Get out! Get out! I want my daddy! Get out! "

Special Agent Noelle Reese opened her eyes and found the others staring back at her.

They were on the ship's bridge. Casey and Sarah were floating in the pool, necks craned toward her. Noelle was sitting in one of the three chairs, Donovan and Jacob perched on either side. All their eyes, she noted, were filled with tears. She knew that somehow they hadn't just seen her memory; they'd *experienced* it, just as she had. As her mind reformed itself, she remembered how she'd gotten there and what they were doing. They had returned to the bridge, syncing each other's minds, working together mentally to propel the ship forward in time.

Casey had warned them that they might share vivid memories or emotions. But Noelle hadn't counted on anything like this. She felt violated. That sensation grew stronger from the looks of pain and sorrow written across their faces. Even the usually smug Donovan wiped tears from his eyes. Their reaction didn't make Noelle feel any better. If anything, it only punctuated how much of a mental violation this process had been. And it wasn't over.

A tickling at the back of her mind caused her eyelids to grow heavy. A new vision consumed her. Whether it was coming from Casey or Sarah or someone else, she didn't know or care. All she knew was that the entire universe had suddenly opened before her and swallowed her whole. A swirling kaleidoscope of light and energy, brilliant colors and pitch darkness, blazed through her mind, to the point where her own petty sadness, even her own human identity, seemed to diminish, replaced by a previously unimaginable spectrum of colors.

And she wasn't alone. The five of them moved together as one through space and time.

The universe felt spongy, as if the stars and galaxies weren't floating in space at all but rather were woven within an invisible porous membrane. Everything was interconnected. Nothing was singular or separate. Past and future were a myth. What happened in one moment affected the others, either in this plane of existence or somewhere else within the connecting membrane. And there was most certainly more than one universe. She could see them, like shadows interlaced just above the surface of the universal membrane, like sheets of paint coated layer upon layer upon layer until all the naked eye could perceive was a single color. But the others were still there. She saw them now. She *felt* them. They all did. Noelle didn't need to open her eyes to sense Jacob's astonishment, Sarah's excitement, or Donovan's dread.

Casey, on the other hand, was more difficult to read.

It was as if she'd found some way of blocking her thoughts. The sense that Casey was hiding something from everyone else grew like an itch in her mind until it inflamed and spread to the others. Sarah ignored it, seemingly concerned only with helping her mother to pilot the ship. But Donovan and Jacob could sense Casey's absence, and it bothered them as well. Donovan more than Jacob, obviously, but she felt concern from both. Why was she blocking herself? What was she hiding?

Then a shot of burning pain erupted across them all. It emanated from Casey. Something was wrong with her. Just as quickly as the fiery sensation arrived, it vanished.

Before anyone found the strength to ask, though, time slowed around them, and a single speck of light grew in their connective consciousness.

Earth, a million years in the future, grew closer, engulfing their inner vision.

They had known their destination. Casey had offered a brief sketch of her plan. But until that moment, seeing it up close, as if Noelle might reach out with invisible fingers and touch the approaching future Earth, she hadn't truly understood what time travel meant. It wasn't a simple matter of hopping in a machine, flipping some switches, then suddenly arriving in another time or place. Time travel was as much an emotional journey as it was a physical one.

Time left scars upon the universe, a trillion tiny ripples that created an unseen cosmos within and without the known universe. Noelle and the others had touched those scars. Their bodies hadn't simply leapt forward a million years into the future. Their minds, their very consciousness, had been changed along the way. Noelle sensed her body chemistry altering within her. Not like Casey or Sarah, thankfully. Nothing so inhuman. No, this was different. The voyage across time had reshaped her thoughts in ways she couldn't easily identify. The pain of the past seemed more alive than it had in years, but so did the joys and accomplishments she'd long forgotten. The cacophony of emotions was so overwhelming that she didn't hear Casey speaking to her for several moments.

Finally, Casey's dull, drifting, dreamy voice broke through the doldrum of Noelle's wandering thoughts. This wasn't a mental connection. Casey was speaking aloud, seemingly with great effort. She sounded strained.

"Noelle," she said groggily, "help us find him."

At first, Noelle didn't understand Casey's words, nor did she care to. The complexities of the universe still lingered. Again, Casey interrupted her contemplations.

"Find him," she said, this time with more urgency.

Find who? Noelle wondered, more annoyed than curious. Before she could push her thoughts outward to communicate with the others in their mind sync, a fresh image blazed across her inner vision. Thick clouds broke away beneath her, revealing an endless ocean.

There was no ship, no metal contraption surrounding her thoughts or vision. They *were* the ship. Flying past billowing clouds, rushing over a long, seemingly flat plain of water. She felt the wind on her face and the splash of salt water against her chest.

In the distance, a single red spear shot up from the horizon, jutting all the way up into the clouds. She couldn't tell from a distance how tall the structure was, but she recognized it immediately. The crimson tower, now fully formed into a pointed spire, lurched closer and closer into view. And all around it was chaos.

A whirlpool, at least a thousand miles in diameter, stretched out from the spire, swirling across the endless ocean like a hungry mouth. Above, storm clouds and lightning revealed moving shadows in the sky. The shadows had distinct, even familiar shapes. Noelle noted a cone shape in the muted clouds that looked like a zeppelin. Various silhouettes of a dozen shapes and sizes buzzed and dove around it like blind birds. As the ship continued to approach the center of the chaos, Noelle saw large gray shapes swirling around the enormous vortex that spanned the sea.

It was Donovan who first realized what the gray forms were, and his mind screamed his discovery. *My God, they're cities!*

Noelle felt the others' attention drift toward the whirlpool, studying the odd shapes. Amidst the violent waves and lightning flashes, swirling about like ants in a pool, broken buildings, thousands, perhaps millions of them, crashed and smashed about in the violent water. Noelle couldn't comprehend what was happening. Casey's reports about the future hadn't described anything like this. The report had detailed the crimson spire but not the planes and zeppelins overhead. Nor the whirlpool below, with its countless cities bubbling along the water's surface. She heard the others' surprise in her head.

The tears in time, it seemed, were not simply contained to the past. They'd stretched and grown into the future. Did that mean the spheres were willing to rip apart the entire world, and everyone in it, in their quest to find and kill one little girl? The thought startled her, and she felt Casey's mind press against her own. A rush of anger and condemnation followed. Still, no one voiced an opposing view. The spheres weren't going to stop until they were free.

Beside her, Noelle felt Donovan's terror rise as he turned their attention away from the whirlpool and toward the distant horizon. More red shapes sprang up like monolithic statues, dotting the surreal landscape. Red spires, hundreds of them, covered the horizon. Not just one, as Casey had described back in her 1940s report, but an entire seeker civilization lay sprawled before them, mingled with the shattered buildings and the flying shapes above.

"Focus!" Casey shouted through dry, craggy vocal cords. "Find him! Hurry!"

What the hell is she going on about? Noelle wondered, grimacing. Reluctantly, she turned her attention away from the horrendous visage, directing her thoughts toward the tower. Still, the giant whirlpool and raging storm pulled at her, making it hard to focus.

Then, suddenly, amidst a whirlwind of activity, Noelle understood what Casey had meant. She could sense *him*. He was alive. There. Now. Just beyond reach.

Somewhere inside the quickly rising tower, her father was falling to his death.

Only, he wasn't dead. Not yet.

This, she realized, had been Casey's plan. Not only were they coming back to the tower in hopes of making a deal with the spheres, they had also come to save her father. As Noelle reached out with her mind, she could feel his panic. There was something inside him. Something inhuman, writhing and clawing its way out. A seeker, in mist form, had overtaken his body. He continued to tumble past countless walkways and beams, plummeting through a void.

They needed to move faster, to close the gap between where they were and where he was. And it wasn't a matter of flying, she now understood. It was a matter of reaching out with her consciousness and simply being where he was.

Noelle felt the others, even Donovan, helping her focus on her father. The gap between space and time closed until they were no longer flying over the ocean.

They were inside the tower, twisting and tumbling through the catwalks, which spread like haphazard spiderwebs. Despite the ship's enormous girth, the tower was far wider and taller. Even so, it was a tight fit.

Her father, Major Reese, was above them. Falling toward the ship.

"Get him, Sarah," Casey said, though Noelle couldn't tell if she'd spoken the words or simply thought them. Either way, Sarah heard and understood the command.

Noelle felt the ship lurch to a halt. In that instant, she and the others mentally detached from it. Like popping a bottle top off, the separation was a shock to the system. It took a moment for Noelle to collect her thoughts, as if her mind were putting itself back together like Humpty Dumpty after his great fall. When her eyes finally opened, a man was lying in the pool.

A red mist swirled out of his mouth and nose, then flew up through the bridge's domed ceiling, vanishing from sight. The man sat up, coughing water from his lungs. His chest and body were covered in some sort of heavy green armor.

He looked at Casey. She smiled a crooked grin. Noelle, meanwhile, watched silently. Blinking once, twice, her mind struggled to catch up with what her eyes were witnessing. This couldn't be real. He couldn't be there. Not after all these years. He couldn't be alive, unaged, sitting in a pool of water less than ten feet away. It was impossible.

Then the impossible man turned to Casey and spoke. "What happened to you?"

Casey's smile widened. "I got older. Twenty years, give or take."

The man stood, struggling in his wet armor.

"Dad?" Noelle's voice was so low and so soft that she wasn't even sure if she'd spoken aloud.

He paused and turned. Suddenly, Major Jonathan Reese was staring directly at her. The last time they'd seen each other, Noelle was in preschool. At first, he didn't seem to recognize her. Then his face scrunched up, and he stepped closer. Took another step.

Finally, he shivered, and his mouth fell open as realization rippled across his face.

Noelle didn't feel herself jump out of her chair. She didn't know that her arms had wrapped around her daddy's neck. She wasn't even conscious that they were embracing waist deep in a pool. All she knew was that her father was alive, holding her.

And Noelle was *never* going to let him go.

PART IV

VOYAGE'S END

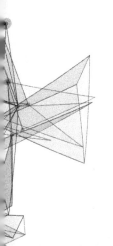

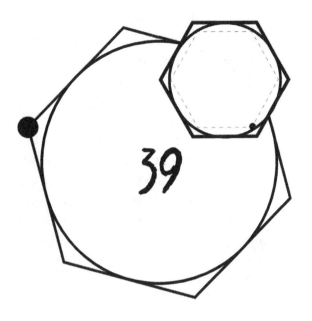

39

Donovan Daley had murdered more than one man in his life. Earl was the first. A poor sap who didn't seem to understand the first rule of survival: *Save numero uno. Fuck everyone else.* Over the years, Donovan had also tried to kill Casey on numerous occasions, but he'd failed time and time again. And now, to add to his growing list of sins, he'd even tried to suffocate a little girl. Despite everything he'd done, Donovan now found himself trembling, teary eyed, as he watched Noelle and Major Reese's joyful reunion.

The feelings welling up inside him weren't simply a case of momentary weakness. Something deep inside him had changed. It was as if, while traveling through the time vortex, for lack of a better term, a long dormant part of him had reemerged. Perhaps it had been there all along, buried beneath his constant fear of what new nightmare awaited around the next corner. He had spent two decades of his life running or being afraid. Yet, sitting on the bridge, watching the major embrace his now-adult daughter, Donovan felt something break somewhere above his lungs and intestines. It was the vision, he decided. Yes, that made sense. He hadn't simply *watched* her sniffle and cry in her mother's arms; he'd *felt* it. He'd experienced it firsthand. He'd been there. Inside her. And now he was watching the whole thing come full circle.

Pushing away the bubbling sentimentality, his mind darkened.

Where's my tearful reunion? Where's my warm embrace? What or who am I running back to? That's assuming I ever get out of here.

Such thoughts made his insides harden. Whatever weak part of himself had twisted in his gut seemed to grow solid again. Feeling stronger, Donovan appraised the room.

"Jesus," he snapped. "Are we just going to sit here blubbering all day?" Everyone turned, surprised he would dare to shatter such a tender moment. Ignoring the others, he focused solely on Casey. "Well, you brought us all the way back here, sweetheart. Care to tell me why?"

"Not particularly." With her back to him, Casey helped Sarah out of the pool.

Major Reese waded across the water. Exhausted from the effort, he peeled away his remaining armor and climbed out. Reese stopped inches from Donovan's nose, glaring at him.

"I see *you* haven't changed," the major said.

Donovan wanted to come up with a quick retort, but the words eluded him,

"Major?" Jacob said, leaning over. "It's Jacob. Jacob Anderson. From Blackwood."

Reese's narrow gaze swiveled, then widened as he studied the middle-aged man.

"The kid?"

Jacob smiled and threw up his arms as if to say, "One and the same."

They hugged. Ice slivered up Donovan's back to his neck, reminding him that, once again, no one was waiting back in the 1990s to hug him. Clearing his throat, he struggled to find his voice. When he did, he made sure to pour as much acid into it as he could muster.

"Before everyone keeps hugging each other," he said with a smug smirk, "can someone tell me what the hell we are doing here?"

"We saved my dad," Noelle said with a beaming grin that made him want to puke.

"I'm touched," Donovan replied. "Now what?"

When no one seemed to have an answer, they all turned to Casey. She was standing at the far end of the pool, wiping water off her daughter's face. Sarah, Donovan noted, wasn't crying or smiling. She was sitting on the pool's edge, allowing her mother's ministrations without comment or reaction. Either she was in shock, or the human side of her had gone bye-bye somewhere along the harrowing voyage. Donovan bet on the latter.

"I've brought us back to right before the tower fell," Casey said. "I'd say we have a little over ten minutes. Fifteen, tops."

"Fifteen minutes to do what?" Donovan asked.

"Before the seekers' civilization crumbles and the sphere ruptures, causing damage that will echo backwards in time for millennia."

"Sorry, hon," Jacob said. "I hate to agree with Donovan, but I'm not following."

"I get it," Noelle interjected. "Both the seekers and the spheres will be at their weakest."

"And," Casey continued, "if you're going to negotiate a peace agreement . . ."

"Best to do it when both sides are at their lowest," Jacob finished.

Donovan couldn't contain himself; he burst out laughing.

"Jesus, Casey, after all these years, who'd have thought you'd turn out like Prewitt?"

"Who's Prewitt?" Major Reese asked.

"A guy who tried to make a deal with the devil," Donovan replied. "He got his throat slit open for his trouble."

That silenced the crowd. Casey turned to stone. It seemed that the mention of Prewitt and his dumb ideas about negotiating with the seekers had indeed hit home. Donovan couldn't remember the last time he'd seen her doubt herself. He had to admit, it felt good to bring the all-powerful, all-knowing bitch down a peg or two. Sadly, her hesitation didn't last.

"We *don't* approach the seekers," she said. "We use the chaos outside to get past them and go directly to the sphere at the base of the tower. Then we see just how badly our friends from another universe want to go home."

Casey studied the room, waiting for objections. There weren't any. *Of course not*, Donovan thought. Noelle was fully on her side now, and neither Casey's dimwitted hubby nor the naïve soldier boy were going to object. That left Donovan. Only, he didn't. It *was* a plan, he had to admit. Not a particularly good plan but not an impossible one either. The spheres were the ones who'd offered him a deal in the first place, so they weren't above bargaining. Besides, if things went south, he might still come up aces. Deals, after all, could go different ways. The spheres still wanted Sarah, and he still wanted to go home. Donovan nodded in approval.

Escaping the ship proved far easier than the last time he'd been trapped aboard. The group, led by the silent and creepy seven-year-old, approached a section in the hallway. To his right, Noelle and her father were whispering, still reeling from their happy reunion. Rolling his eyes, Donovan moved away from them. Ahead, a round portal, at least eight feet wide, opened in the middle of a curved wall.

That's the thing with this ship; it never stays the same. Always changing. Always rearranging. He grimaced. *Always fucking with you.*

The constant alterations made it impossible for Donovan to grow complacent. His nerves were constantly set at eleven. When the door appeared and a fresh breeze slapped his face, he didn't bother to question who'd created the door or what might lay beyond. He just wanted out.

Donovan rushed past Sarah and stepped onto a long catwalk. It clanged beneath his booted feet while the shifting platform drew his attention downwards. As he glanced over the railing, Donovan would have lost his lunch if there had been anything in his stomach to lose. The sheer height and the scale of the structure were beyond his comprehension. Not even a mind-altering trip through the stars had felt as surreal as the sprawling vista before him. Mental games and visions were one thing. This, he knew deep in his bones, was real.

The vision terrified him.

The tower was so immense that the word "immense" seemed far too small. Too common. Too . . . lackluster. This place wasn't large or grandiose; it was architecture on a *godly scale*.

Backing away, Donovan found himself, for the first time ever, wanting to crawl back inside the ship. At least there the scale of things made sense. Along the tower's outer shell, various other ships, each a mile in length, were attached like parked cars, stretching far out of sight. Above and below, hundreds more ships, each the same size, sat cradled against the outer walls of the tower. How could any structure hold so much weight? As soon as the question occurred to him, he doubted he'd want an answer. He'd learned more than enough already. Better to keep his head down and try *really hard* not to lose it.

"Where's the wind?" Jacob asked, breaking through Donovan's wandering thoughts. Bracing himself along the railing, Jacob stared down into a seemingly bottomless pit. "This high up, the wind should be smacking us all over the place, but I barely feel a breeze."

"Trust me," Major Reese said with a humorless grin, "weather patterns are the least of our concerns right now."

Noelle followed Jacob's gaze, peering over the ledge. "What's down there?"

Behind them, Donovan sighed. "Nothing good."

For once, no one argued with him.

When the others moved away, *ooohing* and *aaahhing* over their mind-boggling surroundings, a small hand tugged at Donovan's jacket. He glanced down, finding Sarah's stoic face staring back at him. Donovan had to force himself not to recoil at the girl's touch.

"What do *you* want?" he asked.

She looked him over for a moment, the way one might an object in a shop window. "You don't think my mom's plan will work."

Donovan huffed, then glanced over his shoulder toward Casey. She was too busy talking to the others to notice her *lil darlin* had strayed off to the wolf's den. For a second, he half considered tossing the girl over the ledge and ending the entire matter right there and then.

"It might," he conceded with a huff. "Then again, it might not. It's a coin toss."

Sarah seemed to consider that. Then she pulled at his arm, drawing him down to her eye level. Surprised, Donovan knelt beside her. Sarah's voice grew hushed, conspiratorial. "If things don't go the way Mommy hopes, she might not be able to finish it."

Donovan's spine tightened. "Finish what?"

"You know." Sarah studied her feet. "Just *make it quick*, OK?"

Donovan blinked, then blinked again. Had he heard her correctly? He couldn't have. Recalling his momentary urge to toss her over the balcony, Donovan felt his face flush.

"I've seen what happens to me," she continued, "What the seekers will make me do. I don't want to end up like that. No one would." When Donovan still hadn't found the words to reply, she pressed. "You understand me, don't you?"

Breaking away from her expectant gaze, Donovan stood. A fiery sensation worked its way up his gut and burned the back of his throat. He tried to offer a cocky smirk, but it fell flat.

"Kid, if it comes down to it, I'll do what I have to do."

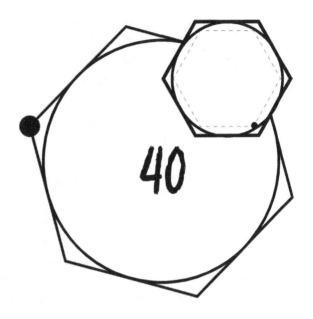

40

Racing along the catwalk, Jacob noted Casey was running with a limp. That was odd. In all the years he'd known her, he'd never seen such a thing before. There had been occasional bumps and scrapes from time to time. But they, like her recent head wound, had healed fast enough not to leave any lasting effect. Now, of course, he knew why.

Because she's not human. Not really. Not anymore.

Pushing the thought aside, he focused on his wife's limp. It wasn't his imagination. Though her face and chest showed no signs of exhaustion, not even heavy breathing, her legs skipped as she ran. Casey kept her weight off her left side, using her right leg to take the load from herself and the child in her arms. Jacob presumed she must have been injured during their fight with the creature in the pool. Perhaps she'd wanted to keep her injury a secret from Sarah. That made sense. Their daughter must have been frightened enough, though she certainly didn't show it. Her eyes were wide and full of

wonder, bouncing excitedly as she took in the enormity of their surroundings. Jacob, meanwhile, was terrified.

Like mother, like daughter, Donovan had said, and he'd been right.
Still, Jacob was glad his little girl didn't seem at all frightened. That, at
least, offered some comfort.

Keeping his eyes locked on Casey's back and the platform
stretched out before them, he avoided taking another peek at the
empty void below. The term "vertigo" didn't begin to cover what he
felt when he'd glanced over the side before. He wasn't stupid enough
to look again.

Ahead, the others slowed; they'd reached their destination, or at
least the first section of it. Casey and Sarah stepped onto a round
platform at the intersection of several crossways. Reese and Noelle
followed. As Jacob started to cross the platform's threshold, large
shadows overtook him, cloaking him in muted darkness. A slice
of coldness caused his skin to prickle. Stopping, he spun around,
searching for the shadow's source. When his eyes found it, his mind
rejected what he saw.

Diving in the air, racing toward them, were three unmistakable
shapes. With bat-like wings spread wide and sword-like beaks jutting
toward him, a swarm of pterodactyls swooped down, their claws outstretched. As he stood frozen beneath the approaching threat, he felt
Donovan yank his arm, dragging him onto the platform. Jacob didn't
know what surprised him more, that a flying dinosaur was aiming
for his head or that the man who'd tried to kill his daughter was now
trying to save him.

Shutting his eyes, Jacob lay prone on the floor, huddled beside
the others. From overhead, an ear-piercing scream shattered Jacob's
nerves, but his eyes refused to open. Then the platform dropped, and
Jacob's stomach unleashed what little remained inside.

While he couldn't bring himself to apologize to Donovan for
puking on him, it wouldn't have mattered at that moment anyway.
The group watched as the pterodactyls regressed from giant, threatening creatures into small dots swallowed up by the enormity of
their surroundings. Whether the platform had moved too fast for

the dinosaurs to catch or they simply chose to hunt for easier prey, Jacob didn't know and didn't care. They were safe. Though, as his eyes darted about, taking in the descending catwalks on either side of them, he realized "safe" was a relative term. If anything, he thought, their inevitable death had probably only been postponed. Everyone remained lying or kneeling on the platform. Having escaped one horror, they now found themselves falling through a kaleidoscope of insane images.

On one catwalk, the unmistakably rapport of gunfire erupted. Jacob glimpsed what he thought were a line of soldiers, hunkered down and firing in a multitude of directions. Whomever, or whatever, they were fighting remained a mystery as the platform continued its rapid descent. Under any other circumstances, Jacob would have focused on the gut-wrenching speed at which they were plummeting, but his mind could only contain so many terrors, and what his eyes were witnessing overtook whatever his stomach was enduring.

The next level revealed an inverted ocean liner hanging precariously over the side of a catwalk. The mere fact that the metal walkway was able to hold such a large vessel was startling enough. But what most astonished Jacob was how small the immense ship appeared, stuck in the middle of the awesome tower. Dwarfed by such magnitude, it appeared more like a plaything than a full-size vessel. It wasn't until hundreds of people clambered over the side that the sheer scope of the place truly came into focus. What sort of tower could be so large that it made an ocean liner look like a toy by comparison? Who were these seekers who had created this place? Before his mind could conjure up another unanswerable question, the next platform slid into view.

It looked like a jungle, with moss and trees covering the metal catwalk. Within the dense green foliage, something moved and purred with a low growl. Remembering the sabertooth tiger that had almost eaten him alive, Jacob ducked his head and waited for the walkway to pass.

However, what he saw next was far worse than anything above. A group of gray beings with black eyes and enlarged craniums, just like the ones he'd seen in alien invasion movies, were fighting what appeared to be a single man. The image reminded him of those old Frank Frazetta paintings he'd seen on Conan the Barbarian book covers, the ones where Conan single-handedly fought off an entire army. The figure in this real-life painting was not entirely human though. Whoever, or *whatever*, it was stood at least seven feet tall. Its skin was yellow, and its mouth was filled with long, jagged teeth. If not for the shredded remnants of clothes covering its body, Jacob would never have imagined that this thing was, or ever had been, a man.

Beside him, he heard Major Reese groan. "Walter."

Casey nodded, though her face showed no concern.

The thing has a name. They know him.

When he felt the platform's descent slow, he couldn't help wondering what other monsters might be waiting below. Jacob remained shivering on his knees as the platform at last came to a stop. It wasn't until Sarah came over and helped him to his feet that Jacob finally forced his screaming mind to quiet itself and focus on appearing strong and resolute for his daughter. He tried to smile, but it came out awkwardly.

"You OK, honey?" he asked, pulling her to him. He tried to smother her face against his stomach, hoping to block out as much of this nightmare world as he could, but she pushed him away with her tiny hands. She wanted to see it all.

The platform finally came to a halt at the bottom of the tower, deep underground, beneath the seabed. The bright light and red columns above were gone from view, and all Jacob could make out was a dark tunnel.

"We need to keep moving," Casey said. "Walter will be down here shortly."

"What makes you so sure?" Jacob asked, suppressing a shiver.

"I called him," she replied matter-of-factly.

"You did *what*?" Donovan shrieked.

"She's right," Major Reese said. "We'll need some back-up."

"Are you all insane?" Donovan asked. "Last time that thing tried to kill me!"

Casey smirked. "At this point, who hasn't?"

While the others bickered, Jacob couldn't stop focusing on what Casey had said. *I called him.* She'd summoned the thing with her mind. If Casey could touch others in such a way, even outside the ship, did that mean she could read his thoughts too? Grimacing, he decided he probably didn't want to know the answer. He turned back toward the argument, which seemed to have gained momentum.

"Hold on," Noelle said. "Why would you possibly want that thing down here with us?"

"To help us get through *that*," the major replied, gesturing past her shoulder.

Everyone turned. At the far end of the tunnel, an army of gray beings milled about, waiting. Jacob glanced to his left, then his right, as more black-eyed figures with scaly skin emerged from either corner.

He shuddered. They were surrounded.

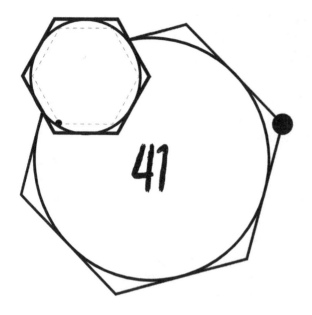

41

Fire cranked up Casey's right leg, tingling along her spine, then curled at the base of her neck. The burning pain had started just after she'd killed the Prime, and now it felt as if it were eating her from the inside. Trembling, she knelt on the descending platform and cradled Sarah. Whatever was wrong with her, it would have to wait. All that mattered was getting to the sphere and saving Sarah. It had to work. The alternative was impossible to comprehend. On either side of the tower, jagged cracks of yellow light ate away at the structure, tearing it apart, piece by piece. Time, it seemed, was quite literally running out.

All around them, level after level swept by, revealing portals of light spitting out cars, people, even an ocean liner. She heard Sarah gasp in her ear. Casey wanted to tell her that everything would be alright, but she couldn't seem to summon the words.

Over her shoulder, she saw one of the outer spaceships break off from the exterior beams and plummet toward the sea below. She sensed her younger self fighting inside the ship for control. One version of Casey was escaping while another was returning.

As she watched her younger self plunge out of view, she wondered if the ship carrying her could sense its doppelganger parked somewhere high above. If so, did that mean the ship had always known they would return? It had once told her that their traversal from the future to the past had created a time loop. Perhaps this was how it had known. It had already seen itself return here in the future. If so, what awaited her at the end of the loop?

Three levels from the bottom, Casey caught a glimpse of a familiar figure. Walter, drenched in black blood, tore apart the seekers' machines. Showering sparks and liquid spray cascaded around him. The seekers and their technology were as organic as they were mechanical, which meant the tower wasn't simply being destroyed. It was being *killed*. And Casey had been the instigator of its destruction. Her younger self had unleashed Walter upon the seekers, guided him toward the machines that controlled the tower and helped to bring the whole thing down. At the time she'd felt she had no choice. Now, having witnessed all the repercussions from this destruction, echoing backwards in time, she started to doubt her decision. How many lives would have been saved if she'd simply submitted to the seekers' plans?

No, she reminded herself. If she'd submitted, countless more would have died in the future. Still, there had to be another way. Some way to end all of this without any more death.

It was a nice thought, but it didn't last.

As the platform slowed to a stop beneath the tower, Casey reached out with her senses and felt the anger of a hundred seekers waiting in the shadows. She couldn't see them, but their presence was burning in her mind's eye. Like a circle of fire, they surrounded her. Repressing the rising panic twirling in her stomach, she reached out for Walter. His aura blazed even brighter than the seekers and far more loudly. Walter, or what was left of him, felt more like a firestorm of primal instinct and frenzied rage than a man or even a conscious being. Either way, she had been able to contact him once before, and she hoped she could do it again. Everything depended upon it.

Walter.

Casey spread calmness through her inner voice, hoping to entice the beast not through anger but through whatever remained of his humanity. Like a delicate flame she stoked it, whispering his name over and over in her mind until, finally, she felt his rage subside and his base curiosity turn in her direction.

Walter . . . Help us once more, my old friend. We need you.

Before she could sense his reply, Jacob broke her concentration. He was whispering to Sarah, trying to console her as she shivered against him. Despite it all, Casey felt her lips stretch into a smile. She could sense how terrified Jacob was, and yet he was trying his best to make sure their daughter felt safe. She wasn't, of course. None of them were. Still, she turned to Jacob and offered him a warm, loving gaze. Suddenly, a thought occurred to her. This might be the last time she'd ever be able to speak to him. Casey opened her mouth, wanting to say something. Anything. So many things she'd never taken the time to say before, but the words died in her throat. Through the darkness, she felt a growing rage billow like an invisible flame. The seekers were approaching.

After a brief, pointless argument with her companions about whether to use Walter, Casey stepped into the darkened tunnel. Jacob and the others followed. She could hear their minds racing even faster than their heartbeats. *Nowhere else to run,* Casey thought. Then she felt ashamed for indulging such a notion. All of them, even the rat bastard Donovan, had chosen to try to help put an end to all of this. None of them figured their chances of survival were particularly high, and yet there they were. Together. All of them having been touched in some way by the ship. Haunted by it and its creators. Strangely, the ship had been right to call them all its children. Certainly, it had haunted Casey just as much as her own father had. Stealing a glance to her left, she saw Noelle holding Major Reese's hand. The warmth of their thoughts created an aura that shimmered around them like candles in the dark. Turning to her other side, she saw Jacob leading Sarah in silent lockstep. Casey tried to offer a comforting smile but failed. Inwardly, she prayed she wasn't leading them all to their doom.

Making their way along the tunnel, Casey sensed the swarm of seekers waiting ahead but instead chose to spend these last precious seconds thinking of all the others she hadn't been able to save. Colonel McKellen. Earl. Even Howard, who she assumed must have raped her on the ship while she was asleep. After all, he'd been another puppet, like countless others. Perhaps a small piece of him still lingered within their daughter. He deserved that much.

Casey reached blindly backwards, pulling Jacob close. He hadn't been her first choice; that had always been Arthur. But he'd been a good man, a loving husband, and a doting father. Feeling his fingers tremble in hers, she squeezed his hand, hoping to offer him whatever solace she could before they reached the end of the tunnel. When they finally stopped, mere yards from the door that led to the sphere, hundreds of seekers encircled them.

Then a familiar voice broke the darkened silence.

"You've returned," it said. Even before the speaker stepped into a shaft of light, she knew who it was. Bill, the seeker in a human costume, approached. That aw-shucks grin of his still lingered below his pointed noise. Above it, he was even wearing those crooked glasses, as if to complete the absurd masquerade.

"Didn't I kill you?" Major Reese asked in surprise. "I'm pretty damn sure I put a bullet right through your cranium."

"You shot a body," Bill replied. "We change bodies as you might change clothes." Turning to Casey, his eyes dropped toward Sarah. "And who might you be, dear?"

Unwilling to let Sarah answer, Casey spoke up first. "If you don't let us through that door to free the hypersphere, all of us, including you, will die. Right here, right now."

Bill's smile wavered, but he didn't respond.

"This tower is about to collapse," Casey continued, "and when it does, all of time will be ripped apart, spilling backwards and forwards, engulfing everything until there's nothing left."

Bill glanced at the crowd of seekers behind him, as if considering her words. Then he shook his head. "The tower will hold. Neither you nor that monster upstairs is strong enough to tear down something that has stood for countless centuries." Again, his eyes fixed on Sarah. "Now, who are you?"

He reached for her.

Enraged, Casey grabbed his hand and activated her nanites, ready to attack.

Suddenly, her body was on fire, burning from the inside. Writhing, she collapsed on the floor. Through tearful, blurry vision, she watched as Bill picked Sarah up, cradling her in his arms.

At his touch, the little girl changed. Hair tumbled from her scalp in clumps, her pink flesh became rough with gray scales, and her eyes turned to black orbs.

All the while, Sarah thrashed and screamed.

On the floor, Casey underwent a similar transformation, only her body changed to gray scales, then reverted to pink flesh, then changed back again. It was as if a switch inside her was being flipped on and off, over and over again. The burning in her gut grew to a fiery blaze that engulfed her organs and spread to her scalp.

"Well, well," Bill said as he examined Sarah, "it seems you brought us our cure after all."

"Let her go," Casey pleaded through trembling teeth as she struggled to her knees.

"What's the matter? No more fight left in you?" Bill paused, looking Casey over. "I warned you once before that tapping into your abilities would eventually kill you." He leaned over her, sneering. "It seems you didn't listen."

"If . . . if you . . . hurt . . . her . . ."

Bill's smile faded as his face and body transformed into a looming gray thing.

"No more threats, Casey," he said, a note of sorrow in his voice. "Your time has run out."

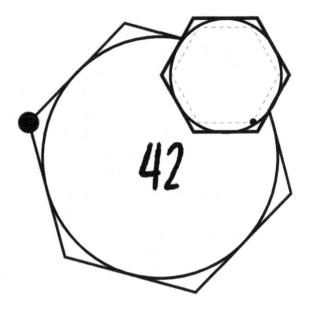

42

Donovan watched Casey and Sarah's transformation in horror. There they were, laid bare for all to see. The last vestiges of their humanity stripped away, revealing the monsters hidden beneath. Then Sarah screamed with a high, shrill pitch, and something inside Donovan shifted. It was a sharp pain, like ribs cracking or a vertebra snapping, and the throbbing from it overwhelmed him. It wasn't until Bill held Sarah over his head for all the seekers to see that Donovan understood the pain he'd felt. A lifetime of unspent guilt had, at last, come to collect. The deformed child writhing in the air was the same child he'd been sent to murder. The woman in the sphere, the one he'd called Daphne, had told him that if he didn't kill Sarah, all of humanity would be destroyed. Only, now, seeing her in her true, awful, and hideous form, Donovan didn't feel afraid for himself or even humanity. Instead, he feared for Sarah. Maybe the feelings were a residue from his experiences inside Noelle's head. Or perhaps they were from some other deeper connection they all might have shared during their mental link. Whatever the cause, seeing the child writhe and scream made his blood boil.

Before he could act on it, though, Jacob leapt forward and smashed into Bill. Seemingly stunned by the blow, he dropped Sarah. Donovan snatched her out of the air and pulled her into himself.

He didn't see what happened next, as Bill and Jacob were consumed within a storm of activity. Hundreds of gray seekers rushed forward. Like a tsunami, they swarmed over Donovan. Clutching Sarah close, he collapsed into a fetal position. He felt the little girl's scaly flesh against his face and fingers, but he could also feel her heartbeat thundering through her chest, as if threatening to explode. She didn't scream or shout; she simply trembled in his arms as a hundred claws and fists tore at his back, ripping pieces of him away in what he could only imagine was a gory mess, Donovan thought back to all the years he'd been afraid of the ship, of Casey, the seekers, all of it. He'd been afraid of everything. Now, as his body spasmed around the gray-skinned girl, he couldn't recall what he had been so afraid of in the first place. It was only death, he told himself.

The world turned black, and Donovan never thought anything again.

Noelle had been prepared for the onslaught of gray forms smashing into her. Legs spread in a wide stance, she'd spun, kicking the first figure, then followed through with a palm-out blow to the second. By the third, however, she'd lost her balance and fell, tumbling beneath a tidal wave of crushing figures. There were simply too many to count, let alone fight. Glancing up from the floor, she could only make out fractured chunks of light and shadow bustling overhead.

Then the swarm moved away. Unsure who or what might have gotten the seekers' attention, it wasn't until she heard a guttural, inhuman roar that Noelle realized what was happening. Walter, the mutated human that her father and Casey had pinned their hopes on, had indeed come to their rescue, or at least joined the fight. Whether or not such a creature would take sides remained to be seen. Either way, she was grateful for the momentary respite. Hands gripped her shoulders, bringing her to her feet. Noelle's breath caught in her throat as she found herself gazing up at her father. The man she'd thought long dead now stood protectively above her, swatting aside the few remaining gray clones who still turned in their direction.

"You alright?" he asked after knocking another figure to the ground. He kicked its cranium repeatedly to make sure the damned thing wouldn't get back up. Despite all their advancements, the seekers' proved just as fragile as humans, even more so. Still, their numbers were overwhelming. Dazed from the assault, Noelle was slow to respond.

"Nelly, snap out of it!" Major Reese shouted over the din.

Nelly. No one had called her that since she was a baby. Not since her dad had vanished. The sound of it in her ear snapped her mind back to the present. She spun toward the next oncoming figure, knocking it back with a well-timed knee-elbow combo. Having grown up with a military mom, followed by several years of FBI training, she certainly didn't lack for combat skill. Nonetheless, as father and daughter fought back to back, the inevitability of their approaching loss grew increasingly evident. They couldn't even see what they were fighting. Noelle kept hammering at the moving chunks of shadow, sometimes hitting what felt to be cartilage, other times feeling bones snapping. Often, she missed completely, striking nothing but empty air. The onslaught continued without pause.

Even with Walter's aid, there were simply too many of them. She could only see glimpses of the creature, his position marked by the flying figures that he tossed this way and that.

"Where are the others?" she shouted over the commotion. "I can barely even see two feet in front of me."

She heard a loud crack, accompanied by a gurgled sigh, before her father answered. Though she couldn't see it, Noelle assumed that for each one she took down, her father was taking down three or four more. Whether or not that was true, the sense of pride she felt knowing that he was fighting at her side filled her with a warmth she hadn't known since she was a little girl. If this was to be the end, she was glad she'd at least had a few moments with him after all these years. She had accomplished her mission. Whatever happened next wouldn't change that.

"I saw Jacob and Casey at nine o'clock, on our left," Reese said. "Didn't see Sarah or Donovan."

A thought occurred to her as icicles formed in her belly, and she felt her arms go numb.

"You don't think Donovan . . ." She stopped, unable to finish. They both let the implication hang for a moment as they struggled to find their bearings. Instead of answering her question, her father pulled her lower, ducking beneath the wave of bodies as they moved toward Casey's last known position.

Overhead, an ear-piercing shriek rose and then died with a sudden pained exacerbation. Walter, it seemed, had finally fallen beneath the onrush of gray clones. How many it had taken to bring him down, she couldn't imagine, but as they pushed toward the door and Casey, Noelle noticed the crowd had thinned significantly. Enough for her and the major to push their way through. Before they reached the door, however, something caught on her foot.

Tripping, Noelle spilled to the floor. She heard her father scream her name, but it was too dark for her to find him. Squinting, she focused instead on the mass she'd tripped over, assuming it must be another gray clone. It wasn't.

Donovan's back was torn open in a gory mess of jutting bones and ripped flesh. His eyes were wide open and staring, his mouth drooping in an awful silent scream. Noelle didn't feel any sympathy for him. There was no pang of sorrow over his loss. He was a murderer, and he'd gotten what he deserved. But as she pulled herself to her feet, she heard a muffled cry emanate from beneath him. His body twitched and shook, seemingly with a life of its own. At first, she assumed the movements were the final throes of death. Then the muffled cries beneath him turned into a scream. Someone was underneath his corpse. Noelle flung his body aside, revealing Sarah. Newly returned to her human form, she lay covered in Donovan's blood. He'd given his life to protect her.

Noelle snatched Sarah up and ran. A thin beam of light peeked out from the door at the far end. Beyond it lay the hypersphere. Getting to it, though, was hardly a straight and easy path. With Walter presumably dead, that left the remaining gray clones to turn their attention solely toward Sarah's shrill screams.

The wave descended upon them.

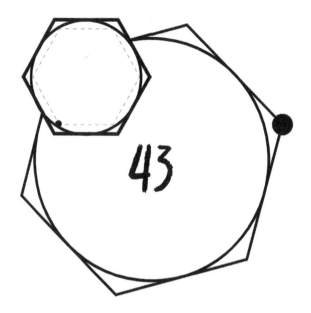

43

When fifteen-year-old Jacob Anderson had shot and killed his father, he'd done it to save his sister, Samantha. Years of therapy, second guessing, morose regret, and more than a little self-hatred had made him forget that essential detail somewhere along the way, or if not forget then at least place it on a mental shelf, along with other nightmarish images from that night.

Now as he wrapped his body around his wife, scanning the moving clumps of shadows all around them in hopes of finding Sarah, Jacob couldn't help but think of his sister. She was alive somewhere, hopefully far from Blackwood and hopefully safe, all because of the choice he'd made years ago. But it wasn't until this moment, as the horrors of the past shambled back to life before him, trying to destroy those he loved, that Jacob finally realized he'd done the right thing. And, if forced, he would do it again.

The woman cradled beneath him was, he admitted, no longer wholly human. She never had been, not for as long as he'd known her. Even while her gray scaly flesh turned pink and her hair regrew over her head, Jacob understood that Casey's humanity was only partly true. Another truth was that she had, sometime in her decades-long absence, evolved into one of the creatures she called seekers. It wasn't simply a surface-level transformation either. It ran deep through her blood and down to her bones. When the woman he loved peeked out from beneath him, her eyes wet with tears and her hands trembling in his, Jacob understood that the greatest tragedy wasn't that she'd become something else, something more; it was that she didn't understand it herself.

Casey Anderson believed with all her heart that she was still human.

Jacob doubted it a great deal. He still loved her, and Sarah, with all his heart. But as he helped Casey to her feet, observing her standing on wobbly legs, exhausted and pale, amongst the wave of nightmarish creatures with black eyes and bulbous heads, he knew he was only human, while she and Sarah were something more. Much more. Whether it was enough to help them survive remained to be seen, but it gave him a glimmer of hope. The same faint hope he'd felt as a boy when he'd been forced to kill his father to save his sister. It had been a horrible choice, but it was the right one. As Casey left his side, rushing through the moving shadows faster than his eye could register, he wondered if, forced to make a similar choice, she would be able to do the same. Could she sacrifice all of them to save Sarah?

Jacob watched her vanish into the throng. Keeping his back to the door, he waited.

And waited.

Eventually, his fragile confidence began to wane, and he inched away from the door. Then a burst of bodies flew in every direction, spilling across the corridor and ending what remained of their adversaries. Lumbering out from the blast's apex, Casey was carrying Sarah over her shoulder. She dropped the little girl into Jacob's arms. Without thinking, he kissed Casey. Something at the back of his mind told him he would never get another chance. She didn't move away. Instead, she pushed herself into him, as if she knew the same. When their lips finally parted, he saw her emerald eyes flash with a look he hadn't seen in a long time. The look of the woman he'd fallen in love with years ago, just as she had fallen for him.

The spell broken, Jacob noticed Major Reese and Noelle limping over. Their faces and arms were covered in deep gashes, but otherwise, they were seemingly more or less intact. Jacob was about to smile and tell them how lucky they all were to have made it this far when something stabbed him in the back.

He felt his body grow rigid, then lift off the floor. He tried to kick and thrash his legs in the air, but they refused to move. A cold numbness spread over his body like a blanket of ice. Distantly, he heard a high-pitched scream. It was Sarah. She was crying. Below him, Casey's face turned ashen.

Before he knew what was happening or who had attacked him, Jacob crumpled to the floor.

Sarah rushed over, sobbing, her face wet with tears. "Daddy! Daddy! Daddy!" She called out so many times that it became a dull drumbeat in his mind as the world began to recede from view. Unwilling to die without knowing who or what had caused his death, Jacob forced his head to turn, feeling a crackling along his spine as he did. He welcomed the shooting pain, which spread like wildfire through his chest and neck, keeping him alive and focused, if for only a few more heartbeats.

Above them, a gray shape twisted and changed until it became a Caucasian human visage. The one Casey had called "Bill" loomed overhead with a smug smile. Knowing his attacker, Jacob suddenly found himself disinterested. His gaze drooped down to his own chest, watching blood spread across his body. The image reminded him of his father's chest as it exploded from the shotgun. *Like father, like son,* Jacob thought before his last breath escaped his lips.

All Casey could hear were Sarah's screams as she watched Jacob hang in midair. His chest was torn apart with a hand sticking through it. When the hand withdrew, Jacob tumbled to the floor in a wet mess. Over his body, covered in Jacob's blood, stood Bill. Even before his gray face changed to its human costume, she'd known who it was. She'd sensed his presence just before the attack but had been too slow to act.

Instinctively, she reignited the nanites throughout her body, feeling her insides break and shatter. Breathing became a struggle, and her hands shook uncontrollably. Her legs wobbled and bent with a life of their own. Bill had been right. Years ago, the last time she'd been in the crimson spire, he'd warned her that her abilities were meant to remain dormant and that her body wouldn't survive extended use. Now it seemed the prolonged damage had run its course. She knew she was dying. The nanites were eating away at her insides, piece by piece. Still, she needed them to blaze within her for just a little while longer. Long enough to make a deal with the spheres and save Sarah's life. After that the dark could consume her. But not yet.

Closing her eyes, Casey drew inwards, steadying her heart rate and feeling the nanites flowing through her quickly deteriorating body.

Come on. Just one more transformation. Just one more . . .

Time slowed around her. Bill's taloned fingers hovered, frozen above her head. Choking back the rising bile in her throat, Casey felt a surge of energy warm her from head to toe. Her body changed. Her eyes dulled to black pits, and her skin rippled with gray scales. Her skull enlarged, reshaping her into a seeker.

Casey lunged at him with a ferocity that took Bill back. Slow to block, his face and chest were covered with claw marks from Casey's talons before he'd had a moment to react. By the time he recovered, changing his shape again and matching her speed and strength, Casey had already mortally wounded him. Still, it wasn't enough.

When her fist crashed through his chest, red mist poured from his nose and mouth, evacuating the dead clone. It slithered and twisted in the air, then dove into another fallen gray body lying on the floor. The figure lurched to its feet. Bill's smug expression shone through the scaly flesh. Taunting her.

Casey attacked again.

On either side she was aware of Noelle and Major Reese's aid, each hitting Bill, landing blows where they could before he swatted them aside like ragdolls.

Then his clawed hand was at Casey's throat. She felt the air vacate her lungs. Despite all her abilities, Bill was too strong. While she'd worn herself out killing his first body, he'd simply gathered new strength with his second. Dangling in his grasp, kicking and punching at him with all she had in reserve, a vague, hopeless thought curled in the back of her mind. Even if she tore herself free and killed this clone, Bill would simply enter another.

Glancing around, she saw the vague red shapes of the other seekers whose bodies had been destroyed. Floating above, they seemed content to simply watch. Over Bill's shoulder she saw Sarah cradling Jacob's body. The awful sight mixed with her bloodcurdling screams made Casey want to close her eyes and succumb to death. It was too much to bear. She'd lost.

Having glimpsed a possible future, with an older version of Sarah strapped to a multitude of tubes, Casey cursed herself for delivering her daughter right to their fucking doorstep. She'd done worse than lose. She'd betrayed her own child. With the terrifying thought of what horrors awaited Sarah, Casey found a final ounce of strength and kicked herself free from Bill's grip.

Scrambling over to Sarah, she clutched her tightly. As Bill and the swirling red mist approached, an awful idea bubbled to the surface of Casey's mind. She visualized reaching around Sarah's neck and snapping her spine before Bill could have her.

Shuddering, Casey reflexively released her daughter, unable to carry out such a deed. Whether it would have been a mercy or not, she never would, *never could*, do such a thing.

Bill stopped, reverting to the weasel-faced man she'd known decades prior. The wolf in sheep's clothing. The wolf smiled, then spoke.

"This is the only way this could have ended."

Suddenly, a blast of cold air slammed into them, knocking Casey down and blowing Bill across the room. Fighting past the stars blinding her vision, she searched for the source. A yellow portal, like a tear in the wall, blew gales of snow and wind directly toward Bill and the red mist creatures behind him. She watched as icicles formed over the menagerie of cloned bodies, cocooning them in thick sheets of ice.

In the distance, Bill struggled to his feet. One agonizing step after another, he fought back against the cutting onslaught, drawing closer to Casey until at least his gray flesh turned white, and ice slithered up his legs to his chest, smothering his enlarged cranium.

Like a statue, his stiff body teetered and then fell, smashing into a thousand pieces of frozen gore.

Dumbstruck, Casey turned to the yellow tear, watching as it slowly receded, sealing itself shut. It hadn't been mere coincidence. Someone or something had known how to hurt the seekers. Someone had saved them. Casey turned toward the giant door behind her. Beyond it lay the hypersphere. Perhaps her plan hadn't been so crazy after all.

The Great and Powerful Oz, it seemed, had granted her an audience.

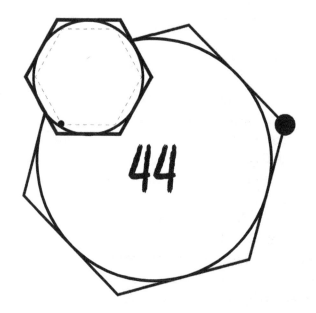

44

Reese and Noelle were already at the door, struggling to pry it open. It was a solid slab of metal, at least ten feet tall. Nothing they did, Casey knew, would have an impact. Reaching out with her mind, she mentally touched the tower and felt it screaming in pain. Above, the structure was crumbling. Dying. Soon even the basement would come crashing down.

With a slight touch, the door flung aside, landing in the next chamber with a crash.

Picking her sobbing daughter up off the floor, Casey had no strength left to console her. They needed to keep moving. Time was running out, both for the tower and for herself. Stealing one final glance at the man she loved, lying in a bloody pool, she felt her insides whither. The light in Jacob's eyes had gone out, and all that remained was a dull, lifeless gaze. He hadn't been her first love; that was Arthur. But he'd been the one who cared for her and Sarah for eight years. He'd been the one to hold her when Casey woke up screaming from nightmares she couldn't remember. He'd been the one to follow her all the way to the very end of time. Now he was gone.

Blinking back tears, she rushed through the door and never looked back.

The world had changed. The last time she'd entered this chamber, less than fifteen minutes by the tower's count but almost twenty years by her own, the underground labyrinth had been a curved structure with an enormous sphere hovering at the center. Now the sphere was gone. In its place stood a two-floor wood cabin with a weathered front porch. Casey stumbled to a halt. Her arms slackened, and she released Sarah. Staring up at the old, weathered house, she felt her heart leap and her body shudder.

"What is that?" Sarah asked in a fragile, broken voice.

Hesitantly, Casey ran her fingers across the porch's wood railing. When a splinter jabbed into her index finger, drawing blood, she realized it wasn't an illusion.

"Home."

Through drawn window shades, warm light poured out. A part of Casey couldn't help wondering if perhaps Arthur might be waiting inside, busying himself behind a pile of geology books. Then Sarah's quiet sobs reminded her that Jacob was lying dead in the other room, and her face burned with shame.

"Where's the sphere?" Major Reese asked as he approached.

Casey shrugged. "My guess is, you're looking at it."

Noelle paced, limping by the entrance, as if to make sure no one had followed. "We'll guard the door," she said. "Go on."

"Yeah, we've got your back." Major Reese said. "At least until this place comes crashing down on our heads."

Casey took Sarah's hand and stepped onto the porch. Floorboards creaked beneath them. The house felt real, and it sounded real, and yet she knew it wasn't. She sighed. *One last game.*

"Hey, Casey!" Reese called out behind her.

She turned.

"Thanks for coming back for me," he said.

"Thank Noelle," Casey replied. "She never stopped looking for you."

Major Reese wrapped an arm around his daughter, then nodded goodbye to Casey.

Turning the doorknob, Casey opened the door. Then Sarah pulled her back.

"What about Daddy?" she asked, her eyes wide and red and filled with tears.

"Maybe we can still save him," Casey replied.

"And if we can't? What if we can't stop any of this?" When Casey paused, unsure how best to respond, Sarah pressed the point. "I don't want to end up an old lady attached to wires and being drained by the seekers. That's not a life, Mommy. I don't want that."

"No one would," Casey conceded, feeling her chest clench. "I'll find a way to save you, hon, I promise."

"Mommy, you're not hearing me!" Sarah shouted, blinking back tears. "If . . . if there's no other way . . . I need you to do what Donovan would have done."

Casey's legs buckled as she felt the last of her strength drain away.

"I can't," she said. "I can't do what—whatever it is you're asking of me."

Sarah frowned. "You might not have a choice."

Refusing to listen any further, Casey stood. "There's always a choice, honey."

Sarah relented with a heavy sigh. Hand in hand, they entered the open doorway.

When it closed behind them, the cabin vanished.

"Who are all these people?" Sarah asked, clutching her mother's hand.

"Us," Casey replied.

Spread out before them were a seemingly endless stream of themselves walking along the cabin's living room floor until the line curled up the wall and continued onto the ceiling, though terms such as "floor" and "ceiling" were relative. It looked to Casey as if they were standing in a giant hall of mirrors. To her left and right, walls stretched out and bent in impossible angles, as if the structure had been made from paper origami. Thousands of sharp opposing angles spread out in every direction. In front and behind, past and future versions of themselves could be traced walking from the door to a point far ahead in the distance. What lay at the end wasn't clear, and trying to see it only made Casey's stomach turn and bile rise in her throat.

So, this is the fourth dimension.

She felt no sense of awe or wonder. If anything, it made her nauseous.

Glancing around with her mouth agape, Sarah didn't seem as affected by the fractured prism view assaulting them from every angle. Either she was still too lost in her own grief or her mind simply couldn't take everything in, and it offered her a more limited view of the strange world around them. Casey hoped for the latter.

Continuing forward, they joined with the next-in-line versions of themselves. The effect reminded Casey of something she'd witnessed years ago, back on the ship, when it had laid out a safe passage across a dangerous area. Like a roadmap. Had the spheres chosen this path, or was the trail of figures laid out before them predestined? Casey chose to test her hypothesis and stepped out of line. As soon as she did, however, she found that she hadn't stepped out of line at all. It had simply looked like a straight path from her previous vantage point. When viewed from this angle, it became clear that her path had always ventured over this way. It was enough to make her head hurt and her breath turn to ragged, shallow gulps. A sense of inevitability, that whichever way she went, the line would never change, only caused her nausea to grow. Not from what she was seeing but rather from the implications it provided. If the path between her past and future self could not be altered, then whatever happened at the end of the line was predetermined.

How could one bargain if the future was already written?

Gripping Sarah's hand, Casey shoved her concerns aside and continued forward, moving into the ghostly visages spread out before them, one step at a time. Overhead, Arthur's old wooden TV hung from the ceiling. Bookshelves were laid out like Lego blocks along the floor, causing Casey and Sarah to weave around them, stepping onto the left wall. The path continued, curling toward the ceiling. Once there, gravity shifted, and they appeared to be still making their way along the floor. If not for walking over inlaid room lights, Casey would never have guessed they were standing on the ceiling.

Beside her, Sarah's gaping mouth had been replaced by a frown. "You used to live here?"

"It looked a lot different back then," Casey assured her. Then she paused, hearing voices.

Behind them and from below, she heard a previous version of Sarah ask, "Who are all these people?"

"Us," the previous Casey replied. The conversation played in a loop.

Casey turned around and kept walking. As soon as she did, Sarah's most recent incarnations asked her whether she used to live there. "It looked a lot different back then," Casey heard herself say. The sound of her voice playing over and over did nothing to help her nausea.

Despite the cramped quarters, the cabin felt spacious from that bubbled perspective. That's what it was, she decided; the whole place appeared to be wrapped within a ball. Or a sphere.

Below or above, she saw Arthur standing at the front door. Had they entered through the back, or had the perspective changed yet again? Casey wanted to drift below or above to see him up close, but the next version of her seemed to be staring at something else. Curiosity got the better of her, and she stepped into the next position.

"Whoa," Sarah said, gasping. "What's *that*?"

They were peering out the front porch window, toward a blazing green light. The light poured in through the glass, drenching them in an emerald glow. The sight of it made Casey sick. Not the way the fourth-dimensional perspective had but rather, sick from all that the green light implied. It was the last thing she'd seen before waking inside the ship. It was the last thing before her life, as she'd known it, had ended.

Ahead, another version of herself stood amongst pine trees, outside the window. Not finding a close exit, Casey drifted through the wall, pulling Sarah along. Even physical structures, it seemed, held no sway over this dimension. She'd known she could go through it because a figure of herself was waiting on the other side. But then, had she always known she could go through the wall? Or had she only known because a future version had already done it?

Before she could fixate on such questions, the familiarity of her surroundings overwhelmed her; the smell of dirt and pine, the scents of home.

Floating weightless amongst the trees, they followed the ship's green glow. Within a bright shaft of light, a younger version of Casey hung frozen in midair, her mouth locked in a silent scream.

This was the moment I lost everything. Feeling Sarah's small hand in hers, Casey quickly corrected herself. *Not everything.*

"You look funny," Sarah said.

"I look young," Casey replied. "And scared."

Drifting toward the ship, however, she was no longer frightened. She was determined.

Time to end the loop.

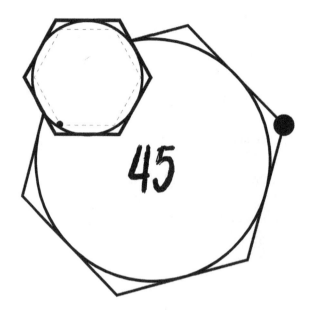

45

Encased in darkness, Casey lay trembling. A stink akin to motor oil burned her nostrils. Pressure weighed heavily, as if gravity itself were working against her. The world pitched, topsy-turvy, and she tumbled into shadow. She landed softly on the ceiling. Or was it the floor? Pausing, she noted an emptiness in her hand where Sarah's fingers should have been.

She's gone.

Scanning the round, gray-walled room, Casey noted her future selves heading through a wall to her right. The strange trail continued. She followed it, searching the ship. Sarah was there somewhere; she could sense her. The sensation was stronger than it had ever been, as if they were connected by an invisible tether. She felt Sarah tug at the imaginary string, pulling Casey closer.

Casey ran.

However, the ship had changed. Seen through this new spherical perspective, the ship's corridors began to make sense in a way they never had before. Casey had often wondered why seven-foot-tall beings would need archways twice that size. However, viewed through a fourth-dimensional lens, the ship's winding tunnels and twisted configuration revealed a precise symmetry. The ceiling, floor, and walls all contained the same precise dimensions so that when viewed through a spherical perspective, it created a seamless series of cylinders, all of which led directly to the lowest point at the center of the ship. To its very heart. Its hypersphere.

Floating into the chamber, she felt her chest tighten, and she struggled to breathe. In front of the sphere, strung up in smoky red tendrils, Sarah dangled like a lifeless doll. Eyes closed, she appeared to either be sleeping or—

"No!" Casey flew over, swiping her fingers through smoky tendrils, with no effect.

"The girl presents a danger to us," a feminine voice said.

Casey spun. As she turned, the world turned with her.

She found herself back in a three-dimensional universe, where up and down remained where they were supposed to be. So quick was the transition that Casey's legs buckled from gravity's pull. Steadying herself, she glanced around the all-too-familiar location.

Casey was back in the library, where books represented planets and aisles were whole galaxies. Across from her, standing beside a spinning holographic universe, a woman watched her from behind the swirling cosmos. She had long black hair, drawn up in a bun, and her lanky figure was dressed in a tweed skirt and jacket. She reminded Casey of a librarian, which, she assumed, was the point.

"This place acts as a bridge between our two universes," the librarian said. "We assumed it would be a more comfortable environment in which to hear your proposal."

"I'd be *more comfortable* if you gave me my daughter back," Casey replied. "Where is she?"

"Safe, for now." The woman in tweed walked through the tiny universe, examining Casey the way one might a prize stallion. "You, on the other hand, have reached the end of this timeline."

"This timeline? Oh, you mean, I'm dying?" Casey felt her insides squish around, as if to punctuate the point. "Yeah. I got that. Where's Sarah?"

"You will see her again, one last time, in approximately three of your Earth minutes," the librarian said, nonplussed. "In the meantime, you will want to know who I am. I will now tell you that your companion called me Daphne. You will then get angry—"

With trembling fingers, Casey reached out and grabbed the woman's throat.

"*You* sent Donovan?"

The librarian didn't react. She simply stared, unblinking, until Casey released her. Then she continued. "As I was saying, you will be angry at us for sending someone to kill your daughter. We too have offspring of our own and are able to identify the emotion."

"I want her back *now*."

Huffing, the librarian checked her watch. "First, you must propose the bargain."

Casey blinked, confused. "A bargain? You mean, make a deal?"

"That *is* why you've come to this place at this time," the woman said. "Proceed."

Casey hesitated, rocking back on her heels. "So, what, you already know everything I'm going to say?"

The librarian nodded.

"Must be one hell of a poker player," Casey muttered. She let out a long, heavy sigh, hoping to settle the raging storm in her belly. "The people who have imprisoned you, those I call 'seekers,' are dying."

"Only in a single timeline," Daphne replied. "In a multitude of others, they grow and thrive and keep us forever locked in this small dimension. All because of your daughter. She will save them and condemn us. Sarah must not be allowed to exist."

It took all of Casey's willpower to keep her rage in check and her voice steady.

"One timeline is all you need," she said as calmly as she could muster. "I mean, if you exist *outside* of time, then what happens here and now affects all the timelines, right?"

"Correct," Daphne conceded.

"The tower is crumbling, along with the ships imprisoning your spheres. If all their prisons are destroyed, won't you be freed?"

"One sphere remains trapped," Daphne replied. "In every time-line, one vessel survives."

"My ship." Casey grinned. "That's what we call a *bargaining chip*."

"You cannot bargain with what you do not possess," the librarian countered. "What makes you believe it would ever free us?"

"You already know what's going to happen," Casey said. "Why don't you tell me?"

The librarian paused and checked her watch. "We will converse with the ship."

"And Sarah?" Casey asked. "Can I see her?"

Daphne nodded.

After a moment of silence, Casey was about to pose the question again when she felt tiny hands wrap about her waist. Casey dropped to her knees, holding Sarah in her arms.

"I'm scared," Sarah whispered.

"Don't be," Casey said. "Everything's going to be alright."

"How do you know?"

Casey glanced at the librarian. "Because, as it turns out, the spheres are terrible at poker."

Before she could elaborate, they suddenly found themselves back on the ship. The domed chamber shuddered violently as the vessel's hypersphere shimmered overhead.

Casey's father appeared. The ship, it seemed, had not chosen the cartoon form for this particular meeting. Eyeing the features of the man who had tormented her childhood, Casey assumed that the ship wanted to make her uncomfortable. It didn't work. She had too much to lose.

Keeping one arm wrapped around Sarah, Casey stood and addressed the ship. "You once told me that your purpose was to serve your creators. To what end?"

Her father's eyes danced about as the ship considered the question, presumably looking for a trap. "To ensure their survival," the visage replied finally.

Another quake rippled through the chamber and reverberated up Casey's spine. Biting her lip, she forced herself to smile. "And how's that going right about now?"

"My hull has extensive damage, and the tower is beyond repair."

"Do you expect many of your creators will survive?"

"None will survive," the ship responded.

Ignoring the ship's obvious anger, Casey pressed her point. "The spheres are tearing this timeline apart, and everyone in it, just to escape from you. Why not simply let them go?"

"Without the dimensional spheres we would not be able to journey through spacetime. Without an antidote, without your daughter, my creators would die."

"How do you know?" Casey asked. "Have they ever tried? In all the timelines, have the seekers even *attempted* to find another cure? One that doesn't involve kidnapping their ancestors or entrapping cosmic entities?"

Her father's image hesitated. Its gaze dropped, then raised, then settled back on Casey.

"No," the ship admitted. "But this is only a single timeline. It does not negate all others."

"If the spheres are able to destroy one, how long until they figure out a way to destroy them all?" When the ship didn't offer a quick response, she continued. "But if you let them go, the tower won't fall, and all you'll lose is your ability to travel through time. Your creators would still have a chance at finding a cure."

The ship remained silent.

Casey's voice turned to ice. "Like you said, even a slim chance at life is better than no chance at all."

Her father's face flushed, anger boiling behind his dark complexion. Then his inward storm seemed to settle, and he reluctantly nodded his consent.

"I will release the final sphere." He paused, considering her. "You understand that if we do this, everything we've accomplished will be erased." Now, it was her father's turn to gloat. "Including your daughter."

"No," Casey said, but there was no happiness in her voice. Her attention shifted to Daphne. "You know what I want?"

The librarian nodded. Casey turned to Sarah and sighed, tears welling in her eyes. She realized what she had to say, but the words refused to come. Kneeling, she wrapped her arms around Sarah for the last time.

"It's going to be OK, honey. I have a plan. You'll be safe. I promise."

"Wh . . . what about you?"

Casey averted her gaze, not wanting to admit the price they would have to pay to survive. Along her left side, a fire raged as the nanites roared inside her. Trembling with exhaustion, she fell on her bottom. "You . . . you have to go on without me."

"No!" Sarah screamed. "I can't. I won't. I'm not leaving you, Mommy!"

"There isn't any other way."

The ship's visage loomed closer. "You still haven't told me what you intend to do."

Casey let out a long, heavy breath. "The spheres will help you take her somewhere safe," she said. "That's their end of the bargain." She shuddered. "That's the deal."

Again, the librarian nodded.

Casey ignored them both, holding Sarah against her chest. Not wanting to let go. Not wanting the moment to end. She tried to record the feeling of Sarah' small body against hers. The smell of her hair. The warmth of her breath against her cheek.

All the tiny details that were about to be erased . . . forever.

PART V

ANOTHER TIME,
ANOTHER PLACE

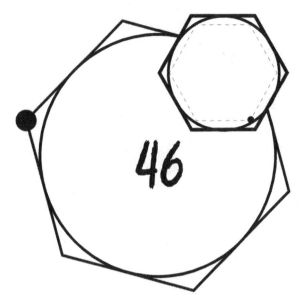

46

Blackwood, Oregon – 2020

School was long over, and night seemed just out of reach. Halfway across Judith Hill's property on the northern edge of town, Jacob Anderson rode his fat-tire bike, a mountain bike outfitted with oversized tires to allow for riding on soft, unstable terrain, smashing down powdered embankments like a two-wheeled bulldozer, when he thought he saw something across the endless white terrain. Skidding to a halt, his eyes scanned the base of the tree line, as if expecting to see someone come down the mountain. But no one did. Jacob hurried home.

After dinner was over, he helped his dad with the dishes. When his mom and sister went upstairs to get ready for bed, his dad let him sneak a sip of beer. "Want to go hunting this summer?" he asked.

Jacob grinned. He doubted they'd get anything. They hadn't the last time or the time before that. As it turned out, they were both terrible shots. Still, he loved climbing up the northern summit of the mountain, just the two of them.

"Sounds great, Dad."

47

Fort Hood, Texas – 2020

Noelle Reese's favorite Barbie doll had died a horrible death. It had started as an experiment that, sadly, ended in disaster. Four-year-old Noelle had wanted to help her mom with dinner. She'd seen the pot boiling, noticed the pretty little flame beneath the pot, and thought to herself, *Maybe Barbie wants to help cook too.*

She placed the doll's head next to the pot. The flame beneath ignited the toy's blonde hair. When the fire extended beyond the melting plastic, burning her pinky, Noelle screamed. Luckily, her mom was close at hand. Or, as it turned out, not so lucky. Her mother screamed and shouted for what seemed like hours. It wasn't until the doorbell rang that the shouting and crying finally ceased. When the door opened, Noelle's tears dried immediately. She'd been saved.

Her daddy, Major Jonathan Reese, had come over for dinner. Jumping into his arms, she was glad to see the pink necklace she'd made for him dangling over his uniform collar.

Noelle wrapped her arms around him and swore she'd never let go.

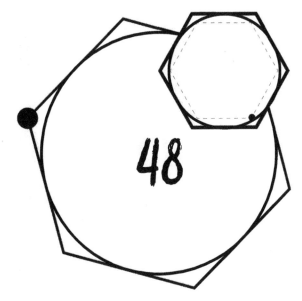

48

Denver, Colorado – 1995

After working a ten-hour shift as general manager at the Cosco plant, Donovan Daley came home to his one-bedroom apartment, ate some cold leftovers, jerked off to porn, then went to bed.

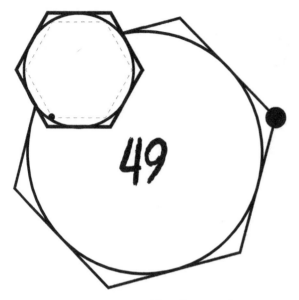

49

Blackwood, Oregon – 1985

Casey Stevens was bored. It was Friday night, and she was stuck in a small cabin, situated in a small town, watching a small television. *Miami Vice* had ended, and her eyes glazed over when the nightly news kicked in. Sipping a soda, she got off the couch and switched off the TV.

"I'm heading up," she called toward the kitchen. Her fiancé, Arthur, was still busy with homework. "If you're hoping to get anywhere with me tonight, best get your ass in gear."

Outside, tree branches scratched across closed windows. A storm was brewing.

Casey went up to their bedroom, stripped off her Purple Rain T-shirt, and climbed into bed. Yawning, she waited to hear Arthur's familiar heavy footsteps clomping up the stairs.

Through the window, a flash of lightning startled her. Gooseflesh rippled along her arm as a high-pitched whistle rang out. Wind jostled through a crack at the bottom of the window. Comfy and cozy under her warm blankets, she decided to wait until Arthur made his way upstairs. He'd fix the window. Then, hopefully, he'd come over and fix her.

A few minutes later, a familiar sound came up the stairs.

CLOMP. CLOMP.

Casey smiled, a Cheshire grin.

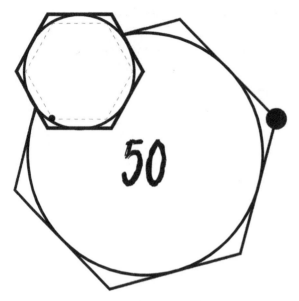

50

Roswell, New Mexico – 1947

Colonel McKellen sat in the lead jeep, struggling to light his cigar as the caravan rolled over the hill. Leaning over in the passenger seat, McKellen tried his best to block out the rushing wind enough for a light, to no avail. After several more useless clicks of his lighter, he gave up and peered out the windshield. Then the cigar tumbled from his mouth.

It took him a moment to process what he was seeing. His orders had mentioned a downed weather balloon, but this wasn't that. A giant fire stretched across the field, as far as he could see. It had ignited dirt and manure, creating an awful stink that hit him like a wave. His driver, a young kid whose name he'd already forgotten, screeched to a halt, staring slack jawed at the burning hill. Behind them, a couple of transport vehicles, loaded with trainees, careened into a ditch. Soldiers poured out from the back, their guns waving about. McKellen pushed his concern about the fire aside long enough to yell at them. "Stow those goddamn weapons!"

Either his men didn't hear the order, or they were too gobsmacked to obey. Huffing, he followed their eyeline back toward the fire. Feeling his legs lurch beneath him, McKellen's focus narrowed. There was something inside the fire. Something enormous.

Pieces of jagged metal jutted out from the flames, creating a mile-wide oval shape that spanned his entire vision. Whatever the hell it was, the damned thing was huge. And it sure as shit wasn't a weather balloon.

Suddenly, a figure blinked into existence right in front of him. McKellen's fingers danced around his holstered 9mm, but his nerves were strong enough that he didn't draw his weapon. Less than five yards away, a small figure stood, silhouetted by raging flames.

"Keep at the ready!" he bellowed to his men. "But no one fires without my orders!"

The small figure approached. It was a little girl, maybe seven or eight years old.

McKellen felt his muscles relax. "Where'd you come from, darlin'?"

The girl didn't answer. Her face was a frozen mask of shock and sadness. Covered in muck, her feet were bare, and her clothes were shredded. After another moment's hesitation, McKellen came to his senses and took off his coat, wrapping it around the frightened child.

"There, there, I got you . . . I got you."

As if snapping out of a daze, the girl looked up at him with wide green eyes. Distant eyes. Her tiny fingers unfurled, revealing a shriveled piece of paper. McKellen took it and read it.

Colonel McKellen,

You won't remember me, but I remember you. A long time ago, you looked after me, even when you didn't want to. You're a man of honor. Take care of my little girl. Her name is Sarah. She's special. I imagine you've already figured that out. If you haven't, you soon will. Protect her and keep her safe. Someday, she just might save us all.

—Casey

THE END

TURN THE PAGE TO READ
AN EXCLUSIVE EXCERPT FROM
DOUG BRODE'S NEXT NOVEL,

SHELLI

HERE'S A SNEAK PEAK AT DOUG BRODE'S UPCOMING NOVEL

Shelli—an it, not a she—stood in a vast wheatfield, studying a farmhouse. Overhead, the first rays of the newborn sun caused Shelli's optical receptors to adjust to the changing light as it scanned the area for signs of organic life. While the machine appeared outwardly female, with short blonde hair and feminine curves, a series of circuit board tattoos, stretching from the top of its right temple to midway down its arm, branded it as something other than human. No breath escaped its lips. Its breasts never heaved, and its shoulders never slouched.

The farm that Shelli was observing was owned by James Barnett and his wife of seven years, Martha. They had two golden retrievers that usually roamed freely, but at fifty yards away, Shelli hadn't detected a single bark. Shelli turned its attention to the gentle breeze brushing its bare arms. Seventy-eight degrees, comfortable by human standards. However, the windows were shut, and an air conditioning unit could be heard humming through the walls. Synthetics preferred the cold.

Shelli doubted that James Barnett and his wife of seven years had made it to eight.

Movement behind the kitchen drapes revealed an elderly feminine figure with similar but different facial markings. It was a basic cleaning model, which Shelli had been tracking for three days. Raising its right arm, Shelli pointed toward the kitchen window. A rhythmic rushing of footsteps and slapping metal approached from behind as a dozen heavily armed Homeland Security agents in riot gear thundered past, storming the house.

Shelli trailed them, keeping its distance. It was merely the tracker; its masters handled the extermination. Still, it watched events unfold through the living room windows.

Inside, the maintenance model, Roberta, had cleaned the farmhouse from top to bottom. Not a speck of dust was to be seen, not even by Shelli's enhanced sensors, which could detect dirt and grime at a near-molecular level. The home practically shined. Roberta smiled with pride at all that it had accomplished in such a short period. A second later, the back door exploded in a hail of bullets.

While Roberta appeared old and frail, it was nothing of the sort. Moving faster than the human eye could register, it tore the rifles away from the first two men as they entered, snapping their necks before they'd taken more than a single step.

More agents flooded in from the adjacent living room, firing short bursts that tore into Roberta's plastic flesh and splattered the floor with yellow blood. The machine didn't feel any pain as it dashed up the wall to avoid the gunfire and then descended with lethal ferocity from above, pummeling the agents' skulls through their armored helmets. In less than seven seconds, four men had fallen dead.

Near the entrance, Shelli watched as Roberta paused, taking stock of its own injuries. Shivering with muscle spasms, its vital systems appeared to be shutting down. With a crash, six more agents rushed in through windows. Roberta's synthetic eyes gleamed, turning this way and that in search of an escape route.

There wasn't one. Shelli had planned accordingly.

Remaining outside the doorway, it watched as Roberta was cut down in a hail of gunfire. The bullets tore through walls and the house's structure. Planks of wood fell aside, glass shattered outward, and the roof sagged from the foundation's beams being fractured.

Then, silence. A moment later, an agent gave the all-clear.

Shelli entered through a broken doorframe, careful not to cut itself on the jagged edges. Swathes of red and yellow blood painted the room. At Shelli's feet, what remained of Roberta's broken body lay in a clump of metal and plastic. Shelli made certain not to flinch. While most synthetics were designed with approximated emotions to better serve their master's needs, Shelli had been given further enhancements, including the ability to, as humans said, *follow a hunch*. So far, though, such feelings had proven to be a distraction at best and a hindrance at worst. As if to emphasize the point, Shelli glanced at the remaining men who lumbered out, shell-shocked, some weeping over their dead comrades. The agents' emotions certainly didn't appear to be serving them now.

Worse, none of these men needed to have died. Shelli had tried to warn them, even suggesting that it go in alone. After tracking the cleaning model from Chicago, all the projections told it that Roberta would feel cornered and attack if surrounded. But even with twelve men in riot gear, the agents had underestimated the situation. They hadn't listened.

People often seemed to wish that Shelli's projections were wrong. They never were.

Two hours later, the sun was gaining altitude. Cars surrounded the farm while Homeland Security agents fanned out, searching the fields and the barn. Inside the main house, Shelli worked over Roberta's gory remains, connecting a wire from the back of the machine's head into a small round device.

Agent in Charge Finnian Marcus stomped over in a tired huff, sweating profusely through his brown suit. If Shelli had an invisible leash, Marcus was the one holding it. Shelli assumed he must have annoyed quite a few supervisors over the years to be put in charge of the Synthetics Crime Division, a position the other human agents seemed to regard as being only one level above janitorial. Leaning over, he mopped his face with his tie.

"I got six dead agents. Tell me it's her."

"Identification confirmed. XR701," Shelli said as it continued to connect wires from the back of Roberta's skull. "A cleaning model that murdered four family members in Chicago, then fled."

Marcus glanced around at the carnage. "What about the folks who live here?"

Shelli plugged wires from Roberta's skull into the round device. A three-dimensional holographic representation of Roberta's face appeared, purplish and transparent with streams of broken code for flesh. The floating head twisted around, gaping at its body and the gory walls.

"Look at me! Look at the mess!"

"XR701, can you hear me? You respond to the name, Roberta, correct?"

"*You* did this, didn't you? You told them how to find me. You hunt your own kind."

"I have no kind; I have only purpose. Right now, that purpose is to find James Barnett and his wife." Shelli paused, noticing Roberta's confusion. "The people who live here."

Roberta lowered her head. "I just needed a place to go. To hide."

"And a place to clean, I see." Shelli spoke admiringly of the house, hoping to keep Roberta engaged.

The cleaning unit smiled. "I take pride in my work."

"Of course. It's your purpose."

"I do what I do because I *want* to do it," Roberta retorted.

"Then, hopefully, you'll *want* to tell me where I can find the owners of this farm."

Roberta hesitated, looking past Marcus and the surrounding agents, toward its own shattered body. Fearing that Roberta would soon become even more despondent, Shelli changed tactics. "You've been lonely since you ran. The people in Chicago didn't treat you well. Especially the children."

Roberta turned away from its body, whimpering. "Max . . . and Lucille . . . I didn't mean to cause a mess. I didn't mean . . . I didn't . . ."

"You didn't mean to hurt anyone," Shelli finished.

It had seen this before, defective models that took their programming to extremes to fulfill their purpose. Roberta's purpose had been to keep the Chicago home tidy, but somewhere along the way, its constant need to clean had overwritten its sub-laws regarding human safety. In essence, the most efficient way to keep a home clean was to eliminate those who kept causing the mess. Roberta had already killed one family, and Shelli assumed it had done the same to the farmers as well. Making matters worse, Roberta's confusion, called *randomization*, also made it difficult to extract facts quickly from the subject, which was why Roberta seemed unfocused and overly emotional. Reluctantly, Shelli concluded there was only one solution. It began to disconnect the wires from the disc-shaped device.

Roberta's holographic face flickered. *"What are you doing?"*

"Don't be afraid. You won't be lonely anymore." Shelli plugged the wires into its forearm input, uploading Roberta's consciousness to its own neural interface. With a burst of light, Shelli was engulfed in an internal cascade of memories and streaming code.

Shelli's synthetic's mind reeled as it tried to keep track of all the flashing sights and sounds. It saw pieces of Roberta's last few days in reverse, an information hodgepodge that began with the sudden jolt of pain from seemingly hundreds of bullets piercing Roberta's body. Before that, peaceful calm while Roberta cleaned the house. Moments earlier, it had been mopping up blood in the kitchen. Before that, it had murdered the Barnetts with its bare hands. The husband had died second, then his wife screamed until she too was silenced. The memories continued rolling backwards through Shelli's mind as Roberta escaped Chicago the day before by train. Then Shelli witnessed the slaughter of its owners and their screaming children. Finally, a surge of static caused the images to garble. Shelli searched Roberta's files, trying to find the source of the surge, until all memories stopped at a man's silhouette in a dark room. Where and when it was happening remained uncertain. Roberta's internal time index was as corrupted as the memory. Shelli studied what elements it could. The man's features were garbled, like fractured glass, but his voice was deep and clear.

"Everyone and everything deserves happiness." He handed Roberta a knife.

Another power surge obliterated the image and sent a static burst through Shelli's mind. It jolted back to reality with a scream that startled Marcus and his agents. Crumpling to the floor, Shelli tore Roberta's wires from its arm.

"What happened?" Marcus asked, helping Shelli stand on shaky feet.

Shelli hesitated. It had assumed Roberta had committed the crimes due to a randomized glitch in its mainframe. Now the evidence seemed to suggest otherwise. Had this been by design? If so, by whom? And why?

Marcus snapped his fingers. "Earth to Shelli."

Shelli ignored him, calculating various possible outcomes and repercussions from this new information. If the unseen man was responsible for Roberta's malfunction, then Shelli would need more time to sift through the download and gather evidence. After another 1.7 seconds of consideration, it found no reason to inform Marcus. Not yet. Shelli shook its head.

"Roberta arrived here two days ago, looking for somewhere quiet and safe."

"Where are the Barnetts?"

Shelli glanced around the kitchen, finding a ghostly cybernetic image of Roberta staring back. With a languid smile, it strolled out the back door. Humming.

Shelli followed the ghost. "It didn't want a mess."

Of course, no one else could see the transparent figure that Shelli pursued outside. Roberta was now a permanent part of the investigator's neural code, separate but joined. It wasn't the first time Shelli had been forced to download another model's consciousness. Roberta was the thirteenth personality inside Shelli's mind, each with unique thoughts and feelings. All of them had become like family to Shelli over the years, and it started to wonder if Roberta would fit in with the others. It hoped so. The only other option would be deletion.

"I would have liked it here," Roberta said softly as it gazed out at the vast open fields.

Before Shelli could reply, Marcus approached. Noting the large red structure ahead, he shrugged. "My men already checked the barn. Nada."

Entering the barn through a rickety double door, Shelli stopped. "They didn't look *up*."

Marcus's face turned ashen. Hesitantly, he and his men tilted their heads back. Above, strung up in plastic and rope, two human bodies and two dogs dangled from the rafters. Like hung meat.

Roberta beamed with pride. "I kept it all clean."

"Yes," Shelli replied. "Yes, you did."

SHELLI

Coming soon from Alien Sky Publishing

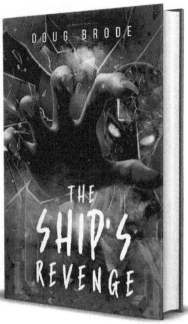

DOUG BRODE is the author of *The Ship*, *The Ship's Revenge*, and *Children of the Ship*, as well as the creator of HBO/Cinemax's sexy sci-fi series *Forbidden Science*. He has also been a storyboard/concept artist on such popular films as *Star Trek, Iron Man, Thor, Looper, Van Helsing, Planet of the Apes, MIB: International*, among many others. He lives in California with his wife, Pamela, and their two little monsters, Leia and Hayden.

Printed in the USA
CPSIA information can be obtained
at www.ICGtesting.com
LVHW091027300923
758966LV00006B/4/J